Here Come the Brides

MICHEALA LYNN

Other Bella Books by Micheala Lynn

At All Costs
Fire Dancer
Jagged Little Scar
Joie de Vivre

About the Author

Writer, Musician, Artist, Habitual Hat Wearer, Cat Whisperer, Guinness Connoisseur, Scottish Highlander, Viking Shieldmaiden, Dragon Slayer, poet warrior and Haggis Lover. A notorious shenaniganizer, Micheala Lynn divides her passions between writing, playing a wide variety of music, wrenching on her Harley, and snuggling with her partner of many years on cold Michigan nights. When not at her desk, she can be spotted blasting down the highway on her motorcycle or at a Renaissance faire speaking Irish Gaelic or Old English and performing on the Scottish smallpipes. Questions concerning her sanity have never been answered conclusively.

Here Come the Brides

MICHEALA LYNN

BELLA
BOOKS

2024

Bella Books, Inc.
P.O. Box 10543
Tallahassee, FL 32302

First Edition - 2024

Editor: Alissa McGowan
Cover Designer: Kayla Mancuso

ISBN: 978-1-64247-532-6

PUBLISHER'S NOTE

Acknowledgements

As always, I would like to thank Kate for without her, none of this would be possible.

Dedication

This novel is dedicated to all who have been touched in one way or another by the COVID19 pandemic. My heart goes out to you all.

CHAPTER ONE

Jess glanced to her left. "How are you doing over there, Legs?"

"Fine, Wheels, just fine," Alex huffed through gritted teeth. "Why? Having trouble keeping up? I could slow down if you need me to."

"You wish." Jess gave her chair an extra burst of speed, hands burning in her black leather gloves. Her heart hammered against the inside of her chest and her lungs burned with every breath, but it certainly felt good to be in a competition again since the world shut down over three years ago. And the Run Thru the Rapids 10K was the perfect race to get back into the swing of things, short and sweet.

A lot had changed during the pandemic. Jess had been out of work for over a year. Infinity Books had been forced to close for several months, and even when they reopened, it was only with a skeleton crew. Without any need for the Espresso Book Machine, Jess had been laid off. As fun as her unofficial vacation had been at first, she'd quickly grown bored. She could only watch *Doctor Who* so many times.

But her woes paled in comparison to what Alex had been through. As an ER doctor, Alex had been on the frontline. For the first six months, she'd lived at the hospital, under quarantine since she worked with COVID patients. The only way Jess had been able to see her was on FaceTime and the occasional glimpse through locked windows. It had taken a toll on Alex, watching patient after patient gasp their last breath alone. Not a moment went by that Jess hadn't worried Alex herself would become the patient.

That was what made today so special. For the first time since it had all begun, it felt as if they had regained some sense of normalcy. Here she was beside Alex, doing what they both loved.

"What do you want to eat tonight?" Alex's voice broke her from her deep thoughts.

Jess glanced beside her. "You've got to be kidding me, Legs. Here we are in the middle of a 10K run and you're thinking about your stomach?"

Alex did her best to look nonchalant as she pushed herself to keep pace. "Sure, why not? I thought maybe we could celebrate."

"Celebrate? Celebrate what? Not keeling over during the race? Are you sure you're feeling okay?" Jess narrowed her eyes, looking for the telltale signs of heat exhaustion—or worse yet, heat stroke. Alex was well known for pushing herself far beyond her limits, so it wouldn't be a complete surprise if she were loopy from dehydration. But Alex looked fine—no blotchy skin, no lack of sweat, nothing.

Alex flashed her a bright, wide smile. "Never felt better. I'm here with my beautiful, loving, and oh so talented girlfriend—what's not to celebrate?"

"Hmmm." Jess slowed up, eyeing Alex skeptically. She was up to something. Jess could tell from the cat-that-ate-the-canary grin plastered across her face. The woman was never good at hiding her feelings. She was even worse at keeping a secret. "I'm not buying it. You're planning something. I can see it on your face. Now, out with it."

Alex slapped her hand to her chest, her mouth open in exaggerated shock. "I would never—"

"Cut the crap, Legs. You can't fool me. You're even worse at keeping a secret than Jordan." Jess's younger sister (by ten months) was notorious for spilling secrets.

"Hey, I'm not that bad, Wheels." Alex feigned righteous indignation.

Jess couldn't keep from laughing as she watched Alex's mock outrage. Even with all her bluster, Jess knew Alex was only joking. This was one of the things that she enjoyed most about their relationship. Though it may not have started out that way, they had reached the point where they could tease without worry of offending.

Alex threw up her arms. "Fine, you win, I'll tell you. I *did* have something in mind."

"Oh? And what might that be?"

With her most salacious grin, Alex leaned in close. "Let's just say that it'll require the removal of your gloves."

Jess's eyes grew wide. Her face flushed in a way that had nothing to do with running a 10K. There was only one reason she removed her gloves.

"That is, if you can catch me." With that, Alex took off like a cat doing a victory lap after using the litterbox, quickly leaving Jess behind.

Momentarily stunned, Jess stared after Alex, who cackled with laughter as she pulled away. With a wicked smile, Jess thrust herself forward with a mighty push. She hadn't seen Alex run this fast before, and this late in a 10K. It was all she could do to pull even with her.

They were on the last kilometer. "You don't think maybe we should ease up a little, Legs?"

Without looking over, Alex pushed on. "Never!"

"Fine, but don't blame me when you can't walk tomorrow." When Alex got like this, there was no reasoning with her. She clearly had something to prove. The only thing Jess could do was try her best to keep up.

Half a kilometer to go. Alex continued to run full out, her focus straight ahead. Jess's hands burned as if she'd set her gloves aflame. How Alex was able to keep up this crazy pace was beyond Jess, but she would be damned if she let up now. She pushed harder and harder, her shoulders and arms begging for mercy.

Two hundred meters. The finish line was right up the street. They continued pushing each other, jockeying for position. Sweat streamed down Jess's face, running into her eyes. Each breath felt like a flame exiting her lungs.

One hundred meters. People lined the sides of the street, cheering them on. Jess barely heard them.

Alex thundered on with a singular determination. "Trouble keeping up, Wheels?"

"You wish! Just try to catch me." Jess pushed with all her might to stay even with Alex.

Fifty meters. Twenty-five. Ten. They crossed the finish line. As Jess rolled to a stop, Alex dropped to her hands and knees, her head tucked down. Jess spun around. "Oh shit, I've killed her."

Jess rolled up to Alex, who was still huffing deeply. Medical staff ran toward them. "Legs, Legs, talk to me. Come on, Alex, are you okay?" There was a note of panic in her voice.

Alex slowly looked up, a bright smile on her lips. She then took a knee and lifted a small box as Jess struggled to comprehend what was happening. Had Alex completely lost her mind? Had she finally succumbed to heat stroke? Then it dawned on her. Alex on one knee, a small box held aloft. Jess clapped her gloved hands to her mouth.

"Will you?" Alex looked into her eyes expectantly.

"Wha...wha...*what?*" All Jess could do was stammer as her mind worked to take in the scene in front of her.

"Will you marry me, Wheels?" Alex flipped open the small box.

* * *

A collective hush fell over the crowd. Alex's pulse thundered in her ears. The moment drew out. She bit her bottom lip. If her legs hadn't felt like jelly before, they certainly did now.

Jess stared back, her mouth slowly opening and closing.

Alex's stomach flip-flopped. Why wasn't Jess saying anything? Oh God, had she read the signs wrong? They'd been together over four years, lived together almost as long. It felt like the time was right, the time was now. Hadn't they even talked about getting married once everything with the pandemic had settled down? If working at a hospital during the biggest health crisis of her career had taught her anything, it was that life was fleeting. So, if not now, when?

She raised her eyebrows. "Well, what do you say, Wheels? Shall we get hitched?"

Jess smiled, tears running down her cheeks—although if Alex were to point that out, she had no doubt Jess would claim it was sweat from the run. Jess reached out and cradled Alex's chin in her palm. "Yes, Legs. A thousand times, yes."

Alex leaped to her feet and pumped both fists into the air. "Woohoo! She said yes!" She shouted at the top of her lungs.

The crowd clapped and hollered. Above it all, Jordan let out a squeal of excitement that carried up and down the block. And before they even had a chance to move, they were besieged.

Jordan threw her arms around her sister and pulled her in tight. "I am so happy for the two of you. It's about time, too. After all that you have been through, both of you, you deserve happiness." Her voice grew thicker with each word, and Jordan quickly blotted away her tears.

"Jordan, don't you dare cry. You'll make me cry." Jess hugged her tight.

Jordan's husband stepped in to lighten the mood. With his big, bear-like voice, he spoke with his usual lighthearted exuberance. "What this occasion needs is a celebration. How about we all meet back at Mom and Dad's for a barbecue?"

Jordan cleared her throat, her voice still heavy. "My husband, the backyard chef. Any excuse to barbecue."

"You know it, babe." Tim leaned in and kissed his wife on the neck below her left ear, making her giggle and squeal like a schoolgirl.

Jess laughed at their antics. Before Alex, she never thought she could have the same. But now, not only did she have a loving girlfriend, but that girlfriend was her fiancée. She smiled. Fiancée. She liked how that sounded. Until Alex, she would never have even hoped to dream. She gave Alex's hand a gentle squeeze. "So, what do you say, Legs? You up for some barbecue?"

Alex's stomach growled as if on cue. "Sure thing, Wheels. But only if I get a shower first. I smell like a whipped swamp donkey."

Jess laughed and eyed her up and down with a fiercely appraising look. "You look like a very cute swamp donkey to me."

Behind Jess, Jordan made gagging gestures. "You two really are too much. My poor innocent ears."

"Like you should talk, sis." Jess playfully slapped Jordan with her gloved hand.

Raucous laughter broke out as Jordan's face flamed red. She shrugged and gave a sheepish grin. "What can I say?"

Tim tapped his watch, clearing his throat. "We'll all meet at five. Don't be late."

With a quick round of hugs and more congratulations, they said goodbye.

Jess pulled Alex close. "What do you say we go home and I can wash my cute swamp donkey?"

Alex ruffled Jess's sweaty hair. "Sounds good to me, my love."

* * *

Alex walked into the bathroom naked after shedding her sweaty running clothes, bare feet clapping on the tile floor. Jess was in her chair, also sans clothing, holding a transfer board and getting ready to slide herself into the shower. Alex rushed forward.

"Hold on, babe, I can help you with that. That is, if you would like me to." She bit her lower lip, waiting. Jess could be very sensitive about receiving help from others, especially if that help involved anything that might compromise her sense of independence.

Jess looked up at Alex and, seeing the uncertainty on her

face, smiled and motioned her forward. "Actually, after a day like today, I wouldn't mind feeling your big, strong arms around me."

Alex bent down and carefully scooped Jess into her arms, thoroughly enjoying Jess's bare skin pressed firmly against hers. She snuck a quick kiss, brushing her lips lightly against Jess's forehead. Once she'd helped Jess onto the shower stool, she went to step back, but Jess clasped her hands tightly on Alex's bare bottom, pulling her back in close. Jess nestled her chin into Alex's little racing stripe of pubic hair and tenderly kissed her along the top of her mons.

Alex tried to pull back, but Jess held tighter. "Oh, Jess, not that I wouldn't like that very much, but I'm all gross and sweaty."

Jess looked up into Alex's eyes, a devilish little grin on her lips. "You're still sexy and beautiful to me. Maybe I don't mind."

"Ewwww. But I do." Alex wrinkled her nose. "At least let me shower first."

"Okay, but you better hurry. You know I don't like to be kept waiting." Jess made a low sound in the back of her throat, halfway between a purr and a growl.

Alex took a step back in surprise, her eyes googling. "That I do, Jess. That I do." Jess's assertiveness had caught her off guard—not that she was going to complain. Even now as she looked into the eyes of the woman she loved, she could see a deep hunger there, causing her own arousal to kick into overdrive. Without wasting any more time, Alex twisted on the shower to a medium cool and fumbled with her favorite lavender-scented body wash, trying not to drop the bottle as her hands trembled.

Jess mirrored Alex's actions, turning on her own shower to her desired temperature. Alex lathered her body, washing away the heat and grime of the day. She watched as Jess did the same, her face turned up to the soft spray. Built specifically for Jess, the shower boasted dual heads and controls, the second of which were designed for a sitting position. The built-in seat made it easy for Jess to shower independently; however, the room for two came in handy also. The brown earthen tiles reminded Alex of a fancy luxury spa, someplace that doled out thick, fluffy towels with matching monogrammed bathrobes. Of course, the best part was sharing the experience with Jess.

"You'd better hurry up there, Legs." With her eyes closed, Jess rinsed her hair. "I'm a woman with needs."

Alex laughed at Jess's boldness. "Hold your horses, Wheels. Didn't your mama teach you that good things come to those who wait?" Maybe it was because she had proposed that Jess was feeling extra frisky. Or maybe it was post-race adrenaline. Or maybe just good old-fashioned horniness. Whatever the reason, Alex was beginning to regret agreeing to a family barbecue.

When she finished washing, Jess beckoned Alex closer. "Come here, you sexy woman." She reached out and took Alex's hand, tugging her near.

"We don't have time for this." The words weren't easy to say. Alex wanted nothing more than to enjoy a fun tryst in the shower after a long day of running. "Seriously, we're going to be late."

"Maybe I don't care." Jess bit her lower lip, giving Alex a deeply sultry look. Then with a giggle, she continued. "What are they going to do, start without us? We're the guests of honor, remember?"

"Still…" Alex was torn. "I don't know… Won't they…"

"You doth protest too much, my love," Jess said cajolingly, slowly turning Alex around until she faced away. She then wrapped her arms around Alex and slid her right hand down over Alex's taut stomach until her fingers rested over Alex's center. With deft, strong fingers, she pushed in deeper, slowly increasing the pressure.

Alex gasped. Her legs suddenly felt rubbery, even more than they had after their run. She threw out a hand to stabilize herself. She was completely at Jess's mercy. She couldn't move if she had to, not that she wanted to. As Jess began to circle her fingers slowly, Alex moaned, pleasure radiating out as her center engorged. "Oh God, Jess, you don't know what you're doing to me."

"Oh, but I think I do." With a laugh, Jess patted her strong fingers against Alex's swollen, throbbing clitoris.

Alex squealed at the explosion of pleasure and nearly fell to her knees. She would have, too, if not for Jess's strong arms holding her up. She wasn't sure how much more of this she could take. At the same time, she didn't want it to end. Jess seemed to know exactly what her body needed. Alex had never had another lover so in tune with her desires. It was almost as if they shared a telepathic bond, an unspoken exchange of sexual give-and-take. Jess increased her pace and Alex bent double, supporting herself against the side of the shower. She drew in quick, short breaths. The sensation was building fast. Any moment now. And then it began, an explosion that radiated out from her center, tingling every part of her body. A deep flush rushed from her small, firm breasts up her neck to her cheeks and forehead. It felt as if she could boil water on her flaming skin. She shuddered, her body still bent in half—once, twice, three times, four—she lost track of how many. She convulsed with pleasure, again and again, her breath growing ragged in her throat, until it began to slowly subside. Finally, she was able to stand upright on her own and turned to face Jess. "That was… That was…"

"Good?" Jess lifted an eyebrow.

"Oh yeah. You can say that again." Alex nodded vigorously. She took a deep breath and quickly blew it out. "Wow. Now it's your turn."

"As much as I would like that, we really should get going or everyone will begin to talk. We don't want to give Jordan any more reason to speculate on our love life."

Jordan was always teasing them about their intimacy. Although a bit too nosy for her own good, there was no one who was more fiercely protective of Jess than Jordan, and since Alex came into Jess's life, Jordan was equally as protective of her. Still, Jordan's greatest passion seemed to be to make her older sister blush. "You're probably right there, Jess, but that's not fair. I really want to return the favor."

Jess smiled softly. "How about later when we get back home. That way we don't have to rush." Her devilish grin returned. "Plus I've got a few ideas I wouldn't mind trying out."

Alex took a step back. "Really? Do tell."

Jess merely grinned wider and shook her head. "I don't think so. It might ruin the surprise."

"Oh?" Alex's curiosity was nearly palpable. In the time they'd been together, Jess had become quite a bit more adventurous and less self-conscious. Their first time together, she'd been reluctant to remove her leather gloves. They had certainly grown a lot together over the past few years. It was hard to believe that Jess was the same person as that angry, highly sensitive woman she'd managed to offend the first time they met. "Come on, Wheels. At least give me a hint. You know how I am with secrets."

Jess laughed and pinched her side. "Yes I do, but as you said earlier, good things come to those who wait."

Alex grumbled, causing Jess to laugh even harder.

"You'll survive, Legs, trust me. Now how about we get out of here and go get something to eat?" Jess gave her a salacious wink and lowered her voice. "You're going to need your strength later. Besides, the sooner we get there, the sooner we can get back home."

Alex didn't need telling twice. She spun around, flipped off the water, and grabbed two fresh towels in one fluid motion. She tossed one towel to Jess. They quickly dried themselves. When Jess finished, Alex leaned forward. "Would you like me to help you again?" She nodded toward Jess's chair. One thing Alex had learned very early on was to never make assumptions. Just because Jess had let her help her into the shower didn't mean she desired help getting out.

Jess thought for a brief second. "Sure, I would like that."

Alex bent forward and Jess threw her arms around Alex's neck. Making sure she had her feet beneath her, Alex lifted Jess, cradling her legs and naked bum in her arms. Very gently, she stepped out of the shower and lowered Jess into her chair. She gave Jess a kiss on the forehead before standing up straight. "Let's get a move on. Like you said, the sooner we get there, the sooner we get back home."

CHAPTER TWO

"Here come the brides." Jordan jumped up and yelled exuberantly as Jess and Alex made their way through the glass sliding door to the wonderfully landscaped backyard. "What took you two so long? Practicing for your wedding night?"

"Jordan!" Linda exclaimed from where she sat on the cedar deck in a comfortable chaise lounge. She waggled a reproving finger at her youngest daughter.

Jess glanced sideways in time to see a deep blush form over Alex's cheeks. She reached out and took Alex's hand and gave it a reassuring squeeze. "Never mind Jordan, babe. You know how she is—no couth whatsoever."

"Hey," Jordan protested, pooching out her lower lip.

"There is no use in denying it, little sis. Everyone knows it's true."

Tim turned from the smoking grill to face them. Wearing an apron and a hat that read "Grill Master," he looked comical in his seriousness as he jabbed the long grill fork in Jordan's direction. "She's got you there, sweetheart."

"Watch it, mister, or there will be no fun for you tonight."

"Jordan! What am I going to do with you?" Linda exclaimed again, this time dropping her head into her hands and shaking it.

Laughter rolled around the backyard. With Alex's hand still in hers, Jess rolled across the deck to the empty lounge chair beside her mom, where Alex took a seat. It was good that Alex was as accepting as she was. Although Jess loved her little sister absolutely, Jordan could be a bit much. Jess was just happy that Alex took it all in stride. Nothing was more important than family to her.

Jordan plopped down on the ottoman in front of Jess and Alex, staring at both of them with a wide, excited smile. "So, have you to come up with a date yet? Maybe a June wedding? Or...oh...oh...I know, what about a fall wedding, sometime mid-October when the leaves are changing?"

Jess stared at her sister, flabbergasted. "Jordan, good grief, we just got engaged today. How about we let it sink in a little bit first?"

Jordan waved her off with a casual flick of her wrist. "You can't start too soon, believe me. There are so many things to do. There's the caterer, the cake, the reception hall—you'd better book that early before they all fill up. Then there's the dresses, or I don't know, will it be tuxes for you two?" Jordan was picking up speed with each word. "There's a DJ, or maybe even a live band. Don't forget to book a church, or are you going to have an outdoor wedding? Oh, an outdoor wedding would be lovely, especially if the leaves are changing. Can't forget the invitations. Oh, oh, oh, you've gotta have mani-pedis for the wedding party, not to mention the flowers..."

"I thought the proposal was going to be the hard part." Alex swallowed, looking decidedly pale. Her voice had a slight tremble to it.

Everyone laughed and Jordan continued unimpeded. "Sweetie, the proposal is just the beginning. Now the real work begins. A wedding is a *huge* deal. You know what you need? You need a wedding planner. Maybe even a whole team."

"Jesus, Jordan, let us let it soak in for a bit. It hasn't even been four hours yet. Let us enjoy being fiancées for at least one day before all the craziness starts." Jess took Alex's hand and gave it another reassuring squeeze.

"But, but—"

Pete turned from the grill—watching Tim suspiciously out of the corner of his eye as Tim beat out the flames that had erupted from the steaks with a grill mitt—and cleared his throat. "Leave them alone, Jordan. It's their wedding, not yours. They'll figure it out themselves, I'm sure."

Jordan pooched out her lip again at their dad's admonition. Jess was grateful though. And her dad was right—they would figure it out themselves, together. And if they needed any help with anything, she had no doubt that Jordan would be right there with wedding bells on.

Just then, Tim called out from the grill, "Steaks are ready. Come and get it."

Jess gave a sigh of relief, grateful for her brother-in-law's timing. It didn't come any too soon either. From the look of it, Alex's head was about to explode. As everyone stampeded toward the grill, Jess held back. She pulled Alex in close and whispered in her ear. "Don't worry about what Jordan was saying. She gets really excited about stuff like this. It won't be that bad, I guarantee."

Alex looked deeply into her eyes. "Promise?"

"Promise."

After they finished eating, everyone sat back in blissful fullness as the sun began to set over the distant trees. It was still too early in the year for bugs. Come July, there would be mosquitoes the size of small sparrows, but for now the yard remained blessedly free of the little bloodsuckers. The air had a bit of a chill to it as the backyard grew darker. Jess shivered and snuggled in closer to Alex, who wrapped an arm around her while they listened to her dad and Tim debate the prospects of the Final Four. Her mom and Jordan were discussing the upcoming Easter holidays. Jess wasn't paying much attention to what was being said. She was busy enjoying the warmth of her fiancée sitting beside her. Thoughts of what she had planned for later danced through her head. She shifted in her seat as the mental images sent her blood rushing south.

Alex stifled a yawn behind her hand. Jess patted her on the knee and sat upright. "I think I should get this sleepy girl home and put her to bed."

"I *bet* you're going to put her to bed. Wink, wink. Nod, nod."

"*Jordan!*" Linda shot a pointed look at her youngest daughter. "You are simply incorrigible. I swear they must have switched you in the nursery at the hospital. My sweet little girl is probably out there somewhere right now, *being behaved!*"

Jordan puffed up her chest, looking pleased with herself. "Then I guess I'm lucky that it's been way too long to give me back."

"Some days, I tell you." Linda merely shook her head. "Some days."

Everyone laughed. Jess wiped away tears. "Never change, Jordan." As far as she was concerned, her sister could be a stand-up comedienne. If Jordan ever took her shtick to the stage, Jess had no doubt that she would be a big hit.

After a quick round of hugs and goodbyes, Jess wheeled down the front walk with Alex at her side. "Did you have a good time?"

"Ye-ah-ah-es. Sorry." Alex stifled another yawn. "Yes I did."

Jess giggled and slapped Alex on the bum as she raced past with a sudden burst of speed. "You'd better stop that yawning, Legs. If there was one thing that Jordan was right about, I most definitely am going to put you to bed." She spun around as she reached the car. "Wink, wink."

* * *

By the time they got home, Alex was no longer tired in the least. All she could think about was Jess's earlier hint at trying something new in the bedroom. What could Jess possibly be thinking of? Once they were inside, she couldn't take it any longer. She took Jess by the hand and spun her around, as if they were dancing a wheelchair version of the foxtrot. They cut a wide circle through the living room.

"I had a great time tonight, Wheels. But I'm glad we're finally alone." She bit her lower lip. The anticipation was making her stomach do flip-flops.

"Me too." Jess spun a complete three-sixty, coming to rest directly in front of Alex. "What do you say to shedding all these clothes and trying a different type of dancing?"

"Oh baby, you know what I like." Alex held out her arm in a grand gesture and bowed toward the bedroom. "After you, m'lady."

Alex followed Jess up the hallway. Her stomach was tense, and a shiver ran through her body. Although they had messed around in the shower earlier—or more precisely, Jess had messed around with her—Alex was looking forward to returning the favor, more than once even. Next to the bed, she hooked her fingers into the hem of her shirt, meaning to tug it over the top of her head.

"No, no, no." Jess held up a finger and waggled it at Alex. "Don't you dare start stripping yet. You're mine, remember? I'm going to do that."

Alex raised an eyebrow. She liked how Jess was thinking. Normally one to take the lead in lovemaking, Alex wasn't going to steal Jess's thunder. No, not at all. Lowering her eyes, Alex chewed her bottom lip, doing her best to look seductive. "What would you like me to do then?"

Jess sat for a second as if thinking. "How about you sit on the bed and get comfortable? Get propped up with a couple of pillows." Jess waggled her finger at Alex again. "But no undressing."

Alex climbed onto the bed and stacked one pillow on top of the other, punching them into a comfortable shape. When they were adjusted to her satisfaction, she turned around and leaned back, stretching her legs out in front of her and crossing her arms behind her head. "Like this?"

"That'll do." Jess wheeled closer and transferred herself onto the duvet, first tugging one leg and then the other until she was firmly seated beside Alex. She then rolled onto her side, propping herself up with her left arm, and slowly traced along the bottom hem of Alex's shirt with her right hand, tickling sensitive flesh beneath the soft cloth.

Alex giggled and squirmed. Jess's fingers brushing over her stomach raised goose bumps over her entire body. The sensation was intoxicating. Alex sucked in a quick breath through clenched teeth. She could stay right there forever. And this was only the beginning.

Jess guided her fingers under the hem of Alex's shirt and slowly, teasingly, worked the fabric up Alex's chest until her green lace bra was exposed. Alex closed her eyes. She could feel the cool air against her warm skin. Jess lightly traced a fingertip up the center of Alex's chest, from her navel to just below her bra. Back and forth. Back and forth. Alex's breath hitched in her chest. Her heart pounded. Jess took the shirt in both hands and lifted. Alex raised her arms to assist and in one swift motion, her shirt was gone, flung to the far reaches of the room.

Still with her eyes closed, Alex felt Jess's hands slide up her sides until they rested over her breasts. She gasped as Jess flicked her hard, erect nipples through the silky green lace of her bra—once, twice, three times. It was all she could do not to throw her arms around Jess and pull her in tight, tearing her clothes off in ragged, torn strips.

Alex leaned forward at Jess's prompting. The cool air felt wonderful against the hot flesh of her breasts and nipples as Jess slid her hands around Alex's back and deftly unlatched her bra with only her right hand, her fingers snapping the clasp in one smooth, fluid movement. Alex's eyes fluttered open for a second, but Jess quickly brushed a hand over her face. "No peeking, at least not yet." Her voice was low, sultry.

Jess traced the back of her hand along the side of Alex's face. With a moan low in her throat, Alex leaned into the touch, hoping for more—more pressure, more sensation—more. As if sensing her intentions, Jess pulled away and Alex whimpered. This wasn't fair. She needed touch. She needed stimulation. She needed Jess.

But Jess wasn't going to rush anything. Good things come to those who wait. She had said that earlier. While that might be the case, Alex wasn't sure she would be able to wait much longer. Her center swelled with arousal, and she could feel the heat even through her jeans and green silk panties. Jess had to know what she was doing to her. Those light touches, gentle caresses. The not-so-subtle promise of more—but when?—and what? Just the anticipation was nearly driving her body over the edge. If she weren't careful, she would climax right there, from only Jess's semi-innocent touches.

With her eyes still closed, Alex waited, wondering what was coming next. Suddenly, her left nipple was sucked into Jess's hungry mouth. The muscles of her stomach and center tensed. Her nipple tingled before the feeling radiated throughout her entire breast, hot and cold at the same time. Or was it cold then hot? Ice then flame. She wasn't sure. She didn't care. It felt wonderful and she arched her back, pushing her chest forward, seeking more of Jess's mouth on her swollen breast. Oh please. Yes. Yes.

And then Jess's mouth was gone.

Alex had just enough time for disappointment to register in her sluggish, besotted brain when her right nipple was drawn into Jess's mouth, this time with more suction. As Jess drew Alex's hard nipple deeper and deeper into her mouth, she reached over and took her wet right nipple between her thumb and index finger. She rubbed the erect flesh between her fingers, working it back and forth, then gave it a firm pinch—a sudden, sharp, piercing sensation.

Alex moaned—loudly, unabashedly, gutturally. Hell, she didn't care if the neighbors could hear. Or even the entire town. None of that mattered. She was so close, just a little more and she'd tip over the edge, pleasure would rush through her body, sweet, sweet escape.

Jess must have sensed how close she was because she drew back, releasing both nipples. "Oh no you don't. No coming yet, my love."

Alex opened her eyes, pleading. This was pure torture. She opened her mouth, but before she could utter a word, Jess silenced her with a finger to her lips. "Patience. Why don't you help me with my shirt."

She didn't need asking twice. Alex sat upright and hooked her fingers under Jess's shirt hem. She gave it an almighty tug.

Jess burst out laughing. "Whoa, whoa, whoa, tiger. Not so fast."

Alex gave a little growl deep down in her throat. She'd show Jess just how much of a tiger she could be. She bent forward and took the hem of Jess's shirt into her teeth, pressing her forehead against Jess's chest and nuzzling her nose between Jess's breasts. Jess snorted a raucous guffaw, grabbing Alex's head, a hand on each side, and thrashing backward. She squealed, much like a young girl who has just discovered that if she goes high enough on the swings, it almost feels as if she can fly for a brief second.

"Down, girl, down," Jess howled through her titters.

Alex pulled back, the hem of Jess's shirt still between her teeth, and looked her in the eye.

Jess wrinkled her nose at her. "I didn't realize I had a wild animal in here with me."

Alex let the soft fabric fall from her mouth. "Wild animal, huh? You haven't seen anything yet, sweetheart." More slowly, she lifted Jess's shirt, first exposing her stomach, taut and muscular from the core exercises Jess did to keep in shape. Next, a no-nonsense black sports bra. Jess lifted her arms as Alex lifted the shirt higher, completely obscuring Jess's face but exposing her shoulders, wide and deeply muscled from her time in her wheelchair. Alex eyed those shoulders with a smile. They were one of her favorite features, along with Jess's strong arms. Jess mumbled as her shirt caught on her chin and Alex gave it a little tug. Suddenly free, the shirt shot off Jess's head. Alex flung it behind her without a second glance.

Before Alex could peel off Jess's sports bra, Jess crossed her arms, snagged the bra with her thumbs, and tore it over her head.

Alex raised an eyebrow. "Who's in a hurry now?"

Jess wrapped her arms around Alex's neck and pulled her in close until their bare breasts were pressed together. "Hush." She laughed softly.

* * *

Jess had been planning this moment all day. Now that the time had arrived, she thought she might chicken out. Would it even be possible? Would it work? Would it be stupid? She didn't know. But as she stared deep into Alex's intense light blue eyes, she regained her courage. She could do this. With Alex, she could do anything.

"Why don't you help me out of these jeans?" Jess leaned back on her hands and lifted her bottom off the bed.

Alex perched herself on her knees and fumbled at the button, doing her best to unfasten the jeans. "Damn, frickin', stupid, come on." She mumbled under her breath as she worked.

"Need some help there, Legs?" Jess laughed.

"No. I can get this." Alex gritted her teeth. "You're probably thinking I failed lesbianism one-oh-one or something." Just then the button released. "Aha!" She let out a whoop of triumph.

"I had total confidence in you, babe. I'm sure you got a very good grade in lesbianism one-oh-one."

"Top of the class." Alex blew on the knuckles of her right hand and then rubbed them against her bare chest.

"You may have gotten the button, but you've left the job half done." Jess was still propped up on her hands. "You don't want me to begin to question that class standing, do you?"

"Absolutely not." Alex leaned forward, hooked her thumbs under the waistband, and in one quick motion, slid both jeans and panties over Jess's hips and down her thighs.

Jess lowered her bottom to the sheets and Alex worked the material carefully over her numb legs. She watched Alex with a smile—the tenderness, the gentleness, the caution—touched by her actions. Alex needn't be so careful. It wasn't as if Alex would cause her pain. When Alex finally whisked the last bit of fabric over her ankles, Jess sat forward, her naked body hot against the cooler air. Her nipples peaked even more, whether from the chill or arousal she wasn't sure.

"Okay, now it's your turn." She licked her lips lasciviously, tracing the tip of her tongue over her bottom teeth.

"Yes, ma'am." Alex hopped up on her knees and in a flash, unfastened her jeans and slid them over her hips, first one side then the other, making quite a show of it, one that Jess could certainly appreciate. Once she'd worked her jeans to her knees, Alex rolled over on her back and pushed them the rest of the way off. She crossed her legs and faced Jess. "How about that?"

"That'll do." Jess smiled. She loved the ease they had with each other. When she was with Alex, there was no reason to be self-conscious. And she knew Alex felt the same. That was very important, especially with her injury. From her experience, disability and self-consciousness were almost constant companions. She eyed Alex up and down, taking in the full beauty of her naked body. "Yes, that'll certainly do."

Before she could lose confidence, she reached out and pulled Alex onto her as she lay back. When her head hit the pillow, Alex tucked in beside her, leaning on her right arm, and smiled down at her. Jess snaked her fingers into Alex's hair and drew her face closer, opening her mouth as their lips met. She sucked in Alex's breath, tasting the leftover tang of the A.1. Steak Sauce Alex had smothered her T-bone in earlier. The garlic and onion tingled on the tip of her tongue. She thrust her tongue deep into Alex's mouth. Alex groaned as she twisted her tongue around Alex's, a swirling dance of slipperiness. Her stomach tightened as she traded places with Alex, this time sucking Alex's tongue inside of her mouth. Her body responded, breasts swelling, the sensation almost painful but at the same time, wonderful. With her free hand, she pulled Alex's hand to her aching left breast. The pressure sent a twinge through her breast and body, but she wanted more, needed more. Jess placed her hand over Alex's and increased the pressure, encouraging Alex to grind her hand against the soft swell of her breast. This wasn't a time to be gentle. Oh no, she didn't need gentle at all. She needed fierce, animalistic coupling—nothing less.

Jess pulled back from Alex, their lips making a loud slurping sound. Her chest heaved as her heart pounded. It was now or never. She wasn't sure her plan would work, but what would it hurt to give it a go? If nothing more, Alex was sure to like it. "Hey, Legs." Her voice was heavy, her heart trying to leap up her throat with each word. "I've got an idea if you're up for it." She held her breath, waiting for a reply.

Alex's eyes were only half open when she looked down at her. "What do you have in mind, Wheels? Is this the surprise you alluded to earlier?"

Jess chewed on her lower lip. "Yeah. But I'm not sure it'll work. It might not. It's just something I've been thinking about lately. I think you'll like it, but promise me you won't laugh."

Alex reached out and cupped Jess's cheek in her hand, giving it a gentle squeeze. "Don't worry, babe. You can trust me. I'd never laugh at you."

Emboldened, Jess took a quick breath and then blurted it out. "How about you straddle me?"

Alex opened her eyes wide. "Like in—one leg on one side and one leg on the other?"

Jess giggled at the look on Alex's face, half serious and half excited. "Yeah, something like that. What I was thinking was to have you straddle me across my hips and we grind our mounds together."

"That won't hurt you, will it?"

Jess appreciated the concern, but this was a time for action. "Not at all. Are you up for it? Give it the old college try?"

"So, what you're saying is..."

"Ride me like a dime store pony, Legs."

Alex burst out laughing. "Really? A dime store pony, huh?"

"Giddy up. Yeehaw!" Jess grabbed Alex by the waist and guided her over until she was straddling her hips. Alex sat straight up on her knees, her legs folded behind her. She slowly lowered her body. Jess felt the increase of weight across her hips. Her injury had left her without much sensation in her lower body. However, with rehab and physical therapy, she'd regained a little bit of sensation. She'd also been trying some new types of therapies that seemed to be showing signs of success. She hadn't wanted to share it with Alex yet. But now was the big test.

Jess placed her hands on Alex's hips, feeling the pressure increase across her own hips and the heat of Alex's center against the top of her mons. Just that little bit of sensation excited her. Having a spinal cord injury could be a crapshoot when it came to feelings anywhere around or below the damage. But this she could feel. Warmth and pressure. And there was something else. Her mind raced. What was that other sensation? Dampness. That was it. She could feel dampness. Whether from her or Alex, she wasn't sure, but there was definitely something there. She closed her eyes, focusing on the feelings.

Slowly, she guided Alex forward and back, forward and back. Their mounds ground together. Alex moaned and Jess's heart rate increased. Alex was enjoying it. But not only that, she was enjoying it as well. With each stroke, a surge flowed through her body, starting from below her bellybutton and traveling up her chest and to her brain. The inside of her head felt like a fireworks show. *Ping, ping, ping.* Little explosions of pleasure.

Alex's breathing became rougher, more ragged. Jess glanced up at her. Alex's eyes were closed, and across her face, the grimaces of pleasure twisted the muscles beneath the skin. She was sure her expression was the same. Suddenly, Alex leaned forward, her hands coming to rest on Jess's breasts.

Jess gasped. The pleasure increased tenfold. Her breath hissed through her teeth. With the rise and fall of her chest, Alex squeezed and kneaded the soft flesh. Jess could barely take it. Her breasts felt as if they were on fire. Or was it ice? She wasn't sure. They were either burning or freezing. Whichever it was, it was intense—and welcome.

As the pace increased, Jess grasped Alex's hips firmer, grinding Alex against herself with more and more pressure. It became more fierce, more desperate. Jess sucked in breath after ragged breath. Air hissed past her teeth like a teakettle about to whistle. The way she felt, any moment and she'd whistle herself.

She stared up at Alex, who still had her eyes closed, but a deep flush was growing across her chest, neck, and cheeks. She was close to climax. It wouldn't take much more. Jess herself was right on the edge. It wasn't as if she couldn't climax since her injury. That hadn't been a problem. But this was different. It included more parts of her body somehow. The grinding pressure against her mons. The friction of their pubic hair rubbing together. The damp heat—she could feel that. Oh the heat. *Mmmm.* She bit her lower lip—hard. She wouldn't be surprised if she had drawn blood, but at that moment, she didn't care.

Alex moaned louder, the sound echoing off the walls. That was all the encouragement Jess needed. She wrapped her hands around Alex, grasped her ass with her strong fingers, and thrust Alex against her center with all the strength she could muster. Alex cried out.

As Alex climaxed, Jess felt herself approaching that cliff. Alex shuddered above her, but she wasn't quite there. So close. So very close. With almost animal instinct, she wrapped her arms tightly around Alex's waist, and with an urgency she had never felt, thrust Alex against her center. Once, twice. Oh god, oh god. Jess slammed her eyes shut. The fireworks in her head became thermonuclear explosions, complete with accompanying mushroom clouds of pleasure. She was sure the sounds escaping her throat were in a range that only dogs could hear. Wave after wave.

Alex fell against her chest, shuddering a little less with each spasm. Jess threw her head against the pillow. She clasped the blankets and squeezed with all her might. Her back was arched, supporting all of Alex's weight. Her muscles were tense. Pulses raced through her body. *Zap. Zap. Zap.* And then she collapsed with Alex still against her, both of them crashing to the sheets. It took several minutes before Jess got her breath back. It was a good thing she was in shape. If not, she would have probably had a heart attack. Finally, she rolled over, Alex sliding beside her.

Jess reached over with her free hand, smoothing a tousled bit of hair on Alex's sweat-soaked forehead. "So, Legs, how was that for a surprise?"

Alex smiled back at her, a look of completely satisfied exhaustion on her face. "You can surprise me like that anytime you want, Wheels. Anytime."

CHAPTER THREE

"So, how was your weekend?" Terra walked up to the Espresso Book Machine cradling a large stack of hardcover novels.

Jess rocked in her wheelchair, balancing only on the large back wheels with the front wheels dangling in the air. It was a favorite pastime of hers. "Not too bad, Terra. Pretty uneventful. Did a 10K run, got engaged, had really good sex—nothing big." She tried her best to sound nonchalant, but she couldn't help the smile creeping over her lips.

CRASH! The stack of hardcovers toppled from Terra's tattooed arms. "Whoa, whoa, whoa. Wait just a blasted second. You got *engaged?*" She bent down to pick up the books all around her on the floor.

"And had really good sex." Jess laughed, still rocking back and forth in her chair.

Terra shot her a wry look. "That's all fine and good, but tell me about getting engaged. Did you know it was going to happen? How did it happen? It *was* Alex, right?"

Jess let her chair thud down on the front wheels with a loud *clank*. "Oh, hardy har. Very funny, smartass. Of course it was Alex. Who else would it be?"

"I don't know. Maybe you met some hot guy and decided to run off with him."

Jess made gagging noises. "That's not funny at all, Terra. You'd better be careful or I'll tell Alex."

Terra stood up with the spilled books in hand and slid them onto the countertop. She turned back to Jess and waved her hands in front of her. "Don't you dare tell the good doctor on me. It was just a joke."

"A bad joke."

"That may be the case, but I don't want her mad at me." She clasped Jess's shoulder. "Now why don't we go over to the café, and you can tell me all about it. I want details."

Jess pointed to the Espresso Book Machine, which was chugging out a special print job in the center of the store. "I'd love to, but I've got to get this order done."

Terra glanced at the printing contraption and waved her off. "Oh, pishposh. That thing can chug along by itself for a while. This is more important. Besides, what are they going to do, fire us?"

Jess laughed. Terra had a point. There *were* benefits to being the owners' child. And Bob and Liz always treated Jess as family too. So, she could take a bit of time and share the good news with Terra properly.

At the café counter, they ordered drinks and snacks—a caramel frappé and blueberry scone for Jess and a macchiato and jalapeño bagel for Terra. They took a table next to the window while they waited for their order. Jess stared out the window at the customers coming and going. The store was doing brisk business for a Monday morning. It probably had to do with the unseasonably warm weather for late April. Without a cloud in the sky, the temperature had soared into the low eighties; however, if the weather predictions were correct, they'd be in for some wicked thunderstorms that afternoon. Jess only hoped they held off until she was home. Having to race to her car in a raging downpour would be a real bitch.

Before she had more time to reflect on possible adverse weather, their order arrived. Jess nodded to the barista, a young woman barely out of high school with pink-striped hair who must be a new hire. "Thanks."

The young woman glanced from Jess to her wheelchair and back before she quickly returned the smile, looking a little uncomfortable. She stammered. "Ah, ah, you're welcome."

Jess was used to the stares, though it still baffled her why some people were so awkward around someone in a chair. It wasn't as if she were about to run them over. And her spinal injury hadn't affected her intelligence. But some people—maybe even most—didn't know how to respond when confronted with someone who was disabled. Jess slowly shook her head as the barista scurried back behind the counter.

Terra was busy slathering an obscene amount of cream cheese on her jalapeño bagel. Jess could barely see the bagel beneath. She'd have a coronary if she ate that much rich cream cheese. "Got enough there?"

With a wide smile, Terra took a huge bite, nodding her head. "Uhhhh huhhhh." She mumbled with her mouth full. After a strained swallow, she pointed the cheese-covered plastic knife at Jess. "Now tell me, how did this come about? How did you get engaged? Did you pop the question?"

Jess nibbled at her scone much more daintily. "Actually, Alex was the one to pop the question. I had no idea she was going to do it either. We had just finished with the 10K and Alex went down on one knee." She laughed as she remembered. "I thought she had overdone it again."

"More like you went all out and she tried to keep up with you." Terra gave her a knowing look.

"Perhaps." She couldn't deny that she did tend to go all out, but this time it had been Alex who had pushed their pace. "Anyhow, there we were, Alex on one knee, me hoping that I hadn't killed her this time, and she looks up and holds out a little box."

Terra let out a squeal. "Oh, oh, oh. You've got to let me see it."

Jess slowly stripped off her leather glove and held her bare hand out to Terra, the engraved gold ring gleaming on her finger.

Terra's eyes narrowed. "What? No diamonds? You'd have thought being a doctor—"

Jess quickly cut her off. "It's not like that at all. We talked about it a long time ago and I told her that because of my gloves and always using my hands to get around, a diamond ring would be impractical. Alex remembered that when she picked this out."

Terra's look softened. "Oh, that's really sweet actually. I knew I always liked the good doctor for some reason."

Jess rolled her eyes. "Yeah, right. Whatever you've got to tell yourself, Terra."

Terra had been adamant to hate Alex when they first met. Jess couldn't really blame her, though. Alex hadn't made the best first impression with her snide, insulting attitude toward the handicapped. She hadn't made the best first impression either as far as that went, flying off the handle and jumping to conclusions.

Terra merely smiled in return. "So, when's the big day? Have you started making plans yet? There's a ton of things to consider, you know. Where are you having the ceremony? What are you going to wear? You need a dress—you'd look so beautiful in a dress. Oh, most importantly, where's the honeymoon? Has to be someplace romantic, like Washington DC."

Jess choked on her frappé, spewing it down her front. She grabbed a wad of napkins and blotted her "I Read Banned Books" T-shirt. "What could possibly be romantic about Washington DC?"

Terra threw more napkins to Jess without missing a beat. "There's the Smithsonian. That'll keep you busy for days. Then there's the Library of Congress. You can't miss that. Not to mention the National Gallery of Art. What could be more romantic than that?"

Jess dropped the sopping napkins on the table. "Sometimes I forget just how nerdy you are." As much as she hated to admit it, those locations sounded exciting to her also. Maybe Terra was onto something. She'd have to put DC on the list.

"Look who's talking, banned books girl." Terra puffed out her chest and gave Jess a knowing look. Her T-shirt read, "I Like Big Books and I Cannot Lie."

After their snack break, Jess wheeled herself back to the Espresso Book Machine. It was still chugging away on a novel by a local author about the history of the rapids in Grand Rapids. It was actually an interesting read, highlighting the use of the Grand River for the burgeoning furniture industry in the late eighteen hundreds. The best part of her work with the Espresso Book Machine was getting to help edit locally published authors, something she'd dearly missed during the pandemic shutdown. But most times, running the book machine gave her plenty of time to think, like now. Her mind was racing with unformed plans for the wedding. As everyone was so kind to point out, there seemed to be a crap-ton of things that needed to be worked out. Who would have guessed a wedding could be such a huge task? With a *thunk*, the completed book slid into the catch tray, mercifully breaking her thoughts. She took a deep breath and started another book printing.

As the machine began churning away again, Jess glanced over her shoulder. No one was looking at her. Great. She could sneak away for a bit and no one would ask. With a big shove, she whisked away, wheels humming on the tight industrial carpet. She pulled up in front of the wedding book section. Her jaw dropped. She had no idea there would be so many books. Where to begin? She ran her hand along the shelf. There were books on wedding planning, budget weddings, wedding photography, wedding etiquette. There was even one on the royal wedding of Kate and William. Good grief. Then she came across a couple of books on lesbian weddings. Miracles would never cease. Of all the possible books she thought she might find, she hadn't expected that. With all the anti-gay sentiment that seemed to have gained strength since the orange buffoon took office, to see books specifically aimed toward her warmed Jess's heart. Maybe there was hope.

Jess pulled the two books on lesbian weddings off the shelf and set them on her lap. She then grabbed a book on wedding invitations for good measure. She could use all the help she could get.

Jess wheeled back to the book machine with the books in her lap. She waited until she caught a glimpse of Terra walking through the store and waved her over.

"Hey, would you check these out for me?" Jess motioned to the books sitting on the table beside her. Then with an apologetic grin, she shrugged. "I'm not ready for everyone to know quite yet. You know how everyone is around here."

"And like they won't think I'm looking to get hitched."

"You're not even seeing anyone at the moment."

"You think that'll stop them? The last time I bought a book on gender studies in the workplace, there were rumors for months that I might be transitioning." Terra let out a raucous laugh. "You know, I'd probably look great as a dude, but that's just not me."

Jess looked up at Terra, her eyes pleading. "Please. I promise I'll make it up to you."

"Fine. Give them here. But when everyone throws me a bridal shower, it will be your fault." Terra took the books up to the cash register and returned a few minutes later with an Infinity Books shopping bag tightly folded shut.

Jess breathed a sigh of relief. At least she could keep it private for a little longer. "Thanks a million, Terra. You're the best."

"I know. I know. That's what friends are for. But you're going to owe me big time." Terra gave a devilish wink.

* * *

Dressed in a white lab coat and with a mask firmly over her lower face, Alex walked through the ER, her legs and back sore and stiff. Wowzers, what a night they'd had. Jess hadn't been kidding about her surprise being worth the wait. Even though she was now paying for it with sore muscles and a couple of contusions, it had been well worth it. The sexiest part had been how Jess had taken charge and communicated what she wanted. She hadn't realized that what they'd done was even possible.

"Hey doc, what's with the big dopey smile?" Maria, Alex's favorite nurse, came up behind her and clasped her on the back. She flipped a lock of long black hair just starting to streak with gray out of her eye.

"How on earth do you know that I'm smiling?" With the masks they all had to wear, Alex rarely got to see any of her coworkers' lower faces.

"It's the eyes, doc. It's the eyes." Maria gave her a wink. "Come on, let's grab some coffee during the lull."

Alex nodded appreciatively. They'd already had one car accident with thankfully minor injuries, a nasty farming accident with a sickle bar mower that resulted in the loss of a pinky toe, and a guy who had somehow gotten a flashlight stuck in a very embarrassing place ("Don't know how that happened, doc, I swear"), along with half a dozen sick kids just that morning, and it wasn't even noon. She stretched her arms behind her back. "That sounds heavenly, even with the sludge they call coffee here."

They sat in the breakroom, each with a cup of the hospital's best instant coffee. Alex kicked her feet up. Her legs twinged, causing her to wince.

Maria laughed. "Rough night, doc? That girlfriend of yours working you over hard?"

"Maria!" Alex hissed in a low voice, face growing hot. It couldn't be that obvious, could it? With the stupid grin permanently affixed to her lips, probably. It also didn't help that Maria tended to be nearly psychic when it came to such matters. She could sniff out a good story better than a Pulitzer Prize-winning investigator.

"Come on, doc. Spill. What's got you all twitterpated?"

Alex sipped her coffee before taking a deep breath. "You'll be happy to know that I finally did it."

"You popped the question?" Maria jumped from her chair and ran over to Alex. She threw her arms around her.

Alex stiffened under Maria's embrace. She had never really gotten the hang of hugs. "Yep. I finally did it right after the Run Thru the Rapids 10K. Had her sister there for the big moment too."

Maria jumped back. Her voice shook with excitement. "It's about time too. How long have you been contemplating that, a year now?"

"Yeah, something like that. Every time I just about got around to it, we'd have another freaking COVID outbreak, or a flu epidemic, or something else. I was beginning to think the universe was against it or something." Alex slowly shook her head. It had been increasingly difficult to keep it from Jess. She'd even had the ring all that time, hidden away at the bottom of the center console in her car.

"Don't worry about that, doc. You two are perfect for each other. It just took a little time to find the perfect moment." Maria nodded firmly.

"Thankfully now that the hard part is done, it should be smooth sailing. I mean, what could possibly go wrong from here on out?" Alex leaned back with her hands clasped behind her head. As far as she was concerned, they could get married anytime, even if it was just a quick trip to the justice of the peace. Hell, they could even do it during a lunch hour if they had to. All that mattered was that Jess was there.

"You think so, huh?" Maria eyed her suspiciously. "Take it from someone who's been through it a time or three, doc. It's never smooth sailing ahead when it comes to a wedding. I could tell you stories. The only thing worse than planning a wedding is maybe getting a mortgage, or bra shopping. With that, there's usually tears involved."

Alex burst out laughing and waved her off. "It won't be like that, not with us." They had gone through way too much for something as simple as a wedding to mess them up. She had seen Jess nearly die in front of her eyes. A wedding would be child's play compared to that.

"Okay, doc, I really hope so, for both your sakes." Maria patted her gently on the knee. "Do me a favor, though, won't you. Whatever you do, don't forget my invitation."

Alex flashed her a wide smile. "Don't worry, Maria, I'll make sure you're the first."

* * *

Jess zipped across the parking lot toward her car, the brown paper Infinity Books bag in her lap. Overhead, the clear blue sky had been replaced with angry, dark clouds. The breeze had picked up, blowing dead leaves and assorted trash across the tarmac. A hint of sour humidity and chill floated on the air. Apparently, the weather forecaster had been correct—there would indeed be a storm that afternoon.

Jess raced to her car. She didn't want to be caught in whatever Mother Nature was cooking up if she could help it. With any luck, she might even get home before it cut loose.

Jess had no more than opened the door to her car when the first clap of thunder rumbled in the distance. She looked up. The sky had a yellow-green tinge to it. "Great. Just what I don't need." She tossed the paper bag with her recent purchase in the passenger seat and transferred herself behind the wheel as fast as she could, sliding her butt in first followed by her legs. She leaned out, folded up her chair, and wrestled it into the back seat behind her. It was times like this where it was a real pain in the ass having to deal with a wheelchair.

With the sky darkening by the second, Jess pulled out of the parking lot and headed toward home. All around her, people were driving like monkeys. She hadn't been on the road ten seconds when someone cut her off. "Asshole!" Jess screamed at the driver and flipped him off. He didn't even notice. He was too busy cutting off another driver. Apparently, the first thunder boomer of the year had driven everyone batty.

Twenty minutes later, Jess pulled into her garage just as the first large raindrops pattered down on her windshield. At least she had gotten home before it started to downpour. She opened her door and was greeted by a loud, long roll of thunder, this time much closer. With a big sigh of relief, she wrestled her chair from behind her seat and opened it beside her car door. The wind was picking up outside and a large blue wheelie bin rolled up the street, its top flopping up and down like a giant gaping mouth trying to gulp in leaves. Jess watched it go as she transferred herself out of her car. If this wind kept up with the coming rain, it was going to be a real gully washer as her grandmama used to say. Another rumble of thunder shook the garage. With a shiver, Jess quickly grabbed the bag of books and wheeled up the ramp into her house, immensely thankful for an attached garage.

Jess rolled through the kitchen into the living room. She glanced up at the clock. Six thirty. Alex should be home anytime now if she hadn't gotten held up at the hospital or on the road. Since COVID, Alex's schedule was all over the place. Jess felt for her and all the other healthcare workers. These past few years had been hard on them all. It was no wonder so many of them were burned out. She wasn't sure how Alex did it, but she just kept chugging along, most of the time with a smile on her face, even when she was so tired that she looked as if she could drop at any moment.

It was now twilight dark, looking as if a weather-generated eclipse were taking place, and the skies seemed to open as the rain battered the house. A quick peek out the window showed the precipitation going more horizontal than vertical. Jess pulled out her cell phone and checked the live radar. Big angry clumps of red crawled over the map. Yellow boxes highlighted dozens of weather warnings throughout the area. Then she saw that most terrifying of all weather warnings. Jess winced, her heart rate increasing at the sight of the word. They were under a tornado warning until late that night. Already there had been some small twisters to the south. She bit her lip and glanced once more out the window. "Come on, Alex," she whispered to herself.

As if she'd been listening, Alex pulled in, her headlights glaring and her windshield wipers slapping at the rain. Jess leaned back in her chair and relaxed as Alex pulled into the garage. Any moment now and she'd come bounding into the kitchen. Jess waited. The thunder boomed. No Alex. A bright flash of lightning split the sky. No Alex. Wind and rain battered the windows. No Alex. What the hell? She should have been in by now. Jess wheeled into the kitchen. Just then, Alex burst through the door, her wet hair plastered to her head and her wet clothes hanging limply on her body.

Jess stared, her mouth gaping. "Wh...oh my God. What happened to you? You look like a drowned rat."

"Oh ha, ha, ha." Alex shook her head and water flew in all directions like a dog after a bath. "I'll have you know, I went to get the mail so it didn't get wet or blow down the street. Shocker, no mail."

Jess stifled a laugh behind her gloved hand. "Oh, babe, that's...that's...that's unfortunate."

Alex shot her a look of complete disbelief. "Ya think, smartass!"

Jess couldn't hold it in any longer. She snorted through her nose and burst out laughing. "I'm so sorry, Alex. I don't mean to laugh, but you should see yourself. It looks like you jumped in a pool with all your clothes on."

Alex lifted her arms, water dripping all over the floor. She made squelching noises with each movement. Alex shook her head, this time slowly. "At least jumping in a pool would have been fun. This is ridiculous."

Biting her bottom lip, Jess regained control. "Come on, babe, let's get you out of those wet clothes."

"Anything to get me naked, huh?" Alex smiled playfully.

Jess wheeled forward and took Alex by the cold, soggy hand. Just as she was about to lead Alex to the bedroom, a sizzling, bright flash of lightning burned through the windows, followed by a massive explosion of thunder that shook the entire house. Jess yelped and Alex jumped, clasping onto Jess's hand. The lights blinked, once, twice. Jess looked around. "That's not good. Maybe we'd better get you out of those clothes sooner than later."

"Yeah, you might be right." Alex was breathing hard, a shake to her voice.

They zipped up the hallway to the bedroom, Jess rolling along beside Alex. Once in the bedroom, Alex quickly stripped out of her clothes, tossing them into the hamper. Jess would have taken advantage of the situation, but with the storm howling outside, she would much rather snuggle into Alex's arms, feeling the strength and safety there.

"Why don't you change into your jammies as well." Alex tugged her favorite baggy sweatshirt over her head.

Jess pulled her eyes away as Alex's breasts disappeared under the soft fabric. Maybe later, maybe if the storm let up, she could set them free again. Jess lifted her arms and tugged her shirt over her head. As the material slid past her eyes, the lights blinked again—on, off—on, off—on. "Uh-oh. I sure hope we don't lose power."

"Jess!" Alex hissed as she slipped into her jammie pants. "Are you crazy? You're going to jinx—"

Another flash of lightning. Another clap of thunder. Another blink of the power—on, off—on, off…off.

"Well, shit." Alex's voice rang out through the darkness. "That's not good."

If her heart hadn't been beating so fast, Jess would have found the situation funny. But it was hard to laugh when every muscle in her chest had decided to contract all at once. With the lights out, lightning cast shadows on the walls like some disturbed funhouse attraction. Ever since she'd spent a hallucination-fueled night outside, clinging to life after crashing her racing wheelchair with only the shadows to keep her company, Jess hadn't liked the dark. Feeling a gentle hand squeeze her shoulder, she took a breath.

"It'll be okay, Jess. I'm here." Alex's voice was soft, sure.

Jess covered Alex's hand with hers. The warmth seemed to fill her, and her chest loosened. "Th…thanks."

"No problem, babe. I'll always be here for you."

With Alex's help, Jess quickly finished changing into her pajamas. The room was still dark, illuminated only by the flashes of lightning that seemed to be picking up in intensity. Jess smiled with her eyes closed as Alex rubbed her shoulders. The muscles underneath were twisted in a convolution of knots. She wouldn't be able to relax until the lights were back on. But when that would be, with all the commotion outside, was anyone's guess. Alex's hand slid down her arm and took her hand.

"Come on, Jess," Alex gently tugged, "let's go find some candles. Then we can snuggle on the couch."

"I'd really like that." Jess rolled herself forward, following Alex down the hall. In the living room, Jess pulled out her cell phone and lit the flashlight. She pointed to the hallway closet. "There should be a bunch of candles in there. There's also a couple of hurricane lamps. Mom insisted on them, said every house should have some in case of a power loss."

Alex shuffled over to the closet and opened the door. "Your mom is right. Never know when you might lose power. We live in Michigan, you know. Crazy weather is just a part of life." She began heaping several large glass jar candles into the crook of her arm.

Jess watched as the stack of jars teetered. "I get that, and I understand what Mom was saying, but do you really think it's a good idea for someone in a wheelchair to roll around in a darkened house with a large, highly-breakable—not to mention highly-flammable—oil lamp in her lap?"

Alex stopped and thought for a moment. "I see your point." She shuddered. "Not a good image."

"Not at all." Talking was helping her anxiety. Something to take her mind off things.

Alex perked up. "Thankfully you have me here with you."

While Jess transferred herself to the couch, Alex dispersed the candles throughout the living room, lighting them one by one as she went, until every flat surface was covered. Next, she pulled out the two hurricane lamps, checked them for fuel, and placed one on each antique walnut end table beside the couch. She removed the glass chimneys and blew out the dust as best she could. She then lit the first lamp's braided wick. The flame crackled for a second and Alex replaced the chimney. A quick adjustment and the room was filled with soft, warm light.

Jess could smell the dust burning off the inside of the glass chimney. The smell reminded her of times during her childhood when they'd lost power—a sudden summer storm, a fierce winter blizzard. When she closed her eyes, she could picture sitting around the fire, reading stories with Jordan. If they got really bored, they would even act out the parts. Jordan always had a flair for the most dramatic scenes. Big surprise there.

Alex lit the last lamp, replaced the chimney, and adjusted the flame. The living room was bathed in yellow light. To Jess, it reminded her of a secluded romantic cabin, somewhere deep in the forest. She patted the couch beside her. "Come have a seat, Legs. You can protect me from all the scary monsters."

Alex puffed up her chest dramatically, reminding Jess forcefully of Jordan. "Anything you say, m'lady."

Jess giggled and shook her head. The raging storm outside barely registered. Even the bright flashes of lightning were no longer as intense now that the room was lit with a dozen different candles, each of the individual scents blurring together into a hodgepodge of floral and spicy aromas. Alex had succeeded in taking her mind off everything. Jess smiled as Alex sat, leaning in close and curling her body beside her.

They sat in silence for a few minutes, enjoying each other's company, until Alex spotted the Infinity Books bag resting on the coffee table. She leaned forward. "Hey, what's that?"

"Oh, I hope you don't mind but I got a few books on weddings today while I was at work. You know, so we can start making some plans." Jess had almost forgotten about the books. Now seemed the perfect time to go through them though.

"Oh, really." Alex's voice rose half an octave. She reached out and pulled the bag from the coffee table, unfolded the top, and pulled the three books from the depths. She spun the books around until they were right-side-up. Her eyes lit up. "There's even wedding books for lesbians. Wow. May wonders never cease."

Jess laughed. "That's what I thought too. You'd never've found books like that only a few years ago, and in this area as well. West Michigan isn't exactly known for its warm embrace of the LGBT community."

"You've got that right. A lot of right-wingers everywhere." Alex huffed, her gaze becoming unfocused for a moment. "Could be worse, I guess."

Jess knew what was going through her mind. Alex's own family had abandoned her—worse than abandoned. They had pushed her away and then rejected her completely. It broke Jess's heart to see the pain that Alex still felt, even if Alex denied it. Jess's family had always been accepting of her. She still wasn't sure if that had to do with her accident or not. It was funny how that changed everyone's perspective.

But it wasn't fair to Alex. How could a parent hate their child? How could a family say you're no longer a part of it? How could love simply stop because of who you were or who you loved? Jess would never understand. Still, she had to believe that love would conquer all.

Alex flipped through the pages of the top book, *How to Survive Your Lesbian Wedding*. Alex opened her arm wide and waved Jess to her. "Why don't we look through these together. Besides, what could be more romantic than planning our wedding by candlelight?"

Jess tucked into Alex's arm, the storm all but forgotten. "I like how you think, Legs."

CHAPTER FOUR

By the next morning, the storm had blown itself out. Alex couldn't remember an early season thunderstorm that bad in a long time. The wind had howled all night, lashing the side of the house with rain and debris. The thunder had been nonstop until around four in the morning when it moved off to the northeast. Even the lighting had lasted to the wee hours. A few times it had struck so close that the flash of light and crash of thunder had seemed to be simultaneous. No one Mississippi, two Mississippi, to see how far away the strike had been. It happened so fast that it was over even before her stomach tried to leap out of her throat.

Alex shaded her eyes from the sunlight streaming through the living room windows. She yawned and stretched. If not for the incessantly chirping birds and the sound of some sort of heavy equipment, she would have much preferred to sleep. She got up and tried the light switch—still no power. Wonderful.

Alex heard Jess zipping up the hallway and turned around. "Good morning, babe. Where'd you go?"

"Bathroom was calling." Jess yawned, looking distinctly bleary-eyed. "What the hell is with all the ruckus outside? It's not like it's a Tuesday or anything."

Alex wrinkled her brow. "What's being a Tuesday have to do with anything?"

"Nothing I guess." Jess snipped. "It's just after last night, I'd have thought we could maybe have had a little bit of a lie-in, but *nooooooo*. That's not going to happen." Jess was on a roll now and Alex hid her smile behind her hand. "And here I was thinking I might even get in a little run before work. Enjoy a quiet breakfast. Drink some coffee."

The high-pitched whine of a chainsaw pierced the morning. Alex turned back to the living room windows. "What in the hell is going on out there?" She strode over and peered through the glass. Her mouth dropped open. Up and down the street, tree limbs littered the neighborhood. Big, car crushing, what-the-fuck-just-knocked-my-house-off-its-foundation limbs. The neighbors two houses up had a big hole in their roof. Straight across the street, the only thing visible of the neighbor's Mini Cooper from beneath the massive maple tree that once stood proud in their yard was the fake English license plate. Alex was immensely grateful they had put their cars in the garage. "Ahhhh, babe. I think you're going to have to cancel that run."

Jess wheeled up beside her. "You can say that again. I'm going to have to cancel everything for the foreseeable future. At least I can get some coffee."

Alex winced and bit her bottom lip. There was no easy way to say it, so she closed her eyes and spilled it. "Ummm. I don't know how to say this, Wheels, but we still don't have any power."

Jess let out a stream of profanity that made even Alex blush. Working in the ER, she thought she'd heard it all. Apparently not. There were words that she had never even heard before. When Jess hit, "…fuck a dead duck…," Alex couldn't take it any longer and burst out laughing. So much for her sweet, innocent girlfriend. She was in a relationship with a Barbary pirate. Finally, Jess stopped and took a deep breath.

Alex raised an eyebrow. "Feel better?"

"Hell no." Jess sat with her arms crossed. "What am I going to do for coffee?"

Alex leaned over and pulled Jess closer until her head rested against her body. "Come on. Let's check outside to see how bad the damage is, and I'll take you to Starbucks. Sound good?"

Jess perked up. "Now you're talking, my Amazonian goddess."

Alex laughed again and puffed out her chest. Amazonian goddess. She liked the sound of that, sort of a cross between Diana Prince and Hippocrates. Dr. Alexandra Hartway by day, Wonder Woman by night. With that image still in her head, she stepped out onto their front deck with Jess and surveyed the street. From the look of it, she'd only been able to see a small fraction of the true toll the storm had taken. Everywhere downed limbs covered the yards, sidewalks, and street. If that weren't bad enough, the street was blocked in both directions by large trees that had toppled over. A crew was busy cutting through the one to the left. The power lines were ripped down in at least a half a dozen places. Various houses had suffered damage anywhere from minor (siding missing or gutters torn off) to major (holes through roofs, windows broken, or trees uprooted and lying where they shouldn't be). Alex blew out a low, soft whistle through her teeth. "Oh my."

Jess stared with her mouth hanging open. "All that happened while we were curled up on the couch looking through wedding books?"

Alex shared her astonishment. "It certainly appears so. Wow." She spun to survey the damage to their house. Several inch-in-diameter limbs were on the roof. That had apparently been the thumps they'd heard. Another limb, this one a good six inches in diameter, lay across the driveway. Their mailbox was also MIA.

Jess stared up and down the street, her eyes goggling. She then looked over their house. "Looks like we got off easy compared to everyone else. Damn." She slowly shook her head, her voice quiet, thankful. "I guess coffee is the least of our concerns. Doesn't look like we're getting power back anytime soon."

Alex rubbed her hand gently over Jess's shoulder. As they stood, still trying to take it all in, one thing became clear—they couldn't stay here. Then the idea struck her. "Hey, Wheels, why don't you give the bookstore a call. Tell them what happened, and you'll be out for a few days. I've got some days off coming up. Let's pack a quick bag and head for the lakeshore. Find someplace with room service and wait for the power to come back on. We can find a Starbucks on the way."

"I don't know. Should we really take off after such a bad storm? Doesn't quite feel right. Plus, we really can't afford a fancy hotel on a whim." Jess was shaking her head slowly.

Alex took a deep breath. Jess could be a little too stubborn sometimes. "Look, Jess. We can't really stay here. Lord knows when the power is going to be restored. That means no cooking, no showers, no lights...no coffee. So, we've got to go somewhere. Why not enjoy it? We certainly deserve to splurge once in a while. Just think of it as a post-engagement celebration."

Jess's face lit up. "I can't argue with that logic. When you've got a good idea, Legs, you've got a good idea."

* * *

After getting off the phone with the bookstore (they were more than understanding) and a quick call to her family (no one else suffered any damage), Jess dashed through the house to pack a bag. She grabbed several changes of clothes along with her toiletries. Lastly, she tossed the wedding books onto the stack and zipped her bag closed. Alex had already finished packing and run her bag to her car. Jess heaved the suitcase onto her lap and wheeled through the house to the garage. She was just in time to see Alex loading her racing wheelchair into the trunk. Alex knew her too well. A good run might be just what the doctor ordered, and hopefully over at the lakeshore the trails would be free of debris.

Looking up, Alex shoved the chair in the trunk and ran up to take the bag from Jess's lap. "Let me get that. Good grief, you could have left it in the house."

"I've got it. Not to worry." Jess smiled. Sometimes Alex forgot that she was as capable as anyone. But she did appreciate the gesture. Jess wheeled herself up to Alex's car and tossed her bag in the trunk. "There."

Alex popped the emergency release on the garage door and heaved it up. It rattled along its tracks. That was something Jess wouldn't have been able to do on her own. She'd have been stranded, unable to get her car out of the garage. Next, Alex jogged down the driveway to the big limb lying on the cement.

Jess cupped her hands to her mouth and called out over the commotion in the neighborhood. "Be careful, Legs. You don't want to go hurting yourself."

Jess watched as Alex dragged the limb down the driveway to the curbside for the city to pick up, then turned around and flexed her arm muscles like a bodybuilder striking a pose. Jess clapped her hand to her forehead. On the way back up the driveway, Alex kicked smaller limbs out of the way. That was another thing she couldn't do in her chair. Not only would picking up the branches prove difficult, but a stick in her wheels could also be extremely hazardous. The last thing she wanted was a trip to the hospital because she flipped her chair.

While Alex walked back up the driveway, Jess slid into the passenger seat, folded her chair, and pulled it into the car behind her. Alex appeared in the driver's side window and mimed keys in her hand before pointing toward the house. Jess smiled and waved back.

This was turning into a delightful adventure. And she had Alex to thank for that. Without her, she'd never be able to drop everything on a whim and take off into the unknown.

A few minutes later, Alex darted out of the house and climbed behind the wheel of her car. "I'm just going to back out and then I can pull the garage door down."

"I can do that," Jess joked.

"Once we get on the road..." Alex began to back up as if she hadn't heard. She stopped suddenly and turned to Jess. "Wait a minute. Did you just say you'd get the garage door?"

Jess smoothed her face into the most serious look she could. "Yeah, I'll just hop out and get it." She sputtered out laughing at the expression on Alex's face, a mixture of incredulous disbelief and wide-eyed astonishment.

"Nice try, Wheels. You had me there for a moment." Alex patted her on the arm and climbed out of the car to pull down the garage door. Once behind the wheel again, she took a deep breath. "Well, here's to adventure and riches!"

Jess snorted through her nose. "We're not pirates, Legs. It's not like we're going to be pillaging any villages."

Alex twisted up her face into what looked like a grimace. "Arrrrr me matey. Batten down the hatches, ye landlubber, or I'll send ye straight to Davy Jones's Locker."

If Jess had had anything in her mouth, she would have sprayed it all over the windshield. If only she had had her cell phone ready to record, that would have made it all throughout the bookstore. Jess grabbed her sides as she laughed, gasping for breath with her chest heaving. Finally, she was able to regain some composure, still snorting through her nose though. "Ye landlubber? I had no idea I was engaged to Jack Sparrow."

Alex threw a hand to her chest, looking shocked. "*Please*, I'm Elizabeth Swann. Besides, the way you were cussing this morning, you're more of a pirate than I am."

Jess couldn't deny Alex's assessment. But there had been coffee involved. Not getting her morning cup of Joe deserved a few well-chosen words. That and she worked around English majors all day. She'd come to realize no one can out-cuss an English major—not even pirates. "Fine, fine. You may have a point. Now let's hit the road. I was promised Starbucks if my memory is correct."

Alex gave a firm nod and backed out into the street. The tree to the south had been cleared enough that they could sneak through if they were careful. Alex weaved around the smaller sticks and branches along with a whole host of various yard ornaments, lawn chairs, and trash bins. The entire street looked like a war zone.

They slowly made their way out of town. As the streets cleared, Jess relaxed. "So, where are we going?"

Alex glanced over, a wickedly sneaky smile firmly plastered on her lips. "It's a surprise, Wheels."

* * *

An hour and a half later, Alex pulled off the highway into the outskirts of Holland, Michigan. Although known worldwide for their Tulip Festival, it was too early in the season yet for the flowers. Alex took a mental note to make another trip when the flowers were in full bloom.

In the passenger seat beside her, Jess was quietly sipping away at her Starbucks Caramel Ribbon Crunch Frappuccino, a sinfully indulgent drink if Alex had ever seen one. But after the night and the morning they'd had, Jess could have any drink she wanted.

According to radio reports, their neighborhood had been ground zero for the storm, a derecho. Alex had never heard of such a thing. Bomb cyclones, derechos—it seemed like there were new types of storms with each event. This one was an intense line of thunderstorms with high winds. On top of that, what had hit the Rockford area was a downburst. That was what had caused so much damage. It would be several days before power was restored and all the debris cleared. Getting out of town had been a great idea.

Jess looked through the windshield. "Holland, huh? I haven't been over here in forever."

"Seemed like a good idea. There're some really nice trails here. I figured you'd like to stretch your arms on a few of them."

Jess smiled widely, a dollop of caramel on her nose. "Ahhhh, Legs, you know the way to this girl's heart."

Alex's chest swelled. Hearing Jess happy was the way to *her* heart. She swallowed the lump in her throat. "I've been meaning to do this for a long time. But with everything going on, the crazy freaking hours at the hospital…"

Jess patted her gently on the leg. "I know it's been difficult. But we're here, and I couldn't think of a better surprise."

Alex grinned mischievously. "Oh, this isn't the surprise." She pointed out the windshield at the tall, brick and glass building coming up on the left. "That's the surprise."

Jess's mouth dropped open as she stared. "Are you kidding? The CityFlatsHotel?"

"You bet." Alex sat up straight in her seat. "I was able to get an accessible king suite."

"Room service?" Jess's voice was so soft that Alex barely heard it.

"Of course it has room service. And a ton of other amenities."

"But…but…"

Alex reached over and took Jess's hand. "Trust me, you're worth it."

* * *

When Jess rolled into their room, her mouth dropped open. She had never seen such a luxurious room, let alone stayed in one. It was huge, bigger than their living room and kitchen combined. And everything was set up with mobility in mind. She could easily wheel anywhere in the room. All the furniture appeared to be a light maple and the tilework a deep, earthen brown. Even the artwork on the walls, a series of abstract geometric shapes, was tastefully done. Jess spun, taking in the décor. It looked more like an apartment than a hotel room.

Alex walked in behind her, carrying their bags. Jess had tried to argue that she could carry her own, but Alex wouldn't hear of it. Since this was Alex's idea and treat, she didn't argue too much. With a grunt, Alex heaved the bags onto the bed. "What do you think, babe?"

"I…I…" Jess sputtered. She didn't know what to say. Part of her felt guilty for leaving after such a storm, like she was abandoning the neighborhood. Another part wanted to slide out onto the bed and show Alex exactly how much she appreciated everything right then and there. In the end, she simply gulped and answered in a soft, low voice. "This is amazing, Legs—just like you."

Alex smiled, looking deeply touched. Her mouth worked silently, as if trying to wrap around something just out of reach. Finally, she lowered her eyes to her hands, which she'd clasped in front of herself. "Thanks, Wheels. You're pretty amazing too."

Jess let the moment draw out, silence filling the room between them. But it wasn't an uncomfortable silence. It was the silence that happens with total contentment. And that was how Jess felt—totally content. Her chest swelled as she looked at Alex, who was still staring at her own hands. Jess recognized Alex's I'm-so-thankful-I-have-no-words posture. She had seen it a lot over the past couple of years, mostly when Alex had an especially trying day in the ER. Alex had been at ground zero of the pandemic, had lost more patients than she would admit, but she always had that look of utter thankfulness whenever she saw Jess.

Finally, Jess cleared her throat quietly, getting Alex to look up. "What do you say we go hit the trails? I'm itching to stretch my arms on some new asphalt."

Alex smiled and nodded. "Beat you to it, Wheels."

Twenty minutes later, they were zipping along Lakeshore Trail, an eleven-mile loop that started out of Holland State Park. The cool breeze coming in off Lake Michigan kissed Jess's face as she pushed her racing wheelchair faster and faster along the trail. Her wheels bounced with a small *thud* each time she ran over a crack in the tarmac. Warmth licked her skin with each sunbeam piercing the trees overhead. The air was filled with early spring blossoms. Was it daffodils, or maybe hyacinths? Or the golden yellow forsythia? Whatever it was, it smelled like spring. Jess inhaled deeply, enjoying the floral bouquet.

"Are you keeping up back there, Legs," she called over her shoulder.

Alex ran up beside her, feet pounding the pavement with a rhythmic *slap, slap, slap*. "Of course, Wheels. Just giving you a bit of a head start." She gave Jess a devious grin.

Jess swerved abruptly in her chair before quickly righting herself. "Oh *really*? You want to go there? You'd better hold on."

Jess pushed harder, working her arms and her chest muscles. She sucked in breath after breath. Much to her amazement, Alex was keeping up right beside her.

They were starting to draw attention along the trail. Jess could just imagine what they looked like—a half-crazed woman in a decked out, top-of-the-line racing wheelchair being paced by a strikingly beautiful woman with a look of intense determination on her face. People were jumping out of the way as they approached. They received more than a few filthy looks, and one shirtless gentleman sporting a hipster beard with matching handlebar mustache, yelled out, "Watch it, you crazy idiots!" as he scrambled out of their way. Jess didn't care. She pushed on, her gloved hands burning with each grasp at the wheels. It felt too good to stop.

Jess pushed harder and harder until she couldn't go on any longer. She pulled off the trail, gasping, hot air passing in and out of her lungs like a blowtorch. Alex stood beside her, bent in two, her hands on her knees and puffing like an old steam locomotive, legs shaking. Britney Spears's voice popped into her head. "Oops, I did it again…" She fought back the laughter crawling its way up her throat, the type of laughter that would raise eyebrows and lead to questions about her mental wellbeing. The kind that once it started, it would not end.

Once she'd recovered enough to speak, Jess called over to Alex, who still stood with her hands on her knees. "Are you okay there, Legs?"

Jess jumped with surprise when Alex quickly stood up and let out a loud whoop of triumph, pumping her fists into the air. Jess stared, beginning to worry. Had she finally driven Alex loopy? Jess leaned forward. "Are you sure you're okay over there, Alex?"

"Whoo-wee, Wheels! That was *awesome!* Talk about a workout. I've really missed this, just going for a run for the sheer joy."

"Alex?" Jess bit her lower lip. The wild, animalistic grin on Alex's face didn't fill Jess with confidence. Passersby were giving them sidelong glances, like people trying to avoid a stray dog that may or may not be rabid.

Alex held up an index finger, still breathing hard. She placed her fists in the small of her back and arched backward, stretching. She then turned to Jess. "Yeah, yeah, I'm okay. Just really pumped."

Jess eyed her suspiciously. "I guess. There for a second, I thought I might have driven you like—" she raised her hands dramatically, waving them about her head, and blew out a raspberry with her lips "—I don't know…wonky or something."

Alex laughed. "Wonky? I don't think I've gone off the deep end that bad yet. Although, you certainly drive me something." She leaned in and winked wantonly.

Jess's cheeks grew warm, but it had nothing to do with the sunshine dappling her skin. She glanced shyly around, suddenly wishing they were anywhere else that wasn't swarming with people. Why had they even left their room? She could be there with Alex at that very moment, sweating in a whole other way. Jess swallowed hard. "Easy there, stud. We're a long way from our hotel. Don't go starting anything you can't finish."

Alex clapped a hand to her chest. "Who says I won't be able to finish?"

"*Alex!*" Jess gasped in shock. Who was this lecherous woman in front of her? "We are in public, for God's sake. You've been hanging around Jordan too much."

Alex twisted her pinky against the edge of her lips in a spectacular Dr. Evil impersonation. "Maybe."

Jess playfully slapped her arm. "Oh, you're just incorrigible. Perhaps we should head back to our hotel before you scandalize the entire city of Holland."

"Now that's an award-winning idea." Alex made as if she were about to take off in a dead sprint. "Race?"

"Oh my God, Legs." Jess laughed. "Tell you what, why don't we take it easy going back and I can think up other ways to burn off this excess energy you seem to have."

Alex stood up straight, a sappy smile on her lips. Jess had no doubt that if Alex could fly, she'd be floating a foot off the ground at that moment. Alex reached out and took Jess by the hand. "Promises, promises."

* * *

Once they returned to their room (it had taken a lot longer than Alex wanted), they locked the door behind them with a resounding *snick* of the deadbolt. Alex stripped off her tank top and sports bra together, tugging them over her head. The cool air of the hotel room hit her chest, raising goose bumps on her arms, stomach, and breasts. She shivered—from the chill against her skin, of course.

Jess spun her chair around, leaning it back on two wheels. They had switched out her racing chair for the regular one down in the parking lot. "I don't know about you, but I'm starving to death." She rubbed her stomach. "I hate to say it, but we should probably take a shower. I'm all gross. Maybe we can try out that shower, then order room service."

Alex couldn't argue with that. She felt grimy too. "Sounds like a plan, Wheels. You want to go first, or do you want me to?" She was quickly losing her bravado. The run had tired her out more than she'd thought possible.

"Oh please. Since when do we shower separately after a run?" Jess wheeled herself into the bathroom. She called over her shoulder. "Now get your sexy little butt in here. I'm going to need someone to wash my back."

Alex raced in behind Jess, kicking off her shorts and panties on the way, nearly causing herself to trip. Luckily, she just ping-ponged off the doorway instead, her shoulder crying out in sudden pain. She slid to a halt on the tile floor and took in the shower. It was much smaller than the one at their house and it had only one showerhead. But they could make it work.

"Do you want me to lift you?" Alex raised her eyebrows.

Jess paused with her shirt over the bottom of her chin. She let the fabric drop as she seemed to think about it for a moment. "Naw, I think I can slide in there no problem."

Alex thought about pushing the matter, but the determination on Jess's face changed her mind. Alex had learned to bite her lip when she saw that look. It would only lead to an argument, and that was the last thing she wanted. "Okay, babe, just holler if you need anything."

Jess pulled off her shirt and worked her shorts over her hips. She was struggling to remove the sweat-dampened material that was clinging to her skin like spilt honey. Alex took a step forward but stopped herself. Once Jess had freed her shorts from her legs (and not a moment too soon or Alex would have bitten through her bottom lip), she tossed them over the top of Alex's head where they landed on the floor in the other room. She then wheeled into the roll-in shower and deftly transferred herself to the chair in the shower. Alex followed Jess in, holding her breath until Jess was safely seated, then moved Jess's wheelchair back out of the shower.

The water felt good against Alex's skin. Unlike the shower that they usually shared, they had to take turns under the water. Since Jess was confined to basically one spot, Alex found herself mostly huddling to the side except when she needed to rinse, but she didn't mind. The cool air helped soothe her overly warm skin. From the feel of it, she'd gotten a bit of a sunburn as well. Never failed, every spring she got a sunburn early in the season thanks to her Irish heritage.

As she lathered her hair, she glanced over at Jess, who sat with her eyes closed and her face upturned to the falling water. She wore a beatific expression and had an utterly relaxed demeanor, as if at any moment she could drift off into blissful sleep.

"Are you going to make it over there, babe?"

Jess slowly opened her eyes and looked at Alex with a lazy smile. "Yeah. I'm just so happy, especially being with you."

"I'm really happy to be here with you too, Jess." A lump formed in her chest. Sometimes she still had difficulty accepting that Jess was in her life.

She closed her eyes and ducked under the water, rinsing her bobbed tresses. While she worked her fingers through her hair, she felt a second pair of hands lightly run up the sides of her belly. She gulped in a mouthful of soapy water, the suds bitter on her tongue, and started coughing. Water flew everywhere as she sputtered.

"I'm so sorry, Alex. I didn't mean to...you know...that wasn't...oh God..." There was a note of panic to Jess's voice.

With tears springing from her eyes, Alex waved her off while she tried her best to regain her breath. Finally, she gasped out the words, "I'm...I'm okay, babe. Seri...seriously. I sw...swear." At Jess's wide-eyed look of horror, Alex started to laugh, triggering another sputtering fit.

Jess didn't seem to share Alex's optimism. She still stared, grimacing with each cough. "You don't seem okay." She bit her lip.

Alex hacked and spluttered some more. Finally, she coughed one last time. Her stomach hurt—that twinging, pulsating, muscles-pissed-off-and-barking sensation. "Holy crap, that sucked."

"I didn't mean—"

Alex held up a hand. "It wasn't you, babe. I got a big mouthful of shampoo. Let me tell you, that shampoo tastes like shit."

The comment had the desired effect and Jess giggled, looking relieved. "I thought you were going to choke to death there for a moment. And I was just trying to be sexy."

Alex took Jess's chin in her hand and rubbed her cheek with her thumb. "You're always sexy to me, Wheels. Hold on..." Alex quickly finished rinsing her hair, then stepped in closer and slowly pulled Jess to her wet chest. Water rained down on them both, a gentle warm pounding. With Jess's face against her stomach, Alex stroked Jess's cheek, letting the moment draw out. She then kneeled and looked up into Jess's eyes. "Have I told you lately how much I love you?"

Jess nodded slowly, a bright smile on her lips. "Yes, but I never tire of hearing that."

"Well, in that case," Alex slowly moved her lips closer to Jess's, "I want you to know, Jess Bolderson, that I love you—in every way possible."

"And I love you too, Alex Hartway."

Alex closed the distance and their lips met. Warm water trickled over their heads, running down their faces and over their bodies. Alex took a breath and opened her mouth wider, sucking Jess's tongue inside. Their tongues twisted together, around and around, fighting for dominance. Alex was careful not to inhale too deeply. She didn't want to accidentally snort in water and go into another coughing episode.

Alex wasn't sure how long they continued kissing, but her tongue and mouth were beginning to feel well-used, in a good way. If it were up to her, she'd never stop kissing Jess. But as good as that sounded, she had other plans, better plans.

Alex pulled away and Jess let out a whimper. Jess licked her swollen lips. Her dark eyes were heavy with desire, making them several shades darker than usual. As Jess began to protest, Alex silenced her with a finger to her lips. "Shhhhhh." She stood and smiled down at Jess.

Without another word, Alex took Jess's hands in hers and guided her forward until she sat on the edge of the stool. Then, careful that Jess didn't slip off (or spill herself on the slippery floor), Alex threw a long, naked leg around her and slid onto the stool behind Jess. She leaned against the wall and pulled Jess in tight until Jess was resting against her chest, her tender breasts poking into Jess's back. Alex opened her legs wider, her long legs wrapped around each side of Jess. She nuzzled her lips just below Jess's left ear, teasing that sensitive spot at the top of Jess's neck.

"Mmmmmm." Jess leaned her head back, opening her neck to more.

Alex softly kissed Jess's neck, breathing in the fresh scent of lavender bodywash. Jess's wet, dark locks that she had let grow out over the winter tickled Alex's nose. Alex closed her eyes, relishing the heat of Jess's body pressed against her. She slowly reached around Jess's side with her right hand, tracing small, loopy circles with her fingers. Jess jittered under her touch, but Alex wasn't wanting to tickle her. Oh no, she had much better sensations in mind.

Finally, Alex's fingers bumped up under the gentle swell of Jess's right breast. The firm weight of that fleshy mound rested on Alex's hand. She turned her hand slightly until she was able to fully cup Jess's breast, a hard nipple against her palm. Jess moaned again, a low, lazy moan, the sort that only happens at moments of near unconsciousness, that time when dreams and reality merge.

Alex slowly moved her hand around in small circles, lightly tracing a fingertip along the edge of Jess's pinkish-brown areola. She slowly spiraled in until she was able to take Jess's hardened nipple between her fingertips. Once Alex had captured the sensitive protrusion, she gave it a firm squeeze. Jess let out a soft cry, barely louder than a whisper. Alex could feel Jess's breath increasing. Her own breath was keeping pace. Still nuzzling her lips against Jess's tender neck, she lightly nipped with her teeth and tugged on Jess's nipple at the same time, tenting the pigmented flesh.

Jess moaned, this time much louder, then made a sound in the back of her throat, an almost constant groan.

Alex nuzzled her lips against Jess's ear. "You like?" Her words were soft, slow, sensual. Her warm breath caressed Jess's earlobe.

"More." One word. That was all Jess managed. But Alex didn't need any more encouragement.

Still teasing Jess's breast with her right hand, Alex reached around with her left and buried it between Jess's legs. Jess covered Alex's hand with hers and guided it to the spot she liked best. Alex could feel the heat radiating from Jess's center, almost as if she had run her hand through the steam of a whistling teapot. But unlike the burning sensation of hot steam, this heat was inviting, welcoming. She had to have more.

As Alex slowly stroked back and forth, back and forth, Jess shifted her weight and scooped her hand under her right leg, opening her legs wider and wider. Alex explored the soft velvetiness of Jess's folds. Jess's center was even hotter to Alex's touch. She ran her fingers through the slippery flesh, each time pressing harder and harder.

Jess was gasping, her eyes closed, and her teeth clenched. Each breath was sucked in with a loud, explosive hiss. Her back arched away from Alex's chest.

Alex increased the pressure oh so slightly and slid deep inside as Jess gave a low, guttural groan. Alex worked her fingers in and out, sinking deeper with each pass. She curled her fingers, stroking, and quickened the pace. In and out. In and out. Alex's fingers passed through the hot dampness, her hand colliding with Jess's slippery, well-lubricated folds. With the slightest adjustment, Alex twisted her hand until her thumb made contact with Jess's swollen clitoris with each thrust. Jess squirmed and Alex held on tighter with her right hand, supporting all of Jess's weight. Jess writhed in Alex's arms, her moaning echoing off the tile shower.

Alex thrust—in, out, in, out, in, out. Jess was close. It would only take a little more to push her over the edge. She squeezed Jess's nipple and tugged while raking her teeth along Jess's exposed neck. Jess cried out and clamped down on her fingers, trapping Alex inside her as she climaxed hard. Alex had never felt this strong of a climax in Jess before. The muscles of her center contracted and released, contracted and released. Jess arched her back so much that Alex thought she might break in half. Finally, with one last contract and release, Jess fell back, her entire body shuddering.

Jess gasped for breath, trying her best to talk. "That…that was…that was…yeah. Wow."

Alex wrapped both arms tightly around her. "You like then?"

"*Duh!* Of course I liked. I think the entire floor knows that I liked." Jess giggled.

"I'm thinking the floors above and below too."

Jess burst out laughing. "You're probably right. I can certainly say this, Legs, you've got the touch. Oh my!"

Alex puffed up her chest. "Why thank you."

"No, believe me—thank *you*." Jess nuzzled against Alex's neck and nipped playfully at her ear. "Now it's your turn, stud."

As much as she liked that idea, they needed something else first. "Tell you what, Wheels, how about a little raincheck, at least until after dinner."

"Room service?"

"Yeah, that's what I was thinking."

"Great, that means no clothes."

"Um, maybe a robe for when it's delivered, you think?"

Jess pooched out her bottom lip. "I guess so, if you insist."

Alex slipped out from behind Jess to turn the water off but then turned back. "Have you ever noticed how we are often overcome while in the shower?"

Jess laughed, the sound like a wild discordant song against the tile. "Legs, I am often overcome with you no matter where I'm at. So why don't you shut that water off and get me out of here. After room service, I'll show you just how overcome I can get."

CHAPTER FIVE

Jess wished their vacation could have been longer. Four days just wasn't long enough. They had gone on walks and a few slow runs, eaten way too much delicious food, and made love, again and again. But they had to come back to reality sooner or later.

When they pulled onto their street, Jess couldn't believe the difference a few days had made. Most of the downed trees and limbs were gone. The neighbor's Mini Cooper was still in the driveway, sans tree, but looking quite the worse for wear with a caved-in roof and hood. Up the street, workers were busy fixing another neighbor's roof. However, the biggest surprise for Jess was a clean yard, free of branches and sticks. Even the limbs and debris that had been on their roof were gone. As they pulled in, she gaped out the window, unable to believe what she was seeing. She'd figured she was going to have to call a lawn care service once they got back home but the yard was spotless.

Jess turned to Alex. "How? What? Did you do this?"

Alex laughed. "Surprise, babe." She grinned like a little kid who had just given an artistic masterpiece in crayon to their mom. "I made a couple of calls while we were in Holland. Didn't figure you'd want to come back to the house and yard being a total disaster."

"But how did you keep this a secret? You're terrible with secrets." Jess still stared in disbelief. "The only one worse at keeping secrets is Jordan."

"Speaking of which—" Alex looked as if she had pulled off one of history's greatest capers "—Jordan actually helped me out with lining up a lawn service and Tim put up a new mail—" Alex stared out the windshield. "What the...oh my God..." Their new mailbox was in the shape of a giant fishing lure, complete with what looked like giant treble hooks dangling from the bottom.

"Tim? *Tim?* Put up a mailbox? No way. The man can barely assemble anything that's not a grill or a videogame." Jess felt as if she had fallen through a portal into some bizarro world. Tim assembling a mailbox, mystery yard service, and here she hadn't even had a clue any of this had been going on.

"Who else would put up a mailbox in the shape of a fishing lure?" Alex stared out the windshield, slowly shaking her head. "From the looks of it, he didn't scrimp either and got the extra-large one."

"You've got a point there. Only Tim." Jess scowled as she took in the kitschy mailbox. She wasn't looking forward to getting their mail from the mouth of a fish every day.

Alex threw the car in park and climbed out, still shaking her head. She turned back to Jess. "Be just a sec."

Jess watched through the windshield as Alex entered the garage via the side door. Seconds later, the large overhead door began to rattle up its track. The power outage map had shown that they'd regained power on Wednesday, but it was nice to see confirmation. It was bad enough that they would have to empty the refrigerator, a job Jess was certainly not looking forward to.

Alex jogged back to the car and jumped behind the wheel. "You know, I was thinking."

"Just now?" Jess teased.

"Yeah, shocking, isn't it?" Alex gave her a wry grin. "Anywho, I was thinking, maybe we should have Jordan help with the wedding plans after all. I mean, she really helped organize the yard repairs. I couldn't have done it without her. Besides, I'm sure she would like the job. Just not Tim. He'd have us doing a Hawaiian luau or something."

Jess laughed and thought for a moment. "Hmmmm. You make a good point. We could even tell Jordan that she would be the official wedding planner. You know how she likes titles."

"Oh, oh." Alex bounced in her seat. "We could make her a T-shirt that says, 'Official Wedding Planner.'"

"T-shirt my ass. Jordan would want nothing less than a full uniform with a large marquee sign behind her announcing her official title: Dame Jordan, First Lady of the Hartway/Bolderson Wedding." Jess tried to inject as much import into her voice as possible.

"I love it," Alex laughed, "except for one thing—it's the Bolderson/Hartway wedding."

"*What?* No, no, no." Jess waggled a finger in front of Alex's face. "It's got to be the Hartway/Bolderson wedding because you're the one who asked me to marry you, therefore you should be first."

"Babe, I don't think it works that way." Alex adopted a voice that sounded much like a parent trying to explain to their obstinate child that watermelon seeds don't in fact sprout if you eat them.

"Well, why should it be the other way around then?" Jess placed a hand on her hip and faced Alex straight on.

"Simple—alphabetical." Alex gave a firm nod.

Jess sat there with her mouth open. She couldn't really argue that. Still, it didn't seem right. Alex should be first. It was Alex who had saved her life when she had crashed her wheelchair. It was Alex who had put up with her bad attitude in the beginning of their relationship. It was Alex who had fought for them, who had seen something in them, and had refused to give up.

Alex leaned in closer. "Tell you what, Wheels. Why don't we leave it up to our wedding planner."

Jess laughed, glad for a more diplomatic solution. "Okay. We'll let the wedding planner decide. What could be fairer than that?" It didn't hurt either that the person making the decision would be her sister. Jordan was sure to see it her way.

* * *

Alex was glad to be home, but there was something else on her mind. The more they talked about the upcoming nuptials, the more her stomach muscles tightened. They had spent each evening in their hotel flipping through the wedding books while Jess took notes on a hotel notepad. As a child, Alex had grown up in the church. Her father was a minister, so she had attended her fair share of weddings, along with funerals and baptisms, and even a few revivals. But as much as she tried to recall, she didn't remember weddings as a huge affair. Perhaps it was being younger, so she didn't see all the behind the scenes. Or maybe things had changed in the past few decades. Maybe weddings now, gay or straight, were a lot more complicated. But bottom line, she wanted Jess happy, so she would go with whatever Jess decided.

Alex sat beside Jess on the couch, where she was busy scratching out something on a legal pad. "Whatcha up to, babe?" Alex leaned over to get a closer look.

Jess continued looking at the list she'd been writing, her forehead deeply wrinkled. "I'm just trying to work up a list of who to invite. Don't want to leave anyone out." She took a deep breath and lowered the legal pad to her lap. "Don't forget, you're going to have to come up with a list also."

Alex waved her off. "That's easy. Jamie and Sue of course. And Maria." She thought for a second. There really wasn't anyone else she was particularly close to except for Jess's family and Jess was already inviting them. "I don't know, maybe a couple more from the hospital. That should be it."

Jess crossed her hands in her lap and took a deep breath. It was a posture that Alex equated with Jess not wanting to mention something, something that she, Alex, probably wouldn't like.

From her experience, these situations worked best with the Band-Aid approach—just rip it off and be done with it. "Okay, what is it? You obviously want to say something."

Jess took another deep breath. "I was thinking...now I don't want you to get mad...but I was thinking, maybe it would be a good idea to invite your family. I mean it's been a long time. Maybe things have changed." Jess bit her lip, waiting.

Alex's vision swam in and out of focus. Invite her family? The same ones who had dumped her in that freaky conversion therapy nuthouse? The same ones who never once looked for her when she'd escaped? The same ones who had written her off as dead? Was Jess crazy? Alex's entire body grew stiff. Her response was simple. "No."

"But Alex, I mean, they are your family."

"*They are no family of mine!*" Alex's voice echoed throughout the room. She hadn't meant to yell. The words had just spilled out. But the thought of her family being there on one of the happiest days of her life made her sick. At the look of shock and fear on Jess's face, Alex relaxed and lowered her voice. "Look, Jess. I appreciate what you're trying to do, but you and your family are the only family I have."

"Okay, sorry." Jess's words were only a whisper.

Now Alex felt like an ass. Jess had only been trying to mend fences in her own way. But some fences could never be fixed, and *should* never be fixed. She was dead to her family, her family was dead to her—simple. Jess just liked to believe the best of everyone, and Alex's experiences unfortunately proved the opposite. She looked over at Jess, noting the mistiness in her eyes.

"Come here, babe." Alex pulled Jess over and tucked her under her arm. "I didn't mean to yell. You're all the family I need."

Jess snuggled in closer. "Let's talk about something different. Do you want to wear a dress or a tux?"

Grateful for the change of topic, Alex stroked Jess's hair while she thought. "Hmmmmm." This was something she hadn't given much thought to as an adult. Of course, growing up, she'd pictured it a thousand times. Strangely, it was always just her. She never pictured who she'd be marrying. The only exception (and it really wasn't an exception per se) had been a recurring fantasy of getting married with her best friend in a double wedding. They'd both wear matching full-length white dresses with cathedral-length trains sweeping the floors behind them. They'd walk up the aisle together, hand in hand. She couldn't ever remember anyone waiting at the end of the aisle for them. It was just the two of them in her fantasy. She figured at the time that it was simply because she didn't know any boys to put in the groom role. Now, it made a lot more sense. There would never be a groom.

Jess craned her neck to look up at Alex. "What are you thinking about, Legs?"

Alex flushed. That had been a silly girlhood fantasy. She was a grown woman now. A grown *gay* woman. But still, the idea wouldn't go away. "I want a dress," she blurted before she could change her mind.

Jess looked surprised. "Oh, I'd've bet on a tux for you, being the professional woman that you are."

"I know, I know." Alex's heartbeat increased. "That's what I was planning but…" She held her breath.

"But?" Jess prompted, drawing out the word.

Alex blew out her breath, the words tumbling out with it. "But I want the gorgeous white dress with the long flowing train and the veil over my face and the garter on my leg, the whole works. I want it all." She bit her bottom lip, waiting for Jess to start laughing. But that laughter never came. Instead, Jess took Alex's hand in hers. "I know I'm just being silly—"

"It's not silly at all." Jess smiled reassuringly. "I completely understand. If that's what you want, that's what you'll get. No need to explain."

Alex gave Jess's hand a tender squeeze. She needn't have worried. Of course Jess would understand. God willing, it would be her only wedding day ever. She wanted no one but Jess, for better, for worse, for richer, for poorer, in sickness and in health, 'til death did they part…a long, long time in the future if she had anything to do with it. Alex leaned over and kissed Jess on the side of her forehead. "Thank you."

"For what?"

"For being you."

"Awwwww, you're so sweet."

Alex smiled to herself. They'd probably sicken other people with their canoodling, but she was with the love of her life and nothing else mattered. She shifted her weight enough to pull Jess over until Jess was fully reclining against her. "Now that you've heard my wedding dress fantasies, what about you? Tux or dress?"

Jess didn't hesitate. "A dress, of course, not that a tux doesn't have its appeal. But there's just something about a wedding dress. Just no train or veil for me."

Alex pondered that for a second. "Why no train or veil?"

Jess burst out laughing. "Can't you just see a long piece of cloth attached to my head getting wrapped up in my wheels? Not good at all. I'll have my hands full just keeping a big fluffy wedding dress out of my wheels without the added risk of whiplash."

Alex felt like smacking herself. How could she have not thought of that? Sometimes she forgot that Jess had to make allowances on a daily basis because of her chair. What else had she missed?

Before Alex could respond, Jess continued. "There is one thing I'm going to do though. They say that shoes make the bride?"

"Really? I hadn't heard that."

Jess gave a crisp nod. "Oh yeah, at least according to Jordan. But instead of shoes, I'm going to have white leather gloves. Well, I'll have shoes too—it would look pretty silly being barefoot—but since my hands act as my legs…white leather gloves it is. What do you think?"

Alex didn't even need to think. "If that's what you want, Wheels, then that's what it'll be."

* * *

Jess called Jordan the next morning, ostensibly to thank her for arranging to have their yard cleaned from the storm but also to float an idea. "So, what do you say, Jordan, will you be our wedding planner?"

The squeal through the phone nearly blew out Jess's ear. She pulled her cell away from her face and stared at it. She could still hear Jordan squealing from three feet away and waited until it was safe to put the phone back to her ear.

"Yes! Yes! Oh, yes, Jess. I'd love to." She squealed again, sounding like a police siren.

Phone at arm's length again, Jess waited until Jordan settled enough before continuing. "Great. Thanks, Jordan. The more I think about everything that must be done, the more overwhelmed I get."

"Oh, don't I know it." Jordan nearly sang the words, pride in her voice. "But I'm here for you, sis. This will be my honor."

This would be the perfect job for Jordan. She had a ton of contacts through her real estate dealings. If anyone knew the ins and outs of greater Grand Rapids culture and events, it was her sister.

"I'll tell you, sis, I don't even know where to begin."

"Leave that to me. I still have all the information that I gathered for our wedding."

"In a big binder, no doubt." Jess refrained from laughing.

"Of course." Jordan sounded as if that was the silliest question she'd ever heard. "Plus, quite a few of my girlfriends have recently gotten married as well. I'll talk to them. But first things first. We've got to find the perfect place."

"What about our backyard?"

"Jess, Jess, Jess." Jordan clucked her tongue. "This is a big deal. You're only going to get married once. You've got to have an awesome place. I'll come up with a couple and you'll just have to choose."

"Okay." Jordan was right—they were only going to get married once. Still, if it were her, she'd just had it in the backyard. Or maybe a park. Someplace peaceful and beautiful. But Jordan was sure to find the perfect spot. "When do you want to get together and get started on all this?"

Jordan hesitated a moment. Paper rustled in the background. "How about today? Are you up for that?"

Since Alex was working and she had the day off, Jess couldn't think of a better time to begin. Besides, the sooner they started, the sooner they'd be done. "Yeah. Yeah, today is good. Where would you like to meet? Here? Or your place?"

"How about Starbucks?" Jordan's voice was close to squeal levels again.

At the suggestion, Jess sat up straight. Starbucks? Oh, hell yes. She just might be able to get through this after all.

Thirty minutes later, Jess sat across from Jordan, sipping a venti (or as she liked to call it, the big ass cup) Caramel Ribbon Crunch Frappuccino, her go-to beverage. What did it matter that it had enough calories for a baby elephant? They were fucking delicious.

"So…" Jordan leaned across the table. She slid a binder nearly three inches thick in front of Jess and flipped to the first page. "I think the first thing we've got to do is shop for a dress. You *are* wearing a dress, right?"

"Yes, yes. I've decided on a dress." Jess took a big sip, looking down at the binder. Jordan seemed to have everything, all neatly organized by topic with little plastic colored-coded tabs. Jess lightly flipped through the pages.

"Good. Not that there's anything wrong with a tux, but you'll look so beautiful in a dress."

Jess glanced at the page she'd stopped on and nearly spit out her coffee when she saw the prices. They were all in the thousands. "I don't know, Jordan. From the looks of it, they're really expensive. Maybe I could just wear yours or get a used one."

Jordan took a deep breath, looking much like someone trying to talk reason to a completely insane person. "Sweetie, you can't wear a used dress. It has to be one that only you have ever worn."

Jess didn't really see the difference—used, new, big deal, a dress was a dress—but Jordan wouldn't hear otherwise. Dress shopping it was. "Okay, you've made your point. Just so it's not too expensive."

"Great. You're making the right choice." Jordan reached across the table and flipped a few pages. "We can go to Elegant Bridal. Angela there is amazing. She's who did my dress. Let me tell you, I wouldn't trust anyone else. We can go there after here."

"Whoa, hold on. We can't go right now. For one thing, Alex is at work."

"So."

"So?" Jess's chest tightened. Having Jordan as a wedding planner was supposed to relieve stress. So far, it seemed to be adding to it. "Jordan, I kind of wanted Alex to be there when I pick out a dress. Plus, she wants to wear one too, so we can both pick out dresses and get fitted at the same time. Two birds, one stone."

Jordan stared across the table horrified. "Jessie-bessie, you can't have Alex there with you. Don't you know that it's super bad luck for the groom...or I guess it's the bride...to see the... well bride...in her wedding dress before the ceremony?" Jordan laughed. "It's a little tricky when talking about two brides. Like which bride is which."

Jess could see Jordan's point. It was traditional for the groom not to see the bride in her wedding dress before the big day. But they were two women. What would be the big deal if they saw each other? "But what about Alex? She needs to pick out a dress and get fitted. Who's going to do that?"

"I'll talk to Alex, see if she wants me to go with her." Jordan nodded. "Or maybe she'll want a friend of hers to go. Whatever, the important thing is that the two of you don't see each other."

Jess held up her hands in defeat. Separate dress fittings it would be then. By the time Jess had reached the bottom of her big-ass Frappuccino, Jordan had scratched down several pages of notes. From the sounds of it, Jess wouldn't have any free time between now and the wedding. It would all be devoted to meeting with florists and caterers, event center hosts and cake bakers, and a ton of others Jess couldn't even remember. But it would all be worth it. She was marrying the love of her life.

* * *

Alex parked in the Monroe Center parking ramp across from the Grand Rapids Art Museum. She had gotten home late last night after Jess was already in bed, fast asleep. This morning, Jess had been gone by the time she'd gotten up. Even though it had been a week since they'd gotten back from their spontaneous vacation, they hadn't had a lot of time together lately, and what time they did have was taken up with wedding planning. Jordan was a big help, although she could get a little too excited at times. It was a wedding, after all, not a mission plan for a trip to the moon. Since Alex had the morning free, she had planned lunch with her best friend.

She darted across Monroe Center, dodging the noontime traffic and shielding her eyes against the sun. The temperature had already soared into the low eighties. As warm as the spring had been, Alex figured they were in for a hot summer. Good thing they'd decided on a fall wedding. That was one of the very few things they had settled on so far. October fourteenth.

Taking two steps at a time, Alex ran up to the front doors. Once she passed through the big glass doors, she stopped, waiting for her eyes to adjust. A group of students, from one of the private middle schools by the look of them, noisily crossed the lobby. They were all dressed the same—girls in skirts, boys in slacks, both with the same shirts, vests, and ties. Alex sighed. She had worn a similar uniform when she was a child.

After the group of students swarmed toward the gallery with their teacher, the lobby mercifully quieted. Alex glanced at the ticket counter. A young woman sat behind it with a book pressed to her nose, most likely a student from the nearby art college. A wave of sorrow swelled in Alex's chest. That was where Lois used to sit, working on a crossword puzzle or sudoku or reading the latest bestselling novel. Alex really missed her.

Lois had been a victim of the early pandemic. She'd gotten sick only a week after the shelter-in-place order. In those early days, it had been utter chaos. There had been so much confusion and panic, no one seeming to know what to do. Lois had arrived, barely able to breathe, while Alex was on duty—not that there was a time in the beginning when she wasn't on duty. Alex had done her best to comfort Lois when she was left with no choice but to intubate. The image would forever be burned into her mind.

Lois had smiled at her. "Don't you worry your pretty little head, Dr. Alex. At my age, I could use a break from talking."

Those had been the last words Lois ever said. She had died three days later. Lois had been one of the first death certificates Alex had signed but sadly not the last. In the beginning, Alex had tried to remember every name from every death certificate she signed, but in the end, there were simply too many. They all blurred together into one long, continuous certificate where she wrote the same thing, over and over.

"Alex!"

Alex looked up at the sound of her name, pushing the memories from her head. Jamie was crossing the lobby, dressed in a pinstripe navy suit and dark blue pair of perforated leather wingtips with rainbow laces that clashed horribly with the rest of the ensemble but somehow cried out Jamie.

"Sorry, I'm a little late." Jamie rushed up and gave Alex a big hug. "It's been bonkers around here this morning."

Alex returned the hug, taking in Jamie's new haircut. It was much longer than it used to be. Had it really been that long since they'd seen each other? Alex stepped back. "It's okay, Jamie. I've only been here a couple of minutes. Just—" She waved a hand toward the ticket counter.

Jamie swallowed and took a deep breath, looking sadly at where Lois used to sit. "Yeah. I miss her too. She was as much of a fixture at this museum as the art itself."

Alex tore her attention away from the young woman who was starting a crossword puzzle by the looks of it. Lois would be proud. She turned to Jamie. "What do you say to Mediterranean?" It was their go-to lunch.

Jamie clapped her on the shoulder. "You know me. I don't need an excuse for Mediterranean, or any food for that matter."

Alex eyed Jamie up and down as they walked through the doors to the bright outside. Jamie had put on a little weight since the pandemic, but hadn't they all? Alex, who must have put on a good twenty pounds herself, could attest to that. Too much crap food, not enough exercise. But hopefully she would be able to remedy that now.

They walked across the street to Parsley Mediterranean Grill. Jamie got a tabouli salad and Alex a hummus Fattoush wrap with feta, the same thing they always ordered. At least they were consistent. And to prove the point even more, they both ordered Turkish coffee and settled into a table near the window where they could watch the cars zipping up and down Ottawa.

Halfway through their meal, Alex broached the real reason she had asked to have lunch together. "Jamie, how would you like to be my maid of honor?"

"Maid of honor?" Jamie looked perplexed, her fork floating an inch from her mouth. "Wait! Hold on! You and Jess aren't getting married, are you?"

Alex sat up straight, puffing up like a peacock. "As a matter of fact, we are."

Jamie's fork clattered to her plate. She jumped from her seat. "Oh my God, when did this happen?" She threw her arms around Alex, nearly knocking her out of her chair.

Alex could barely speak with Jamie holding her in a beartrap-like embrace. "It was a couple of weeks ago, right before that big storm."

Jamie pulled back, giving Alex a stern look. "And you've kept that from me all this time?" The serious look dissolved into manic smiling and Jamie leaning in for another hug.

Once free from Jamie's hug attack, Alex took a sip of her coffee, trying to order her thoughts. "I know. I should have called you sooner, but it's been a bit crazy. So, would you like to be my maid of honor?"

"Ah, duh. Of course, I would." Jamie sat down across from Alex, a toothy grin still firmly on her lips.

Alex relaxed. This was one item she could check off the ever-growing wedding to-do list. "Excellent. There's not a lot that has to be done. At least, I don't think so. But I do have one request if you don't mind."

Jamie snapped to attention. "Just name it, Alex. I'm here for you no matter what. It's not like my best friend is getting married every day."

"Don't answer too quick." Alex hated asking, but of anyone, Jamie would be the best. "I need to go dress shopping. Would you go with me?" She cringed.

Jamie laughed. "As long as I don't have to wear it, sure."

"I wouldn't make you do that, Jamie. I'm not that cruel. I'd go with Jess's sister, but Jordan can't keep a secret. She'd end up blurting out what my dress looked like to Jess."

"I understand. Preserve the mystery until the big day, huh?"

"Something like that." Alex knew she was being silly, but she still wanted the fairytale wedding, complete with all the customs and traditions. She leaned back and took a bite of her wrap. "I'm surprised you and Sue haven't gotten married yet."

Jamie waved her off with a lazy hand. "Oh, we've talked about it, but what's the point? We've been together so long it seems a bit…I don't know…anticlimactic." She quickly changed tack. "Not that you shouldn't get married. You two are perfect for each other and you're going to be such beautiful brides."

"Thanks, Jamie."

Before their goodbyes, they set up a date to go dress shopping. As she drove home, Alex leaned back and relaxed behind the wheel of her car. She took a deep breath, feeling a big load lift from her shoulders. One thing down—ten thousand to go.

CHAPTER SIX

Jess wheeled into Elegant Bridal with Jordan at her side. She clenched her teeth as the door closed with a resounding *thud* behind them. Jess didn't know why she felt so nervous. It was just a dress fitting. Big deal, right? But for some reason, the more excited Jordan got, the more uneasy Jess felt.

They had barely entered the shop when a loud voice with what sounded like a French accent (or was it an affectation?) called out, "Jordan, darling!" A trendy woman in her mid-thirties, wearing a crisp pair of slacks and a long-sleeved shirt with the sleeves rolled to the elbows, threw her arms around Jordan and kissed her, once on each cheek.

"Angela, dear, it's so good to see you again." Jordan returned the hug and cheek kisses.

Jess looked on, her chest growing tight. Hopefully Angela wouldn't want to hug and kiss her.

Angela released Jordan and turned to Jess. "And this must be your beautiful sister, Jess, no?"

Jess held out a leather-gloved hand. "Yes, I'm Jess...or no? I'm not sure what to answer."

"Ah, she's a funny one, your sister, no?" Before Jess could respond, Angela stepped forward and knelt, pulling her into a hug, complete with cheek kisses.

Jess didn't know how to respond so she quickly gave a peck to each of Angela's cheeks. When in Rome, or however the saying went, right? However, Jess would give just about anything to be a fly on the wall when Alex met this woman. Maybe she should warn Alex first. Jess thought about it for a second. Naw. That would ruin the surprise. She giggled to herself. Alex deserved the whole experience.

Angela stood and clapped her hands together. "So, shall we get started?"

Jess immediately liked the woman, rambunctious personality and all. She hadn't looked once at Jess's chair. That was usually the first thing people saw. Jess figured it would be doubly so during a dress fitting. Her chair would be a natural obstacle, wouldn't it? But if it was, Angela certainly didn't show it.

"First off, what does the lovely bride have in mind?" Angela took her chin in her hand, eyeing Jess up and down like an artist evaluating a sculpture that was only half carved out of the marble.

Jordan spoke right up. "I was thinking something long and flowy. Maybe lace—"

Jess spun in her chair to face her sister. "Jordan, it's my dress, not yours."

Jordan laughed, completely unfazed. "Oh yeah, I forgot."

Angela smiled at Jordan then focused directly on Jess, her focus intense. "What is your dream dress, chéri? What's the first thing that pops into your mind?"

Jess thought for a minute. What *was* it that she had always dreamed of? Part of the problem was that she hadn't allowed herself to dream that someday she would get married, at least not since the accident. She tried to picture herself in a white dress, but that was all she could muster—just some generic white dress. Finally, she lowered her eyes to her gloved hands, clenched together in her lap. "I...I don't really know. Sorry."

"No, no, please no apologies." Angela patted Jess on the shoulder. "Many women come in and have no idea. We will just look around and find the perfect one for you."

At least she wasn't the only one who had come in there with no idea what they wanted. Still, there was the proverbial elephant in the room. She was sitting in it. From the look of most of the dresses, she'd look like a big white cloud piled into a chair. It would be a miracle if she would even be able to see over all the material in her lap. She bit her bottom lip as she looked from one dress to the next. "I don't know. They are all so...I don't even know how to put it. Because of my chair..." She trailed off, simply shrugging instead.

"Not to worry, chéri. That is something we can take into account." Angela waved Jess and Jordan over to a desk covered in photo albums. "Come, come. I show you. We have made dresses for brides with...how to say?...unique challenges."

Jess rolled up to the desk with Jordan at her side. She looked down at the page that Angela had flipped open. A woman in a wheelchair, just like her, was in the most gorgeous dress. It wasn't bunchy or puffy at all. In fact, the dress looked as if it were cut specifically to look best from a sitting position. "Wow." Jess couldn't think of anything else to say.

"We have more. Look, look." Angela slowly flipped through pages of different dresses, each worn by someone in a wheelchair.

The first thing that struck Jess was how many there were—dozens. Of course, she knew there were a lot of women with her same injury. But since she had written off the possibility for herself, it hadn't occurred to her that many of them would still want to get married. Unlike her, they hadn't shied away from romance.

Angela flipped another page and Jess's eyes flew open wide. "That's it! That's the one!" Jess pointed at the page, her voice shaking. If she had to picture her dream dress, this was it.

Jordan leaned in to get a better look. "Are you sure, Jess? That's the one?"

"Oh yes, definitely." Jess hadn't realized she would get so excited. It was just picking out a dress. But she shivered as if she had a big chill blowing down her back.

"We can do that, no problem." Angela pulled out the picture from the page. "That's a very popular dress, and it works great for women sitting down. You will look beautiful. I promise."

Jess couldn't tear her eyes from the picture. She smiled widely, feeling as if she had drunk one too many glasses of wine. As much as she wanted to show Alex right then, she knew she had to keep it a secret. And that was going to be so hard. Alex was going to love it, just like she did. She turned to Jordan, her voice firm. "You cannot tell Alex. You hear me, Jordan? You cannot tell Alex no matter what."

"Sure, sis. You can trust me." Jordan gave her a wink.

Angela pulled out a chair and began to take notes, going over the process of fitting and customizing. Jordan fielded the questions, which was for the best. Jess barely heard what Angela was saying. Finally, one last question. "Is there anything specific that you can think of that needs to be changed? Any modifications?"

Jess nodded, her smile growing even more. "Yes, just one."

* * *

Alex sat on a rolling stool in trauma room two across from a young man in his late twenties. He was dressed in Carhartt coveralls and a blue checkered flannel shirt along with big, chunky brown steel-toed boots and had a bushy red beard that would make any lumberjack proud. He winced as Alex tugged a stitch snug, the twelfth so far on the gaping incision across the palm of his hand.

"And what have we learned, Bill?" Alex glanced up from her work, a smile lighting her face.

Bill lowered his head like a boy who'd been caught smuggling a frog into school in his pocket. "To not put my hand in the table saw." He let out a long sigh.

"That's right." Alex prepared the next stitch. "I'm no expert but I'm pretty sure table saws are for wood and not hands." Her voice was light, teasing.

"Yes ma'am." Bill shook his head. "It just happened so fast. I'm not even sure *how* it happened."

Alex looped the curved needle through the skin, starting yet another stitch, hopefully the last. "That's how it always happens. You wouldn't believe how many times I've heard that. But let me give you a piece of advice—the table saw always wins."

Bill laughed, flinching again as Alex drew the suture tight. "I'll have to remember that, doc."

Alex snipped off the remaining thread and leaned back, examining the long line of sutures. It was the best she could do under the circumstance. Table saws and flesh didn't mix. But if he was lucky, he'd only have mild scarring. Alex took a deep breath and smacked her hands against her thighs. "Good, then my job here is done. I'll have a nurse come in and we'll get you discharged as—"

CRASH!

Alex jumped, spinning around on the stool. "What the heck?"

Loud shouting came from down the hall, an angry male voice. And then again—*CRASH!* The sound of breaking glass filled the air along with the banging of what sounded like stainless steel sheet metal hitting the hard linoleum floor. Alex glanced back at Bill, who looked on, wide-eyed. Just as Alex turned back to the door, Frank, one of the security officers, ran past the room.

"Stay here. I'm going to go see what's going on." Alex leaped from the stool without a backward glance and slid the door open on its track. More shouting came from down the hall and around the corner. The nurses station. Alex slid the door closed behind her—she didn't need a patient involved in whatever commotion was going on—and sprinted down the hall.

She reached the corner just in time to see Frank quarterback-sack the unruly gentleman, not a light matter considering Frank's two-hundred-and-fifty-pound frame. They both went down in a hail of paper and coffee cups, knocking a large metal medical cabinet askew in the process.

Heart hammering in her chest, Alex raced up the hallway. Frank had pinned the man between himself and the floor, muffling his protests. Coffee pooled on the floor beside them. Alex heard more running coming up the hall behind her. More security had arrived, although Frank seemed to have neutralized the threat quite effectively. The two other security officers ran up and took the unruly man by the shoulders as Frank rolled off. They then pulled the man to his feet. He had started to yell again, struggling against the grip of the officers. "Conspiracies! Fake news! Fascist lefties!"

Alex stepped up. "What's going on?"

While security struggled with the man, Maria popped up from behind the nurses station. "Hey, doc. Just another fun afternoon in the ER."

Alex stepped beside Maria as security wrestled the man out of the ER. "What in the blue hell happened here?"

Maria looked around at the mess scattered across the floor. "I don't really know, doc. The guy snuck in when someone was going out and started yelling that we were hoarding all the good medicines and it was a conspiracy against true Americans." She turned to Alex and shrugged.

Alex leaned back against the wall, taking a deep, frustrated breath. She closed her eyes for a moment before rubbing her temples with her thumbs. "Good God. I don't know about you, Maria, but I'm sick and tired of all this conspiracy crap. First it was COVID's a hoax. Then it was all the anti-mask blowback. Not to mention all the supposed *alternative* treatments. You can't reason with these people." Alex hadn't meant to sound bitter, but it was frustrating dealing with this almost every day. She took another deep breath, forcing herself to calm down. "Sorry."

"Hey, don't sweat it, doc." Maria clapped her on the shoulder. "I totally agree. How many doctors and nurses have hung up their stethoscopes the last couple of years? It's almost impossible to keep the hospital fully staffed. I'm not sure I'd want to be a nurse nowadays if I was just starting out."

"Oh please, Maria, you've got nursing in your blood. You wouldn't be happy doing anything else and you know it." Alex looked over at her friend. Although there was hardly a better nurse than Maria, Alex could see the toll the past few years had taken on her. More than a few wrinkles and more than a few gray hairs. But hadn't that happened to all of them? Whenever Alex looked into the mirror, she could see lines around her eyes and mouth that hadn't been there a few years ago. She could try to chalk it up to natural aging all she liked but deep down she knew stress was really to blame.

Housekeeping arrived, busily cleaning up the mess of coffee, papers, and assorted detritus from the confrontation. Surprisingly fast, the ER shifted back into gear as if nothing had happened.

Maria gathered a stack of charts. "Whelp, excitement's over, back to work."

"Yep. Fun, fun, fun." Alex kicked off from the wall. Hopefully that would be the only excitement they'd have today. With one last deep breath, she walked back to trauma room two to discharge her patient, longing for the days when a hand in a table saw was the most exciting thing to happen in the ER.

* * *

Jess smiled as the garage door rattled up, revealing Alex's car. She'd been hoping Alex would be home when she got back. Alex's schedule could be unpredictable at times, especially if an emergency came in right before she was off. Today must not have been one of those days. Jess pulled up the ramp. They should be able to share the evening together—always a treat.

Once parked, Jess pulled out her chair from behind her seat and wheeled her way into the house. As she rolled into the living room, she came to an abrupt halt. Alex was asleep on the couch, her head flopped to the side. A snore escaped her mouth with each breath and a little trickle of drool ran down her chin. Jess smiled at the scene. Alex looked so peaceful and beautiful.

Jess watched until she figured it was venturing into the land of creepy. Who liked to be watched while they were sleeping anyway? That was like the height of stalker behavior. One last moment to take in the scene and then Jess rolled up beside Alex, gently nudging her leg.

"Hey, Legs, wakey, wakey." Jess jostled her again, and the snoring came to an end in a final almighty snort.

With heavy eyelids, Alex blinked herself awake. She stretched, her arms over her head, and yawned widely. "Oh hey, hi. When did you get home?" She yawned again.

"Just a few minutes ago." Jess wasn't about to tell her that she had been watching her sleep for the past ten minutes. "I wasn't expecting you this early."

Alex blinked again and sat up straighter. "Ah, I actually got to leave on time. And after today, I wasn't going to argue."

Jess raised an eyebrow. "Oh? Bad day?"

Alex shook her head and patted the couch beside her. "Not really. Just a bit of craziness."

Jess slid from her chair to the couch. She took Alex's hand in hers and gave it a tender squeeze. "Anything you can talk about? You know I'm here for you."

Alex returned the squeeze along with a soft smile. "Thanks, Wheels. It's nothing big really. Some guy went bonkers in the ER."

Jess covered her mouth with her free hand. "Oh my. No one was hurt, were they?"

"No, no," Alex leaned her head against Jess's shoulder, "nothing like that. It was just the same old crap—government conspiracies and fake news—blah, blah, blah. Smashed up the nurses station. Same ol', same ol'. Security took him down quick enough."

Jess sucked in a breath. Whatever Alex said, someone tearing up the ER wasn't same ol', same ol'. At least it shouldn't be. "I don't get it. How many does this make?"

"What, this week?" Alex laughed but it sounded more bitter than amused.

Jess frowned. "That's not funny, Legs. It really isn't."

Alex let out a long, weary sigh. "Yeah, I know. You're right. It just gets so exhausting, trying to treat people who don't want to be treated. I swear, it's like trying to talk to a wall sometimes. They think they know best."

"But why?" Jess slowly shook her head. None of this made sense. "Why would people come to the hospital if they won't listen? Why are they so hostile? What's causing it?"

Alex turned to face Jess. "I wish I knew for sure. Ever since COVID, people have been paranoid and aggressive." She paused for a second. "Actually, that's not true. Some were like that before. It's just gotten a lot worse, a lot more blatant. All this conspiracy crap and misinformation spewing from every direction. It's all preyed on the fears of people. They're afraid and angry. They'd rather be dead than right."

"That's sad." Jess cringed. "But I've even noticed a difference in people. People are just more angry, more aggressive, more…I don't know…entitled. And that's just a bookstore. We haven't had anyone bust up the store because *The Great Gatsby* was out of stock. Now maybe if it was *A Tale of Two Cities*." She nudged Alex in the ribs.

Alex smiled, the reaction Jess was aiming for. "'It was the best of times, it was the worst of times.' If that doesn't sum up my life at the moment, I don't know what will."

"So, are you saying being with me is the worst of times?" Jess pooched out her lip, trying to act offended.

Alex laughed and pulled her in tight, placing a kiss on Jess's forehead. "You're my best of times, you goof. Don't you ever think any differently."

After a long moment in Alex's arms—she couldn't think of a better place to be—Jess pulled back and stared directly into her eyes. That twinkle that had been missing earlier had returned. But still, she worried. What if someone did more than smash up the ER? She took a deep breath, pushing that thought from her head. Instead, she lifted Alex's hand to her lips and gently kissed it. "I'm very glad to hear that. You're my best of times too, Legs. Never forget that."

Jess snuggled against Alex, soaking in the warmth of her body, better than any electric blanket. If she could stay there forever, she would, wrapped up in Alex. The only thing better might be if they were naked. Jess fought back a giggle. She'd never pass up a chance to be naked with Alex. But as nice as that thought was, her stomach growled. She probably shouldn't have passed up the chance for lunch earlier, but after the stress of dress shopping, Jess just wanted to go home.

"Is that your stomach I hear? What, didn't you eat?" Alex leaned over and put her ear to Jess's stomach.

Jess chuckled. "Of course not. I've been starving myself just to get you to put your head in my lap. Didn't you know that?"

Alex sat back upright, eyes wide. "Oh really. Just to get me to put my head in your lap, huh?"

Jess stirred in her seat and lowered her voice to a purr. "Uh-huh. That's just where I want it."

Just then, Jess's stomach growled again, this time much louder.

Alex began laughing. "As much as I'd like to show you what I'd do if I kept my head in your lap, from the sounds of it, you need to eat. I wouldn't want you passing out from exertion because your blood sugar crashed. You're going to need all the strength you have."

Jess bumped her shoulder against Alex's. "Promises, promises. I'm going to hold you to that later, so you'd better be prepared."

Alex winked salaciously. "I like a challenge," she purred.

"I know you do, Legs." If they didn't get up from the couch soon, it would be a long, long time before Jess got to eat. She gritted her teeth and slid forward. "Okay, we'd better get some chow then. What do you say—eat in or go out? Or maybe takeout?"

Alex dropped her chin into her hand. "Tell you what, Wheels, after the day I've had, I'm not sure I'm up for cooking. And I'm definitely not up for a loud, crowded restaurant."

"I'm not either."

"So, what do you think of—"

"Pizza!"

Alex huffed. "Hey, that's what I was going to suggest."

"That just goes to show what a good idea it is then." Jess pulled out her cell. "The usual?" She hit the speed dial to Rogue River Pizza, their favorite pizza joint, and ordered their usual—mushroom, ham, and green peppers.

Twenty-five minutes later, they sat on the couch, paper plates on their laps and a pizza box between them. NPR's *Fresh Air* played in the background, something about a shipwreck and mutiny. Jess was only half listening as she tore into her third piece of pizza.

Alex jabbed her slice at Jess. She swallowed. "I almost forgot to ask you, how did the dress shopping go?"

Jess waved it off. She didn't want to give anything away. "Oh, you know, no big deal. Easy-peasy."

"What did Jordan think?"

Alex was clearly fishing, but she wasn't going to give in. "Jordan was a big help."

"So, it went well?"

Jess smiled. "Oh yeah. Just wait until you go."

Alex pursed her lips, staring down at the pizza in her hand. Her brow wrinkled.

Jess glanced over and dropped her pizza to her plate. She scrubbed her hand on a napkin, removing as much pizza grease as she could, and reached over to take Alex's hand. "It'll be fine. Don't worry. Angela who works there is amazing. She'll get you all set up."

Alex took a deep breath. "It's not that. I…I guess I'm just nervous. I never thought I'd be shopping for a wedding dress let alone getting married. After coming out…well, you know how that went."

Jess gave her hand a squeeze. She forgot sometimes how much Alex's past still caused her pain and doubt. To be raised the way Alex had and then kicked out—Jess shuddered. It was no wonder she was experiencing some anxiety. "Hey, everything's going to be okay. Trust me. You're going to be the most beautiful bride at our wedding."

Alex looked up, a smile creeping across her lips. "The second most beautiful bride at our wedding, especially with the dress I bet you picked out." She lifted her eyebrows.

Jess gave her a gentle shove. "Nice try, Legs, but I'm not telling you anything."

* * *

Alex walked along the sidewalk, staring down at her feet. A warm breeze blew her loose hair out behind her, but she barely noticed. Her stomach rolled. She was not looking forward to dress shopping.

"Are you okay, Alex?" Jamie squinted over at her, leaning in for a better look. "You seem a bit preoccupied."

Alex smirked. Preoccupied was an understatement. She'd thought of nothing else the past few days. She closed her eyes for a second before turning to Jamie. "I guess I'm a little nervous. I mean, this is a big choice, isn't it?"

"Hon, just relax. You're working this up too much in your head. It's only a dress, after all. A billowy assembly of white material and lace. Jess would think you're beautiful even if you were wearing a potato sack. Now maybe if it was a tux…" Jamie laughed loudly and clapped Alex on the back.

"Yeah, yeah. Good one. I'll let you wear the tux this time." Alex chuckled. She was working this up too much in her head. It didn't help all the emphasis put on being a bride when she was growing up. The dress was supposed to be a symbol of purity and virginity. It wasn't for unnatural homosexual fornication as her dad liked to call it. He'd been wrong back then and she wasn't going to let his views run her life any longer. Alex reached for the door at Elegant Bridal with a renewed sense of purpose. She was doing this for them, for Jess.

The moment she walked through the door, Alex stopped dead. She took in the wall of white. Everywhere she looked, wedding dresses hung on racks, on hangers, even dangling from the ceiling.

Jamie stepped up beside her and softly whistled through her teeth. "Whoa. That's a shit-ton of dresses."

Alex merely nodded. A shit-ton of dresses it was. Alex had figured maybe a couple dozen but nothing like this. How on earth was she supposed to pick something from so many? She'd be here all day.

Jamie leaned in and whispered, "Dear God, this is a butch's nightmare."

Alex snorted through her nose. She could see Jamie's point. "Darling!"

Alex jumped at the loud voice. She'd been so focused on the multitude of dresses that she hadn't seen the small, tanned woman who bustled out from the corner. This had to be Angela.

"You must be Alexandra."

Before Alex could answer, arms were around her shoulders and *smack, smack*—a kiss on each cheek. She froze. What the hell had just happened? Had she really been kissed on the cheeks by a stranger? Why hadn't Jess warned her? Alex pulled back, wide-eyed. "Actually, it's just Alex."

"Alex it is." Angela released her and turned to Jamie, going in for a hug. "And you are, chéri?"

Jamie took a step back, waving her hands in front of her as if she were fending off a mountain lion attack. "I'm Jamie and I'm good right here."

Angela merely laughed, taking no offense whatsoever. *"C'est très bien*, chéri. It's fine, it's fine. No hug needed."

Jamie continued to eye Angela, clearly ready to make a break for the door if the threat of a hug presented itself again. "Okay. Just so we've got that clear."

"Of course, darling." Angela talked rapidly, her hands constantly moving. "Come, come." She turned and waved for them to follow.

Alex gave a sideways glance to Jamie, raised her eyebrows quickly, and then followed. Seriously, why again hadn't Jess given her a heads-up? She pursed her lips, picturing Jess laughing her butt off. Paybacks were hell.

Suddenly, Angela spun around as if she were on a turntable. "Jess and Jordan say you're going to have a fall wedding. How lovely. I just love the fall, all the colors. Very beautiful, just like your bride-to-be."

Alex wasn't sure how to respond. She wasn't used to someone so unflappably buoyant, like the syrupy sweet bubble tea she'd tried once and nearly spewed everywhere. "Yes, thanks. That's why we chose October. It's Jess's favorite time of year."

Jamie stood directly behind her, keeping Alex between herself and the manic dressmaker.

"Good, good. Now let's see. Hmmmmm." Angela eyed Alex up and down, her chin in her hand. Finally, she dropped her hand and gave a crisp, firm nod. "Yes, yes, I think a size eight, no?"

Alex almost fell over, deeply impressed. Angela had nailed her dress size. However, with the number of dresses Angela fitted on a regular basis, she could probably guess everyone's dress size, much like one of those barkers at an old circus, shouting out people's weight. Alex stifled a laugh as she thought of Angela wearing a top hat and tails. *Come one, come all, and see if the amazing Angela can guess the tall lesbian's weight.* "Ah, yeah. Size eight. Good guess."

"No guess." Angela looked over Alex's shoulder at Jamie.

"Don't even think about it."

Angela laughed again. She seemed to be enjoying having fun with Jamie. "No worry. I wouldn't dare."

Jamie muttered, "Damn right," under her breath, making Alex smile. She owed Jamie big-time for this.

Angela settled down to business. "Do you have any idea what you are looking for? I find that most women have an image in their head of the perfect dress. It's my job to make that image a reality."

Alex took a deep breath. She *did* have an image in her head. She'd had that image most of her life. But would it be possible? Or was it just a little girl's fantasy? Finally, Alex opened her mouth. For the next ten minutes, she described the dress, every little detail. Angela took note after note, nodding at each item. Jamie stood by the whole time, looking as if Alex were speaking a foreign language. When Alex finished, she held her breath, waiting.

At long last, Angela looked up and smiled brightly. "No worry. This we can do. You'll be just as beautiful as that fiancée of yours. Promise."

CHAPTER SEVEN

Alex drove up Hudson Street in Lowell, going a good fifteen miles per hour over the speed limit and still wearing her scrubs. She put a little more pressure on the gas pedal and held her breath. Please dear God, don't let there be a cop around. She was running late—very late. Why was it that when she needed to be somewhere at a specific time, something inevitably came up? Alex let out a laugh. She was an ER doctor, that was why.

With the speedometer easing itself past the range of even marginal reasoning, Alex let off the gas. A speeding ticket would only make matters worse and her even later. She hated being late. That had been what had gotten her into trouble the first time she'd met Jess. Alex snorted. If she were being totally honest, it had been her mouth that had gotten her in trouble, but running late hadn't helped matters.

Alex rounded the corner into the parking lot of The Royale Event and Banquet Center, tires screeching against the pavement. Jess's car sat in the lot—empty. Not good. Not good at all. Her fiancée was not going to be happy. Alex parked in a cloud of dust and sprinted up the stone pathway. With her heart thundering in her throat, Alex busted through the front doors.

"I know, I know. I'm late. I'm really sorry." She gasped for breath.

Jess and Jordan both looked up—Jordan from the large, overstuffed couch in the lobby and Jess from her chair. From the looks of it, they'd been deep in conversation.

Jordan waved her hand high in the air. "Better late than never, huh?"

"Something like that, I guess." Alex rolled her eyes. Her shoes slapped against the marble floor, echoing off the high walls. She sat across from the sisters and slumped back against the couch, heart still bouncing around her chest like an unruly puppy. She glanced over at Jess, half afraid to see her expression, but she needn't have worried. Instead of anger, Alex was met with concerned amusement. Or was it amused concern? Whatever it was, it was the look Jess reserved for those times when Alex had done something silly—like falling to the ground because she had pushed herself beyond her limit running.

Alex finally leaned forward. "So, what have I missed?"

Jess shook her head with a smile. "Don't worry about it, Legs. We haven't gotten started yet. We've just been waiting."

"Oh no, you haven't been waiting on my account, have you? I'm so sorry." Alex closed her eyes. It was worse than she thought.

Jess wheeled over and placed her hand on Alex's knee. "Seriously, babe, don't worry about it. It's no big deal. We were just talking while we waited. But you might owe me a Frappuccino later."

Alex lifted her head, meeting Jess's deep brown eyes with her own. "Deal."

Jess slapped Alex twice on the thigh. "Excellent. I'm going to hold you to that, you know."

Of that, Alex had no doubt.

"What was up, anyway? Traffic bad? You didn't get caught in that construction on the expressway, did you?"

Alex shook her head. "No, nothing like that. Just a disruptive patient."

Jess sucked in a quick breath through clenched teeth. "*Again?* What's that, twice this week?"

Alex pursed her lips. "Something like that, yeah. Seems to be happening more and more all the time."

"Whoa." Jordan slid to the edge of her seat. "Someone go throwing bedpans around the ER?" She giggled.

Jess swatted her sister on the arm. "It's not funny, Jordan. It could be serious."

Jordan looked properly admonished. "Sorry. You're right. Bad joke. I didn't realize...you know...wow. Like people are really going nuts in the ER?"

If she hadn't been so tired, Alex would have laughed at Jordan's comically apologetic expression. As it was, she just wanted to forget about it. "It sure seems like it. I don't know, maybe it's the same but everyone is so burned out that it seems a lot worse than it is." Although part of her wanted to believe that, she knew deep down that things had gotten worse.

"Hmmm." Jess focused on Alex, her eyebrows knitting together. She opened her mouth, but Alex cut her off.

"Say, why don't we focus on something a lot cheerier." Alex looked around the lobby. "This place seems nice. I could see having our reception here."

The distraction seemed to do the trick. Jess sat up straighter, the look of concern gone for the moment. "I was thinking the same thing. This place is gorgeous. I'm just not sure if we can afford it."

Jordan jumped in. "Jessie-bessie, you're only going to get married once. You need to splurge a bit. Go a little wild. You know, live a little."

Jess smiled sheepishly.

Alex could tell that Jess really liked the place. But she also knew Jess wouldn't come right out and say that. "Jordan's got a point. Let's go a little wild." She gave a devious little wink.

* * *

Jess looked up as a tall, skeletally thin man entered from the far end of the event center, followed by the receptionist they'd met earlier. He was dressed in a dark navy suit, white shirt, and blazingly bright red tie. To Jess, he looked more like a funeral director than an event center coordinator, except for the tie. That tie would border on obscene at a funeral. Jess stifled a laugh and Jordan elbowed her in the ribs.

"Shhh," she whispered out of the corner of her mouth and stood.

Jess stared at her sister in disbelief. Alex stepped up beside Jess, placing her hand on Jess's shoulder. Jess clapped her hand over Alex's, giving it a squeeze.

The tall man stopped in front of them with a crisp click of his heels and held out his long-fingered hand, first to Jordan, then Alex and finally Jess. "Hello, I am Fyodor Kobylik. You may call me Fyodor."

Jess stared for a moment as she took his hand. She wasn't sure what else they could call the man. You couldn't very well shorten that name. Besides, what kind of parent would name their child, "Fyodor?" Then it dawned on her. His parents were probably literature majors. They were always naming their kids strange things. One of her co-workers had named her daughter "Seven" after the *Star Trek Voyager* character. Compared to that, Fyodor seemed quite tame.

Fyodor turned and gestured for them to follow him. "Come, let me give you a tour."

Jess glanced over to Alex and raised her eyebrows. Alex gave a small shrug in return. Jess waved Alex and Jordan on, taking up the rear with her chair. Her wheels glided easily over the marble floor. Jess was impressed. If only everywhere had floors as nice as this place.

Fyodor led them into a large, open room. He flipped on the lights, although they were hardly needed. Bright sunlight poured in through the high skylights, leaving large squares of diffused light on the floor. "This is the main banquet room. We can accommodate up to three hundred—more if we open the side vestibules."

Jess whistled softly, shielding her eyes from the brightness. Three hundred seemed like overkill. They would be lucky if they had a hundred. But the place was gorgeous. And they could have a huge dance floor.

Jordan stared. "Wow." Her voice was only a whisper.

Alex nodded. "You can say that again."

"Wow."

Fyodor continued as if nothing had been said. "We also provide full catering and an open bar so there is nothing to worry about on your big day. We make sure everything is perfect."

Jess liked the sound of that. She wanted everything to be perfect. And this place certainly checked off many of the boxes. There was just one thing she needed to ask. Rolling forward, she turned to Fyodor. "How is the accessibility? Are you set up for a wheelchair?"

Fyodor smiled widely, the first since they'd met him. "We pride ourselves on being accessible for everyone. The entire facility is set up for ease of access. The lower levels have elevators, and there are ramps at every set of steps. Even the paved pathways through our back gardens are specifically designed for ease of use."

Jess was impressed. Most times accessibility seemed more of an afterthought. This place had gone out of their way to include it. She caught Alex's eye and Alex gave a small nod.

They continued with the tour although Jess's mind was already made up. It was perfect in every way.

After the tour, they went through catering options. Jess's head was spinning. How could they narrow down the choices? Everything sounded delicious. They finally decided on buffet-style dinner so their guests would be able to choose their own meal items. When all that had been decided, it was the moment of truth. Jess found herself holding her breath as Fyodor calculated the price.

Finally, he cleared his throat. "For a fully catered buffet and open bar for one hundred and twenty-five guests, plus the venue rental, you're looking at thirteen thousand, five hundred, and that includes the mandatory twenty-two percent service fee."

Jess nearly fell out of her chair. Nearly fourteen grand. Dear God. If her head had been spinning before, it was now stuck in a full-blown tornado. The room swam in and out of focus. And then a warm hand touched her knee.

Alex leaned forward. "If you could give us a minute…"

Fyodor merely nodded and stood. He walked to the office without a backward glance. When he disappeared through the door, Alex turned to Jess, her voice lowered. "Are you okay, Wheels? You look like you're about to pass out."

Jordan spoke up. "I think I'm about to pass out too. Holy shit!"

Jess smiled at Jordan. Her sister had summed it up perfectly. Five thousand? Okay. Six thousand? Ouch but doable. But thirteen thousand, five hundred? Holy shit! Her mouth had grown dry.

Alex slid closer. "What are you thinking, babe?" Her brow was furrowed.

Jess laughed. Part of her wondered if a potluck in their backyard might not be the best idea after all. Baked beans and meatballs. What could be better? But another part agreed with Alex. This was a once-in-a-lifetime event. They should go a little wild. She looked up into Alex's blue eyes and shrugged.

Alex smiled back, the warm, sweet smile Jess had fallen in love with. "I know it's a lot, Wheels, but you're worth it. It's not like we're going to get married every day. We can splurge a bit."

Jess bit her bottom lip. This wasn't splurging. This was insanity. Thirteen thousand, five hundred? How could she justify that? "I don't know, Legs. That's just so much. Can we even afford that?"

Alex patted her on the thigh. "Sure. Might as well put all that overtime pay to good use. That's at least one good thing that came from the long hours at the hospital."

Jordan bounced in her chair. "Come on, Jess. You two can afford it. I say go for it. I mean, just look at this place." She waved her hand around the room.

Alex sat up straight and nodded. "Jordan's right. We've got to do it up."

Jess took another deep breath, holding it until her lungs began to burn. She finally blew it out and nodded. "Okay, okay. Let's do it." Her heart trip-hammered in her chest.

Alex leaned in and gave her a huge hug, almost pulling her from her chair. Alex's heart was beating as fast as hers.

Jordan whistled loudly, the sound echoing off the walls, and called out. "Yo, Fyodor. We're ready."

Jess blushed. Jordan lacked all sense of decorum. But she was good at getting things moving. Fyodor trotted from the office as if he'd been waiting to spring out at the slightest notice.

"Have we decided?" He held his hands out wide.

Jess sat up straight, still holding Alex's hand. "We have. We're going to go for it."

Fyodor rocked onto his toes before settling back on his feet. "Excellent. A very good choice."

Jess hoped so. For nearly fourteen grand, it had better be a good choice.

Fyodor sat across from them at the table, pulled out some more forms, and slid them over. Alex scanned through them quickly. Jess's head was still spinning too much to focus. It was just rental agreements and such, no big deal. After they signed all the forms, Fyodor slid one last piece of paper over—the down payment. "There's a fifty percent nonrefundable deposit due at the time of booking." Without a trace of apology in his voice, he continued, "We take Visa, Mastercard, and Discover."

Alex pulled her debit card from her wallet and with a swipe and a signature, they were booked.

Once outside, Alex rubbed her shoulder. "We did it, Wheels."

Jess looked up at Alex, the light breeze teasing her hair. The sun was silhouetting Alex from behind. The smell of freshly mowed grass drifted from somewhere, mixed with the acrid smell of asphalt coming from the parking lot as the late spring sun cooked the dark surface. She took one last deep breath and squeezed Alex's hand. "Yes, Legs, we did it."

* * *

Alex walked through their slider to the back deck, a glass of Tabor Hill Demi-Sec in each hand. She slid the door shut with her hip. "Thought you'd like some wine."

Jess looked up. "Oh, that sounds stupendous. It's like you read my mind." She patted the chair beside her.

Alex slowly walked across the deck, careful not to spill. She handed a glass to Jess and sat beside her, taking a long sip and savoring the wine's bouquet—crisp, sweet, a taste that made her think of late October. Or maybe it was because their wedding was constantly on her mind.

"What are you thinking about, babe? You seem a million miles away." Jess leaned over and placed a gentle hand on Alex's leg.

Alex covered Jess's hand with her own. "Just thinking about our wedding, I guess. Plans, plans, plans." Alex laughed but it sounded fake even to her.

Jess slowly bobbed her head. "You can say that again. Plans, plans, and more plans. I'll tell you what—there's a part of me that wishes we had run off and eloped—you know, plain and simple." When Jess laughed, the sound was much more genuine.

Alex chuckled, this time sounding more sincere. "I like how that sounds, Wheels—plain and simple."

"You don't think we're going a little overboard with all this, do you?"

Alex took a deep breath. "Probably but it'll be worth it. We're only going to—"

"—get married once. I know." Jess narrowed her eyes as she took in Alex, her face wearing concern. "Are you sure you're okay, Alex? Is it just what happened today?"

Alex sat up straighter. She hadn't meant to worry Jess. She was just tired. That's what it was. Between the ER and all the planning, she was beat. She took a deep breath. "That's probably a lot of it right there. That added with the planning and it's a little overwhelming."

Jess swung her chair around to directly face Alex. "I know what you mean, babe. I feel the same way."

"Remember Holland? What I wouldn't do for a little getaway like that right now." Alex stared off into the rapidly darkening hedge behind the house.

"Let's do it then." Jess slapped her gloved hands against her thighs, the *crack* making Alex jump. "Let's just drop everything and run off to Holland for the week. We won't even tell anyone where were going."

Alex was halfway out of her chair, ready to go pack a quick suitcase, when she froze. As much as she loved the idea, she couldn't up and leave with no notice. They were already short-staffed in the ER. She couldn't abandon them. And then there were the wedding plans. Alex slowly sank back into her chair. "As much as I would love to do just that, I'm afraid that now just isn't the best time. We've still got a lot to do yet."

Jess wrapped her arm around Alex's shoulder. "You're right, of course. But it was a good idea. Maybe after the wedding."

"Yeah." Alex stared off into the darkness. Maybe then things would settle down permanently.

Jess took a deep breath, her voice overly upbeat. "Besides, we've got the venue picked out. That's a big step right there. Now we can get the invitations around. Before you know it, we'll have more free time than we know what to do with."

"Yes, we've at least got the venue picked out. That's probably the hardest right there. What's left shouldn't be too difficult. As long as nothing goes goofy—"

"Oh, don't go saying that. You'll jinx us."

"That's okay, I don't believe in jinxes." Alex smiled, thankful for Jess trying to cheer her up. And Jess was right—they'd have more time once everything was completed. She just had to survive until then.

CHAPTER EIGHT

Jess wheeled through the door to her physical therapist, taking in the slightly antiseptic smell to the room. For some reason it reminded her of the blue disinfectant barbers use to sterilize their combs and scissors. She'd barely cleared the door when a voice called out her name.

"Hey there, Jess. How ya doing girlfriend?" Jerome put a hand on his hip and struck a pose.

Jerome, who was getting a little gray around the temples, reminded her of Samuel L Jackson with just a hint of Morgan Freeman to boot. "Hi, Jerome. How's it hanging?"

"Oh, you know, girl, low and to the left." Jerome let out a high-pitched laugh, one more appropriate to his drag persona, Roxy Rocket.

"Glad to hear, Jerome. Wouldn't want to lean to the right." Jerome was much different around her than with his other patients, able to be more himself.

After their greetings, Jerome turned serious. "Now tell me, have you been doing your stretches?"

"Of course." Jess hoped she sounded sincere. With all the plans, physical therapy had been relegated to the back burner.

Jerome pursed his lips, eyeing her up and down. "Uh-huh. We'll see. You know you can't keep anything from me."

Unfortunately, Jess knew that to be true. She just wasn't looking forward to being chastised.

With his lips still pursed, Jerome motioned to the padded table. "You know the drill—hop up here and we'll see how much of a liar you are."

Jess wheeled herself over to the therapy table, giving Jerome a deep scowl. Most people would probably be offended by Jerome's brazen honesty, but Jess found it refreshing. She'd much rather someone tell her to her face what they were thinking. Jess slid from her chair to the table and settled back, her legs straight out in front of her. She supported herself with her arms behind her, her leather gloves pressed against the tabletop. "Okay, let's get this over with."

For the next forty minutes, Jerome pulled, pushed, twisted, massaged, and stretched her leg muscles. Even though she couldn't feel it, Jess could tell that her muscles were tight and knotted. When Jerome focused on her hips, she could feel the movement, but just barely. She winced.

"Can you feel that?" Jerome narrowed his eyes.

"A little bit. It's more the pressure, if that makes sense."

Jerome smiled. "Good. That means the new protocols have been working. You're getting a little sensation back."

"How much do you think I'll get back?" Jess didn't want to get her hopes up but that was hard not to do.

Jerome patted her on the shoulder, his look serious. "From what I've heard, these new protocols have been getting good results with restoring some nerve impulses from just below the point of injury. For you that means mostly the impulses in your lower core and upper hips. I know that doesn't sound like much but it'll really make a difference with your core strength and stability."

Jess nodded. That made sense. A stronger core would help with sitting in her chair and with racing. However, she was going to keep the added sensations she'd been feeling in her more intimate areas to herself. As she thought about that, her cheeks grew warm. Before Jerome could notice, Jess turned away and cleared her throat. "So, how much *more* feeling do you think I'll get?"

Jerome paused, tapping his finger to his chin. "It's hard to say. Just a few years ago, any restoration of feeling with your injury would have been unheard of. But things are changing all the time. They're making breakthroughs almost every day."

"I know. I know." Jess sat up straight and let out a long sigh. Those breakthroughs, as good as they may be, would never give her her legs back. She'd accepted that a long time ago. Still, not a day went by that she didn't think about walking again. Jess was sure that was only normal for someone with her injury.

Jerome sat down beside her, threw his strong, muscular arm around her shoulders, and pulled her into a side hug. "Don't lose hope, girlfriend. You've already made amazing strides. I couldn't be prouder of you."

"Thanks Jerome. You always know just what to say." Jess turned and smiled. Jerome had always been one of her biggest cheerleaders. She stifled a laugh as she pictured him in a tight cheerleader's outfit, complete with a short little skirt.

Jerome clapped her gently on the back. "Whelp, if there's nothing more, I'd better let you get on home to that *hot* little number you're marrying." He laughed loudly and bumped his shoulder against Jess's.

As Jess was about to slide back into her chair, she paused. There *was* one more thing she had to ask.

* * *

Alex arrived home to find the house empty, which wasn't surprising on such a pleasant evening. On the kitchen table, a sticky note simply said, "Out on the trail." Alex smiled. Where else would Jess be?

With a toss of her car keys—they landed beside the sticky note—Alex scurried up the hallway, pulling her scrub top over her head as she went. She kicked off her scrub bottoms and dug fresh clothes out of the dresser. As quickly as she could, she slipped into a pair of running shorts—black with purple stripes—and a matching racerback top. When she slid her feet into her running shoes, she had to fight the urge to moan out loud. After being on her feet all day in the ER, the change of shoes felt amazing, a true foot nirvana.

Without a backward glance, she bustled out the door and minutes later, was pounding south along the White Pine Trail State Park. Alex took a deep breath, taking in the heady scent of lilac and freshly mown grass. The trees had leafed out a lot in the past week, shading the trail and casting moving shadows in the light late spring breeze. Alex wasn't sure how far Jess had gotten down the trail, but since she hadn't taken her racing chair, Alex knew she was out for a leisurely stroll and not an all-out power run. She should be able to catch up easily.

Alex jogged along at a lazy pace, taking in the beautiful setting. After a long day in the cold confines of the hospital, this was a welcome respite. She didn't get to do this nearly enough, especially since all the planning had taken up much of their free time. Alex jogged on, barely paying attention to where she was going. It felt great to just run without having to think. She had gone a little over three miles when she spotted Jess coming toward her. Even from a distance, she could see the wide smile on Jess's face. Alex waited until Jess was only a few dozen yards away. "Hey, stranger."

"Hey yourself, Legs. What are you doing out here? I thought you had to work." Jess pulled up beside her, a look of giddiness on her face.

Alex leaned down, her hands on her knees, breathing hard. Now that she'd stopped, she realized just how fast she must have been jogging. "I…I was." She huffed out the words. "It's nearly eight o'clock."

"*What?*" Jess looked at her Apple Watch, a gift Alex had given her last Christmas. "Oh my God. I had no idea it had gotten so late."

"Lost track of time, huh?"

"Yeah, something like that."

Alex laughed. "Nothing wrong with that." It was easy to lose track of time on this beautiful trail. She'd done it a time or two herself. Alex clapped a hand on Jess's shoulder. "What do you say we head on back and get something to eat."

Jess rocked her chair up on its back wheels. "I'll tell you what, Legs, you really know how to win a girl's heart."

Slowly, they walked back toward their house as shadows crawled longer over the paved trail. For a long while, they strolled along, side by side, in companionable silence. Overhead, birds called out in the trees—a few robins, a cacophony of red-winged blackbirds near the low marshy spots, and somewhere in the distance, a crow was cawing with all its heart. Jess's wheels hummed along, and Alex's feet slapped the hard surface. Alex tilted her head back, taking in the floral-scented breeze. If this wasn't heaven, she didn't know what was.

"What's on your mind over there, Legs." Jess gave her chair an extra hard push, making it zip a little ahead.

Alex snapped out of her daydream, blinking back to reality. She laughed nervously. "Oh, nothing really. Just a bunch of silliness."

Jess accelerated once again and made a quick U-turn to face her. "Alex, what you think is not silliness. Come on, you can tell me anything."

Alex shuffled her feet. "Sorry, Jess. You're right, I know you are. It's just that I was thinking about how moments like this are perfect. It's the simple things in life, you know what I mean?"

Jess thought for a moment. "Yes, there's something to be said about simple things. I think we could all use a little more simplicity in life."

Alex nodded slowly. "Exactly, but life is rarely like that."

"Well, you can't get much simpler than a walk along the trail." Jess again rocked up on her back wheels. "Except maybe delivery pizza and a movie and then…"

Alex opened her eyes wider, a slowly growing smile curling her lips. "And then what?"

Jess lowered her voice and leaned closer. "And then we'll make love and I promise you, there'll be nothing simple about that."

Alex burst out laughing. Of that, she had no doubt. She waved her arm out in front of her. "In that case, Wheels, lead the way."

* * *

The next morning, they sat out on the deck. It was one of those rare late May mornings where the temperature had just the slightest chill to it but promised a perfect day later on. And as luck would have it, they were both off that morning, an increasingly rare event. Jess cradled her coffee, inhaling the pungent steam. A half-eaten blueberry bagel sat on a paper plate in her lap. Alex sat beside her, lost in her thoughts, a tall glass of orange juice beside her, forgotten. Alex seemed to be in deep thought a lot lately. Between the wedding plans and her increasingly busy work schedule, Jess wasn't surprised. But it wouldn't last forever. Before they knew it, they'd be on their honeymoon, and this would all be a distant memory. After a long moment, Jess leaned in and stroked her fingers lightly up Alex's arm.

When Alex looked up, Jess smiled. "Hey, babe, I was thinking, now that we've got the venue picked out, we should get the invitations around."

Alex shooed a bee away that was threatening to take a swim in her orange juice. When it returned seconds later, she grabbed her glass and held it in her lap with her hand over it. She turned to Jess. "Yeah, we can do that."

Jess continued playing her fingers over Alex's arm. She paused for a long moment, taking a large sip of her coffee. "Say, I was wondering, babe, would you like the invitations to say, '*Dr. Alexandra Hartway?*'"

Alex immediately wrinkled her nose. "I don't know about that. Makes it seem like I'm putting on airs or something. Besides, everyone that's coming already knows I'm a doctor."

Jess had figured that would be Alex's response. But sometimes Alex was too humble for her own good. Jess turned to face her directly. "Babe, that's not putting on airs. I'm proud that you're a doctor. You worked very hard to be a doctor. Believe me, you deserve the acknowledgment and respect."

Alex still didn't look totally convinced. Now she pursed her lips to go along with her wrinkled nose. After a long moment, she groaned. "Fine, if you think that's best."

Jess laughed. "Great. Middle names too?"

Alex rolled her eyes; however, she couldn't quite hide the grin forming. "Good grief, that too? Nobody needs to know that my full name is Alexandra Joy Hartway."

"At least your fool parents didn't name you Jessica Tandy Bolderson. I mean, she was a great actress, but how would you like being named after *Driving Miss Daisy*?" Jess grumbled.

Alex burst out laughing. "I see your point. But if I've got to have 'doctor' in front of my name, I think it only fair to include our middle names."

Jess scowled. "Fine. You win, but don't complain when people start asking if you're going to be driving me around." She then broke out laughing too. On second thought, Alex could take her for a drive anytime she wanted.

Alex lifted her orange juice to her lips. After a big sip, she smiled rakishly. "Y'am."

Jess gaped. "Oh no, you didn't." She picked up the remaining bite of her bagel and chucked it at Alex, hitting her squarely on the forehead.

Instead of retaliating, Alex merely laughed, picked up the piece of bagel, and tossed it out into the yard for the birds. She leaned back in her chair, a wide smile still on her lips.

Jess watched Alex out of the corner of her eye. Although she was smiling and seemed in high spirits, Jess was concerned. Whenever Alex didn't think anyone was watching, she became pensive, a deep crease furrowing her forehead. Jess didn't know what to do to help. The last thing she wanted was for Alex to have more stress in her life.

After a long, quiet moment, she cleared her throat. "Hey, Alex, tell you what, I can get the invitations around if you'd like."

Alex perked up, leaning forward. "Are you sure? I mean you don't have to do it all alone."

Jess waved her off. "It's no biggie." When Alex raised an eyebrow, Jess continued, "Seriously, no biggie at all. I can get them off to the printers and then address them. I've got a bit more free time than you."

"That would be tremendous." Alex let out a deep sigh and seemed to melt into her chair. "You're the absolute best, Wheels. With everything going on, you know…"

"I know." Jess patted her thigh. "You've been so busy. Are you still understaffed?"

Alex let out a strained chuckle. "Understaffed is an understatement. We're short on nurses. The lab is backed up constantly. And we still haven't replaced Dr. Orlowski. The only thing we don't have a shortage of is patients, and bitchy ones at that."

Since Jess couldn't do anything about that, she would try her best to relieve the stress where she could, and if that meant addressing invitations until her fingers cramped, so be it. Jess leaned in closer. "Sorry, babe. I wish there was something I could do."

Alex chuckled again; this time it sounded more genuine. "Thanks, Wheels. I know you do, and I really appreciate that. It is what it is, unfortunately. But knowing you're here really helps."

"I'm glad." Jess took Alex's hand in hers and sat back. The sun was peeking over the trees, bathing the back deck in welcome warmth. Jess closed her eyes. The light turned the inside of her eyelids red, but the feeling of the sun on her face felt too good to turn away. It wasn't until someone in the neighborhood fired up a leaf blower, ruining the tranquility, that she opened her eyes again.

Alex looked over her shoulder toward the offending noise. "I guess it was too good to last forever. Damn leaf blowers."

Jess laughed. She felt the same way. But as nice as it was on the deck, the leaf blower was a reminder that they had things to do. Alex had to get to work soon—there was some sort of in-service—and she had invitations to design. "Are we still on to go to Jamie and Sue's later?"

Alex slowly nodded. "As far as I know. Sue's really looking forward to it. She said something about a surprise."

Jess sat up straight. "Oh? A surprise you say."

"Don't get too excited. You know Sue. A surprise could be anything. There was this one time she tried to make a traditional Nordic meal, complete with lutefisk. Have you ever had lutefisk?" Alex wrinkled her nose.

"Can't say that I have." From the look on Alex's face, Jess was pretty sure she never wanted to either.

"Trust me, you'd remember." Alex had a bit of a green tinge to her complexion. "It's a cured fish dish that has a gelatinous texture not much different than snot."

Jess felt her coffee and bagel rising up her throat. She covered her mouth as a small burp escaped her lips. "Let's just hope that Jamie and Sue's surprise isn't too surprising."

"Amen." Alex stood, grabbing her empty orange juice glass from the end table. She also picked up Jess's coffee cup. "As much as I'd like to sit here all day, I'd better get ready."

"Yeah, me too." Jess wheeled around to follow.

When Alex walked back into the living room ten minutes later, wearing a set of black scrubs, Jess looked up from the list she was perusing. "Hey, Legs, I hate to say it but I'm going to need a guest list from you pretty soon."

Without a word, Alex bustled over to her satchel and pulled out a legal pad with a list of names and addresses. She turned around and handed it to Jess. "Here you go. Already got it."

Jess stared, amazed. She still had at least half of her list to go yet. "Wow. You're really on the ball."

Alex shook her head. "Don't be too impressed. Like I said, I don't have a lot of people to invite."

Jess bit her bottom lip. Should she ask? If she was going to, now was as good a time as any. She took a deep breath. "Um, have you given any more thought to maybe inviting your fam—"

"No. I'm not inviting my family. I've told you, I'm dead to them and they're dead to me." Alex stomped across the room and through the door.

Jess sat staring at the door long after Alex had left. Maybe she shouldn't have brought it up. But what if Alex's family had changed? Wouldn't it be worth at least seeing? Alex might be surprised. Wouldn't it be wonderful if Alex could have the same relationship with her family that she had with hers? Besides, what's the worst that could happen?

* * *

Alex leaned in to punch the doorbell at Jamie and Sue's. Jess sat beside her, looking around at the small flowering lilac at the corner of the porch. As she waited, Alex turned and inhaled the sweet floral fragrance coming from the lilac. It was a smell that instantly took her back to childhood—the end of the school year and the promise of summer right around the corner. It was birds chirping and frogs croaking down in the marsh, helping turtles across the road and the first mosquito buzzing in her ear, longer days and shorter nights. It was late spring going into summer. And what a welcome it was after such a cold and exhausting winter.

Jess wheeled over and stuck her nose right into the blossoms. "God, I love lilacs. I wish I had a bush like this at our house."

Alex silently agreed. There was nothing more relaxing than the smell of lilac. What she wouldn't give to have a huge flowering bush ready whenever she had a trying day at the hospital. Thankfully, this wasn't one of those days. The in-service had been painless if dull. Still staring at the light purple bush, Alex jumped when the door opened.

Jamie stepped out and threw her arms around Alex. "Cool. You guys are here." She let go of Alex and drew Jess into a warm embrace. "Sue's been driving me nuts." Jamie laughed as she let Jess go and waved them into the house.

Alex leaned in and lowered her voice as they walked up the hallway. "Why, what's up? This isn't about Sue's surprise, is it?"

Jamie laughed again. "You have no idea. Sue's been experimenting with cooking again. This time it's a traditional Scottish meal, complete with haggis."

Jess chimed in. "Haggis as in boiled sheep's guts?" Her face turned a decidedly green color.

Alex's stomach churned. She loved Sue and wanted to support her in her cooking, but this may have finally crossed a line. She took a deep breath as they stepped into the kitchen, the aroma of basil and garlic heavy in the air. "It doesn't smell bad."

Sue turned around from the stove with a large wooden spoon in her right hand and a glass of wine in her left. She wore an apron that read, "Kiss the cook, dammit!" with some sort of red sauce splattered all down the front. "Hey, here come the brides."

Alex groaned. "Haven't heard that one before." Her voice dripped with sarcasm.

Jess sat up tall, her chest puffed out. "Why thank you, Sue. That never gets old."

Alex wasn't so sure about that. It may have been cute the first dozen times, but the last thing she wanted to think about was wedding plans.

Jamie walked to the kitchen table and plopped down on a chair. She pointed to an empty chair on the opposite side. "Here, have a seat, Alex. I'd offer you a seat too, Jess, but you brought your own."

"Always the witty one, Jamie. Hardy har har." Jess stuck out her tongue and rolled over to the table.

"Don't you know it." Jamie looked proud of herself. "We can have some wine while Sue works on her surprise."

Alex filled two glasses with the open bottle of Round Barn Redel Doux and took a sip. It was a sweet red wine with a big, round, full-bodied taste, just what Alex liked best. It reminded her of cool autumn nights sitting around a campfire, the stars twinkling in the brisk night sky. She swirled her glass and took another sip. "This is a really good wine. I haven't heard of it before."

Sue held up her own glass. "It's from Round Barn Winery, down in Niles, Michigan. I thought it would pair well with dinner."

Alex wasn't sure anything would pair well with haggis, except maybe scotch and a lot of it.

Jess leaned over and whispered into her ear. "It doesn't really smell like I thought it would."

Sue had the ears of a bat. "Why? What did you think I was making?"

Alex cringed. How to say it without hurting her friend's feelings? "Well, you see, it doesn't smell how you'd think haggis would smell."

Sue gaped for a long moment, looking completely nonplussed, the wooden spoon in her hand slowly drooping. "Haggis? Who said anything about haggis?"

Jamie burst out laughing. She pointed a finger at Alex and Jess. "I got you soooo good. You should have seen your faces."

A dinner roll bounced off Jamie's head. Sue stood with her hand on her hip, a scowl deeply lining her face. "Keep it up, smartass, and you can have P B and J for dinner." Her face began to twitch then Sue broke out laughing.

Alex snorted, blowing wine out of her nose. As she coughed, Jess patted her on the back, giggling. "So, if it's not haggis or any other Scottish delicacies, what is that because it really does smell delicious."

Alex dabbed the corners of her eyes with a linen napkin. Her sinuses screamed in protest. Wine of any sort didn't feel good when it went up the nose.

Sue looked from Alex to Jamie and scowled once again. "Look what you did to our guests. I swear, we can't have anyone over."

Jamie merely shrugged, a mischievous grin on her face.

Sue shook her head and turned back to Alex and Jess. "We're having spaghetti and homemade meatballs. I figured a little comfort food wouldn't hurt anyone."

* * *

After dinner, they made their way onto Jamie and Sue's back deck where they had their hot tub. Although they'd gone for a soak many times with Jamie and Sue, Jess still felt self-conscious getting naked in front of them, not that anyone stared at her—well, except for Alex, and she stared anytime Jess was naked. Unlike her more able-bodied friends, getting undressed and then from her chair into the tub was a big ordeal.

Jess slid into the warm, bubbling water and guided herself into the underwater seat, settling in with the water nearly to her chin. The wine immediately went to her head, giving her a floaty, swoopy feeling. Steam rose into the rapidly cooling late-spring evening. The heat and the bubbles felt great against her skin, particularly her shoulders and upper chest, the areas that took the most abuse from being in her chair. She turned to Alex. "You know, we should get one of these things for us."

Alex laughed, the bubbling water barely covering her bare breasts. "You say that every time."

Jamie splashed water at them. "You really should. Believe me, it's been a real life saver."

Sue chimed in. "I don't know about 'life saver' but I can tell you that it has certainly helped my bad back and sore muscles."

"Gee, I'm not sure. These things are really expensive." Jess cringed. That seemed like all they did anymore—add more and more expenses.

"I don't know, Wheels. I could get used to this. Maybe we should look into it." Alex nudged Jess's arm under the water with her elbow.

"We'll have to put a pin in it, Legs." Jess certainly felt the water working its magic on her sore muscles—there was no denying that—but now was not a good time to think about luxuries like hot tubs.

They discussed a wide range of topics over the next hour. With her neck rolled over the headrest and her face turned to the cool, refreshing night sky, Jess felt as if the hot tub had melted her body, usually a mess of knots and sore muscles. It wasn't until the topic of their wedding came up that Jess tensed. She'd been hoping to avoid the subject, at least for one evening.

"So, how are preparations going for the happy couple?" Sue leaned forward, the bubbles rising between her submerged breasts.

Alex let out a long, low groan. "They're going. We finally nailed down the venue, and the invitations should be going out soon. I'll tell you what, I'm counting down the days until this is behind us and we can get to the real fun."

Jess squeezed Alex's upper thigh under the water. "Yeah, shouldn't be much more other than the cake and some odds and ends."

Jamie sat up straight, only millimeters from exposing her whole chest. "Just wait until you see what Jordan and I have planned for your bachelorettes' party. You know, a night of wild debauchery before you two slap on the ol' ball and chain."

Jess looked to Alex and raised her eyebrows. From the look on Alex's face, that particular ritual had slipped her mind as well. As far as she was concerned, a nice quiet evening with some barbeque and a little wine out on the back deck would make a wonderful bachelorettes' party.

Jamie looked from Alex to Jess and back. "Don't look like that. You guys are only going to get married once. Besides, I could really use a night out."

Alex slowly closed her eyes, looking as if she were about to slide under the surface of the water. Jess felt like doing the same. One more thing to do. But they were only getting married once. As long as they kept telling themselves that, things should be fine.

Jess let out a deep breath. "Just let us know when and where."

Jamie bounced like an overly excited child entering an amusement park, her breasts splashing out of the water. Jess tried not to stare. She turned to Alex, who, from the look of it, was contemplating drowning herself.

Sue pulled Jamie back into her seat. "Good God woman, calm down. You're giving everybody a peep show."

"So?" Jamie settled back in, completely unabashed. "It's just hard not to get excited. This is going to be the best bachelorettes' bash ever."

Alex groaned again, blowing bubbles with her lips. "That's what I'm afraid of."

Jess squeezed Alex's thigh again under the water. That was what she was afraid of also. But together, they'd get through it.

* * *

Later that night, Alex lay awake in bed, staring up at the moonlight dancing across the ceiling. It had been a welcome break visiting friends—a break from work, from wedding planning, from everything. What she wouldn't give to be sitting in their own hot tub, the stress of it all behind them. She took a deep breath and turned her head to the side. Although the moonlight shone through the window, Alex couldn't tell if Jess was asleep or not. After a long moment, she rolled onto her side and propped herself up with her arm, the sheet falling away from her breasts. "Hey, babe. Are you awake?"

"Mmmmm huh." Jess's voice was thick. "What's up?"

Alex paused, considering the question. Finally, she let out a long, soft sigh. "Feels like we're going a little overboard with all this wedding stuff, don't you think?" She bit her lip, waiting.

Jess rolled over to face her, eyes slowly opening and closing. "Yeah, I know what you mean but we're only going to—"

"—get married once. Yeah, yeah, I know." Alex hesitated. She didn't want to hurt Jess's feelings. "It's just...well...I was thinking that...you know..."

"Is it that bachelorettes' party that Jamie brought up?"

Alex nodded. "Ah, yeah. That's a lot of it, I guess."

Jess chuckled in the darkness. "I don't blame you. The thought of galivanting all over town doesn't really appeal to me. I'd rather have a quiet evening in the backyard with friends."

"Yeah, me too. All this craziness is just...well crazy." Alex laughed softly. "But I guess it'll all be worth it. We're only—"

"—getting married once."

Alex closed her eyes and flopped onto her back. She couldn't argue with that.

CHAPTER NINE

Jess was looking forward to today. Compared to all the other wedding plans, this one should be the most fun—or at least the most delicious. Today they'd get to pick out their cake, and the cake lady (as Alex liked to call her) had cooked up several samples for them to taste. Jess had no doubt that everything would be scrumptious. This was the same baker who had made the cake for Jordan's wedding.

Jess zipped through the living room, the wheels on her chair squealing on the hardwood floor as she made the turn into the kitchen.

"Careful there, Mario. You're liable to crash into the fridge." Alex laughed as she jumped out of the way.

Jess grabbed the right wheel and spun her chair quickly around like some sort of pirouette. She came to rest with her front wheels off the floor, balancing in the middle of the kitchen on her back wheels. "That would be a hard one to explain. Here I came flying through the kitchen and took out the entire fridge."

Alex laughed harder. "Actually, anyone that knows you would have no trouble believing that. You're like Evel Knievel in that thing."

Jess polished her knuckles against her chest. "Why thank you, Legs, that has to be the nicest thing anyone's said to me in a long time." She had to admit that she was a bit of a daredevil in her chair but that was just who she was. She rocked back and forth on her rear wheels. "Vroom vroom. Are you ready to go?"

Alex grabbed her keys from the kitchen counter. "As I'll ever be. Lead the way."

Jess zipped out the door to the garage with Alex at her metaphorical heels. She had just reached the passenger door of Alex's car when a phone went off. Jess whirled around.

Alex pulled her phone from her back pocket and held up a finger as she answered it. Jess watched as her smile quickly disappeared, the lines on her forehead getting deeper and deeper. Jess didn't need to be psychic to know that something had gone wrong.

Alex nodded as she talked. "Uh-huh. Uh-huh. Uh-huh. I see. Okay, be there in a bit."

Jess's heart sank as Alex slowly lowered her phone. "You got called in, didn't you?"

"I'm afraid so. Dr. Bryce has a wicked case of food poisoning." Alex looked up, sadness and disappointment warring each other on her face. "Dammit, I really wanted to go with you. This fucking sucks! I'm so sorry."

Jess wasn't sure what to do. They couldn't very well cancel the appointment with the baker. Cake lady had made samples. "Hey, babe. It's okay. Don't sweat it. I can bring some home for you to try. Jordan's going to be there anyway."

Alex gritted her teeth. "I guess, but I still feel like I'm letting you down. We've been planning this for weeks."

"It's okay. I understand. When work calls, right?" Jess wheeled over and took Alex's hand in hers. Although she'd been looking forward to picking out a cake with Alex, this was more important. She gave Alex's hand a shake. "Go. Save the world."

At that, Alex smiled. "Thanks, Wheels. I'll make it up to you."

Jess kissed Alex's hand before she let it go. "No need, Legs. You already have."

Alex ran around to the other side of her car and opened the door. Before she climbed in, she called over the roof. "Save me some cake, babe."

"You bet, babe." Jess waved as Alex backed out of the garage. She watched Alex's car disappear and sighed. She was proud of Alex. Being a doctor was an amazing accomplishment. But still sometimes she wished that it didn't take her away so often. Jess finally turned and wheeled back into the house for the keys to her own car. She'd have to drive herself. At least Jordan would be there with her. Besides, it was just a cake tasting. Nothing horrible ever happened at a cake tasting, right?

Jess met Jordan outside the bakery, a cute brick building in downtown Grand Rapids with several wedding cake demos in the large front windows. Fancy gold painted letters spelled out the name of the business—Cakes by Karen—along the top of the glass.

As Jess wheeled up, her sister gave her a quizzical look. "Where's Alex? I thought she was coming along." Jordan looked professional in her gray tweed pants and matching vest.

Jess came to a sudden halt, her gloved hands pressing firmly against the pushrim, which was hot against her palms. She looked up, shielding her eyes from the bright sun. "We were just about to get in the car when she got a call from the hospital."

Jordan placed a hand on Jess's shoulder. "Hey, sis, are you okay?"

Jess waved her off with a laugh although she couldn't quite keep the bitterness out of it. "Yeah, I'll be fine. I was just looking forward to doing this one thing with Alex."

"I understand, sis." Jordan leaned down and kissed Jess on the top of her head. "I know Alex would be here if she could."

"I know, Jordan. I know." Jess nodded. There was no point sulking about it. "What do you say we go get this over with. I promised Alex that I'd bring home some samples."

Jordan straightened up, bouncing on her toes. Her hair bounced on her shoulders. "Sounds good. I've been looking forward to tasting cake all morning."

Jess chuckled. How Jordan could maintain her slim, athletic figure with her love of all things sweet was a mystery she'd never solve. It would go right down there with other great mysteries, such as where the Ark of the Covenant went and what happened to the lost Roanoke colony. She waved her arm toward the door. "After you, sis."

They were met by a woman in her early fifties—presumably Karen of Cakes by Karen. She looked like a cross between Martha Stewart and Dame Edna with her cool blond bob and cat-eye glasses. But it was the crisp apron she wore over her flower print blouse that really completed the picture. Jess wouldn't have been surprised if this woman had fallen right out of *Good Housekeeping*, the wedding edition.

Jordan held out her hand to Karen. "It's been too long."

"Ah yes, Jordan Poremski. Chocolate fudge six-layer cake with whipped frosting." She turned to Jess. "That was such a beautiful cake for such a beautiful bride."

Jordan blushed, something she didn't do often. "Thanks Karen." She spun around and waved Jess forward. "Let me introduce you to my sister, Jess. She's getting married in October."

Karen took Jess's hand in hers and gave it a limp shake. "Pleasure is all mine." She then looked over Jess's shoulder as if expecting more. "Your fiancé won't be joining us?" There was just the hint of accusation in her voice.

Jess quickly bristled. Who was this woman to judge? But as fast as her irritation rose, she pushed it back down. She put on a wide smile, hoping it didn't look as fake as it felt. "I'm afraid not. Alex, who's a doctor, got called into the hospital at the last minute."

"Oh, a doctor. You lucky girl." Karen opened her eyes wider and gave a firm nod.

There was something about Karen's voice that set Jess on edge. Of course, she considered herself lucky to be marrying Alex, but it had nothing to do with Alex being a doctor. Hadn't society gotten past the notion that a woman should pick her spouse by their financial success or the job they did? Jess took a deep breath, doing her best to calm down. She knew she was being overly sensitive. However, she didn't need any reminders of why Alex couldn't be here. When Jess finally answered, she tried her best to put on a happy face. "Yes, I am very lucky to be marrying Alex, thank you."

With the niceties out of the way, they got down to business. Karen led them into the kitchen at the back of the store. Jess shielded her eyes at first as the bright overhead lights reflected off every surface—sinks, tables, counters, ovens, cupboards. The entire room was made of stainless steel. When her eyes adjusted, she noticed a half dozen small cakes lining the stainless-steel center island, each on a small, clear glass serving plate, the type that was sold through Avon in the sixties and seventies, that staple of every American grandma's pantry.

Jess rolled up to the counter. She could barely see over the top, but she was used to that. Karen began her presentation as if each cake were a contestant in a beauty contest. She started with the cake farthest to the right. "I wasn't sure what you had in mind, so I went with some of our most popular choices." She picked up a knife and cut into the cake. The surface resisted for just a second before the knife passed through. She doled out a small wedge onto a paper plate and slid it over to Jess. Another wedge slid in front of Jordan.

Before Jess took a bite, she looked from the slice of cake to Karen. "Is it possible to take some home so Alex can try it too?"

"Why of course, Jess. Anything for the bride." Karen smiled brightly, her voice saccharin sweet. Jess found it more creepy than welcoming. Karen pointed to the cake with her own fork. "Since you look like a traditional young woman, we'll start with a confetti cake."

Jess wasn't sure how traditional she was, but she would go with it. It was just a cake, after all.

Karen continued. "This is a twist on the old standby, yellow cake. It has rainbow sprinkles in it, always a crowd-pleaser."

"Oh, I love rainbows." Jess stabbed the slice with her fork and raised it to her mouth. The cake melted on her tongue. It was light and fluffy with just a hint of lemon. The real treat was the little rainbow sprinkles that exploded with sweetness on her tongue. "Oh my, this is so good." Jess tried to cover her mouth with her hand as she spoke.

Karen smiled, a knowing look on her face as if she had expected no other reply. She quickly cut wedges out of the next cake in line and slid them in front of Jess and Jordan. "This is another popular choice—our chocolate decadence cake. It's a dark chocolate cake with Amaretto, chocolate buttercream, and to finish it off, dark chocolate ganache."

Jess took a bite and moaned. The cake was so creamy, she didn't even have to chew. The chocolate drizzled down her throat. "This is so rich."

Jordan looked over, a smudge of chocolate beside her mouth. "If I'd known about this, I'd have done it for my cake."

Karen laughed. "It's new, especially for chocolate lovers."

"I can see why it's popular." Jess licked her lips, feeling as if she were going into a sugar haze.

They continued through the next two—a hazelnut praline cake which nearly caused Jess to roll out of her chair and a red velvet cake with thick cream cheese filling. Although delicious, Jess was getting overwhelmed with the sweet treats. Her blood sugar had to be through the roof.

The next cake was a surprise. When Karen cut into it, it had a deep orange color and crumbly texture. "This is one of the newer trends and since you're having a fall wedding, it would be perfect. Carrot cake with cream cheese frosting."

"Carrot cake? I'd have never thought of that." Jess watched as Karen cut out two slices and slid them over.

"Yes, this is popular with those who are looking for something a little out of the ordinary." Karen smiled at them over the cake, eyeing Jess up and down as if to determine how out of the ordinary she might be.

Jess took a bite. The cake was super moist with a hint of something else. Was it cinnamon? But it was the cream cheese frosting that really made the cake. It was like eating an old-fashioned sweet bread combined with a New York cheesecake. "Mmmmmm. Wow, I really like this."

Jordan leaned over. "Yeah, me too. Although that chocolate decadence cake was to die for."

Jess wasn't surprised. If Jordan could eat chocolate morning, noon, and night, she would.

Karen merely laughed and pulled the last cake in front of her. "Still going with the fall theme, this is a great cake for an October wedding. It's our pumpkin spice cake, but it's not like any pumpkin spice you've ever had." She cut two wedges and slid them over.

Jess took a bite. Karen was right—this wasn't like any pumpkin spice treat she had ever had. If she closed her eyes, she could picture crisp autumn air, crunchy apples right off the tree and long, horse-drawn hayrides while snuggled under a warm wool blanket with Alex. It was the perfect picture of fall in Michigan. She wiped the crumbs from her bottom lip. "Oh man, this is so good too. I don't know how we'll ever choose."

Karen smiled from across the counter, looking like the Cheshire Cat. "Perhaps you won't have to."

Jess looked from the cakes in front of her back to Karen, trying to figure out what the baker was getting at.

Seeing her confusion, Karen pulled out a book of wedding cake designs. She dropped it on the table, spun it around to face Jess and Jordan, and opened to a page marked by a dog-eared corner. With a long red nail, she pointed to the picture on the page.

Jess leaned in closer with Jordan right beside her until their shoulders touched. The cake on the page was made up of several small cakes around the base holding up three larger layers of cake above it. It reminded Jess of a flowing waterfall. "That's absolutely gorgeous."

"Nothing is too good for a bride. That's what I always say. You're only going to get married once." Karen tapped her finger to the small cakes at the base. "What we can do is make these cakes into several different types. That way, everyone can have what they like. It's very popular."

Jess liked the idea, and she was sure Alex would too. That way they wouldn't have to narrow the choice down to a single flavor. "You wouldn't mind doing that?"

Karen waved her off. "Like I said, it's really popular, and nothing is too good for the bride."

Jordan bumped Jess's shoulder with her own. "I wish I had known about this when I got married. It would have made everything easier. Tim and I couldn't decide. We even got into a tiff, and he had to sleep on the couch for a couple nights." Jordan laughed loudly.

Jess joined in. "Poor Tim."

Karen nodded. "Believe me, we've had more than a few arguments over the cakes. That's why this is the perfect option. Guaranteed argument free."

Jess relaxed. This was going to be easier than she had anticipated. She liked the design of the cake, and with the multiple flavors, it was the perfect option. Jess pulled the book closer and leaned in. "There's only one thing. We're going to have to change the topper." She pointed to the small bride and groom atop the cake.

Karen dragged the book away from Jess, shuffling through the pages at the end. "That's not a problem at all. We can get toppers with different hair colors for the groom, different hair styles. There's also different skin tones. I do believe we can even get one with the bride in a wheelchair."

Jess laughed and pointed to the groom, tapping her finger on the picture. "Actually, we'll be needing a second bride."

Karen looked stumped, as if trying to solve the quadratic equation in her head. "A second bride? You mean there's going to be two weddings at once and you need two toppers?"

Jess could see the confusion. Although same-sex marriage had been the law of the land for the better part of a decade, it still wasn't widely spread in conservative West Michigan. She smiled, taking on the demeanor of an elementary teacher. "No, just one wedding. I'm marrying my girlfriend."

Karen slowly shook her head, her lips pursed as if she'd sat down on the back deck with a big pitcher of lemonade only to realize with the first sip that she hadn't put in any sugar. "But I thought you said your fiancé's name was Alex."

Either this woman really didn't get it, or she was trying to be deliberately dense. As she looked over at Karen, Jess had the sinking feeling it was the latter.

Jordan chimed in. "That's correct, Karen. Jess's fiancée is named Alex, as in Alexandra. You're going to love her."

Somehow Jess doubted that. Karen's face had taken on a shade of puce that resembled a plum three weeks past its prime. She'd seen that look before enough times to know this wasn't going to end well. And sure enough—

"You're marrying another *woman*?" Karen spit the words out.

Jordan was just beginning to catch on. "That's not going to be a problem, is it?"

Jess could have told her sister that was a stupid question. Of course it was going to be a problem.

Karen jumped up, her arms crossed over her substantial bosom. Her face had moved from puce to the blotchy red and yellowish mottled sickliness of a corpse that had been under water for a few months in the hottest part of the summer. "I'm afraid I don't believe in such wickedness. The good book says that marriage is between one woman and one man, not some perversion like two women. That's as bad as a woman marrying a goat."

"A goat? Wow." Jess couldn't believe what she was hearing. She glanced over at Jordan and from the look on her face— mouth hanging open and nose crinkled—Jordan couldn't believe it either.

Before Jess could say anything else, Karen began beating her hand against her chest. "I cannot be a part of such sick perversion. My religion says homosexuals are a sin and God hates sin. My cakes are a part of me. They are my creation, and I won't let my creation be twisted to the devil's purpose. Now leave." She pointed to the door.

Jess stared, unable at first to move. There was only one word that came to mind. "Wow." She repeated it again. "Wow." Quickly regaining her faculties, Jess turned to Jordan and tugged her by the hand. "Let's get out of here."

Jordan stared at Karen as if unable to tear her eyes away. Finally, her voice not much more than a squeak, she uttered one last thing. "But you made my cake for my wedding."

Jess felt for her sister. In that one simple statement, she could hear both the disbelief and the hurt. She squeezed Jordan's hand to get her attention. "Come on, sis. Believe me, it's not worth it."

In silence they both walked out the door. Jordan flinched when the heavy door banged shut behind them. She turned to Jess, tears beginning to well in her eyes. "Oh Jess, I'm so sorry."

Jess clenched her teeth, too angry to cry. That would come later. But for now, she just wanted to get out of there. "It's not your fault, Jordan. It's nothing I haven't gone through before." She spun around and wheeled away up the sidewalk, Jordan following with her shoulders slumped.

* * *

Alex was anxious to see how the tasting had gone and looking forward to sampling some of the cake that Jess had promised she'd bring home.

When she rounded the corner onto their street, Alex spotted Jordan's car parked behind Jess's and Tim's car parked in front of the garish fishing lure mailbox. Alex stared out the windshield, a sinking feeling in her stomach. "Uh-oh. This can't be good."

Although she'd half-expected Jordan, the addition of Tim, especially on such a beautiful day where he'd most likely be out on a golf course somewhere, did not bode well. Alex pulled into the driveway, drove past Jordan's car and parked in the garage. Alex sat behind the wheel for a minute, taking a deep breath before she threw open her door.

When she walked into the living room, Alex found Jess sitting on one end of the couch and Jordan on the other. Tim sat across from them, his head bent forward as if he were staring at his shoes. Alex's heart painfully skipped a beat. Had someone died? Surely, Jess would have called her if something like that had happened. Alex stopped in front of the coffee table. "What's going on?"

Everyone looked up slowly. Jordan's eyes were red. Tim's brow was furrowed. But the biggest shock was Jess. Not only did she look tired, but also beaten down, defeated, angry. Jess leaned back against the couch. "Well, we've had an interesting day. How was yours?" Her voice dripped with sarcasm, a sour, humorless tone.

Alex walked over to Jess and kneeled in front of her. She placed her hand on Jess's knee. Although Jess was putting up a strong front, Alex knew from Jess's rigid posture that she was doing her best to hold it together. "What happened? I thought you were going to that cake tasting."

Jordan sniffled on the other end of the couch. She wiped her nose. "That's what we did. But it...but it..."

"It didn't go well." Jess laughed and snorted at the same time.

Alex was completely baffled. "I don't understand. What do you mean it didn't go well?"

Jess gritted her teeth, making a nasty creaky sound. Alex winced, shivers going up her spine. The sound was like nails on a chalkboard.

Tim spoke up for the first time. "Apparently cake lady is a raging homophobe. When she found out that Jess was marrying you—" he nodded toward Alex "—she went ballistic and kicked them out."

Alex turned on her knee, gaping at Tim. "Are you serious?" In this day and age, that type of bigotry was still alive and well? Same-sex marriage had been legal for so long that she thought most people had gotten used to it. Then she thought about her own family. She really shouldn't be surprised. Alex turned back to Jess. "Are you okay? I mean, what are you going to do?" She felt stupid asking but couldn't think of anything else to say.

"Oh, I'm as right as rain." Jess laughed. It sounded more than a bit like Heath Ledger when he played the Joker.

At the other end of the couch, Jordan teared up. "I'm so sorry, sis. If I knew Karen was like that at all, I would never have suggested her. I would never have used her in my own wedding." She sniffled again.

Jess softened. "It's not your fault, Jordan. How could you have known?"

"Exactly. It's not like these people go out of their way to advertise their hatred." Tim stood and pulled Jordan into a firm embrace.

Jess scooted the length of the couch and reached out to take Jordan's hand as she cried in Tim's arms. "Hey, sis. Don't you go beating yourself up over this. Really, it's nothing we haven't had to deal with before."

Alex sat beside Jess. She hated to admit it, but Jess was right—this was nothing they both hadn't dealt with before. She could picture her own father praising cake lady for her Christian convictions. She took Jess's free hand in hers. "Look, fuck her. We'll just get another baker. She's not going to ruin our wedding."

Jordan seemed to be calming down. She even cracked a smile. After giving Tim a big hug, Jordan sat down beside Jess, no longer crying outright. "What are we going to do about this? We can't let her get away with it, can we?"

Alex wasn't sure there was anything they *could* do. The woman had refused to bake their cake, end of story. However, Tim had retaken his seat and sat stroking his nonexistent beard. He seemed to be giving it quite a lot of thought. Finally, he leaned forward, tapping his index finger against the side of his head. "Well…there are a few options." His voice had taken on his professional lawyer tone. "It all depends on what you're willing to go through?"

Alex was about to speak up when Jess beat her to it. "What do you mean what we're willing to go through? Haven't we been through enough already?"

Tim continued tapping the side of his head. "Well…yes you have. And if you want to forget about this and put it in the past, I completely understand."

Alex found herself nodding in agreement.

Jordan slapped her hands against her thighs, making a loud *clap*. "But then she gets away with it. We can't let her do that."

Tim smiled his best lawyer smile. "In that case, there's a couple of other options. I have a friend who'd love to handle a case like this. I'm no expert, but what this Karen did is against the law. The Michigan Supreme Court has ruled that LGBTQ people are protected from discrimination in the areas of employment, housing, education and public accommodations under the state's civil rights law. That means if you're a business that is open to the public, you don't get to pick and choose who your customers are."

Jordan bounced in her seat. "Then that's what we need to do. We need to sue the crap out of Karen."

Alex groaned quietly so that only she could hear. The last thing they needed was to get embroiled in some lawsuit.

With a moony schoolboy grin, Tim watched his wife. "And that is why I love you so much, Jordan, my own social justice warrior. But I'm afraid that wouldn't be up to you. You weren't denied service. As far as that goes, neither was Alex. She wasn't there. So, this would be all up to Jess."

Jess chewed on her lower lip. "Damn, I don't know. What's the downside? If I do this, will there be consequences?"

Tim laughed, back to his lawyer self. "The downside is that this could—or probably even would—turn into a media circus. These types of lawsuits are big news, and you can bet that Karen the cake lady will have a ton of fanatics on her side, painting her as the victim in all this, as well as some pretty high-priced conservative lawyers taking this case pro bono. They'll more than likely try to turn your life upside down. As much as I hate to say it, it's anything but a slam dunk."

Alex didn't like the sound of that. They had enough going on without the entire world getting involved in their business. And the last thing she wanted was to deal with any religious nutjobs like her own family.

Jess threw her hands in the air. "Shit, I don't know. Part of me would love to really stick it to that bitch but another part doesn't want our life upended. What else could we do?"

Tim thought for a few seconds, back to stroking his imaginary beard. "There's always filing a complaint with the City's Office of Equity and Engagement. They would do an investigation to see if cake lady's policy violates the City's Human Rights Ordinance, which I can tell you right now that it does. However, that doesn't mean they can do much other than issue a civil infraction penalty and seek injunctive relief. Even if they levy fines on cake lady, chances are someone will start a crowdfunding campaign and she'd actually come out smelling like a rose, at least financially."

Jordan fumed. "That's not right."

Tim laughed bitterly. "No, it's not right but that's the world we live in. It happens all the time, I'm afraid."

None of the options were great. If they filed a lawsuit, their lives would get turned upside down. If they turned it over to the City's Office of Equity and Engagement, even if the woman was found guilty, she might actually come out ahead. Or they could do nothing, try to put it behind them, and the bitch would get away with it. She turned to Jess. "What do you think, Jess?"

Jess dragged her fingers through her hair, causing it to stick up in several places. Instead of answering, she turned to Tim. "We don't have to make any decisions right now, do we?"

Tim smiled and leaned forward. "Of course not. Why don't you two talk it over and let me know."

Jordan spoke up. "But—"

Tim cut her off before she could protest too much. "We're going to let them talk it over. And we're going to go home and give them some privacy."

With that, Tim stood and took Jordan by the hand. After a quick round of hugs, Tim and Jordan left. Once they were gone, Alex wrapped her arm around Jess's shoulders. "I'm sorry I wasn't there for you today."

With a deep sigh, Jess collapsed against the back of the couch. "It's not your fault, Alex. It would have happened whether you were there or not."

"Still…" Alex turned to better face Jess. "So, what are you wanting to do, you know, with all this?" Alex waved her arm around in the air.

Jess thought for a minute. When she answered, she sounded exhausted, as if she had just done a full marathon. "To be honest,

Alex, I simply don't know. I mean it's a lot to take in. At first blush, I really would like to stick it to good ol' Karen from Cakes by Karen—make her really suffer. And I don't want anyone else to go through the same thing. But is that the right thing to do?"

Alex rubbed the back of her neck, smoothing out muscles that had grown as tight as if she'd just finished a double shift in the ER during the worst of the pandemic. "I see what you're saying, babe, but is it worth all the hassle? Don't we have enough going on already?"

Jess sat up straight, her nostrils flaring. "But we've got to do something. We can't just roll over and let someone treat us like this. We've got to stand up for what is right."

Alex closed her eyes. This was what she was afraid of. Jess had always been a fighter, that was one of the things that had attracted her to Jess in the first place, but should this be their battle to fight? Wouldn't it be much easier to just find another baker? Finally, Alex let out a sigh and slowly opened her eyes. "You're absolutely right, Jess. Don't get me wrong. But sometimes what's right isn't worth it. The cost is just too great."

"*What?*" Jess exploded, her chest heaving. "You know as well as I do, Alex, that our community faces discrimination and hatred constantly. Where would we be today if others hadn't stood up and said, 'this is wrong'? What would have happened if those at Stonewall hadn't said, 'enough is enough'? I would have thought you of anyone would see that?"

Alex bristled, her anger rising like bubbling acid filling her slowly from the inside, a churning maelstrom of sour bitterness. "And what the hell is that supposed to mean?"

Jess's face was turning red. She squared her shoulders and faced Alex straight on. "I would have thought that was obvious. With your family—"

"Don't you dare go there, Jess. My past has nothing to do with this. It's in the past. How many times have I told you that I have no family." Alex could taste bile in the back of her mouth.

Jess threw her hands in the air again. "Whether you want to acknowledge it or not, they are your family. They helped shape who you are—"

"Goddammit, Jess. *ENOUGH!*" Alex's voice echoed off the walls. Little droplets of spittle flew out of her mouth. Her chest heaved up and down and her vision had little lightning bolts flashing around the edges. The time had come for her to put her foot down. She didn't want to talk about her family. They were dead to her. She was dead to them. Why couldn't Jess get that? Alex tried her best to regain control before she continued. "Look, you can do whatever you want but don't drag me into it. I've got enough going on without that added to it."

"Fine," Jess snarled. She stared daggers at her for a long moment. "Fine. I won't ask you to do anything." She crossed her arms over her chest, her jaw set.

"Fine." Alex crossed her arms over her chest as well and turned away. She couldn't think of anything else to say. And here she had thought this was going to be a good day. If she weren't so pissed, she might have laughed at the absurdity of it all.

They sat on the couch, each with their arms crossed and facing in different directions. The minutes ticked away. Alex was exhausted. It was hard to believe that only an hour ago, she had been heading home, looking forward to sampling different cakes. Now all she wanted to do was rewind the past hour and pretend it never happened.

Jess finally pulled her wheelchair over in front of herself. "I think I'll go for a walk on the trail." She sounded calmer yet sadder at the same time. "Would you like to come along?"

"No, I don't think so. You go." Alex knew Jess was extending a proverbial olive branch, but she wasn't ready to take it. Jess needed to learn that some things were best put behind and forgotten about. Not every battle needed to be fought.

Jess transferred herself to her chair and silently wheeled out of the room. Alex watched out of the corner of her eye. Any other day she'd love nothing more than to go for a walk with Jess. But right now, maybe a little space would do them good.

CHAPTER TEN

The next morning Jess reached out in bed only to find it empty. When she had gotten back from her walk the night before, Alex had already gone to bed, which was probably a good thing. They both needed some time to cool down. They hadn't had a dustup like that in a long time.

Not able to stay in bed any longer, Jess slid to the edge and transferred into her chair. Wearing a white tank top and matching tighty whitey panties, she rolled down the hall to the living room in search of Alex. Now that she'd cooled off, she did owe Alex an apology. Her words had come across as a personal attack and she hadn't meant for that to happen.

But Alex was nowhere to be found. She wasn't in the bathroom or the kitchen. Jess peeked out into the garage. Alex's car was gone. "Well, that's just great." Jess spun around and wheeled herself back through the kitchen. Just as she was about to rant some more, Jess spotted a sticky note on the coffee table. She zipped over and plucked up the bright yellow square.

Gone to have lunch with Jamie. Didn't want to wake you. Love you, be back soon.

Jess suddenly felt a wave of guilt rise up. Had Alex mentioned that before? Something rattled around in the back of her head. After yesterday, Alex could have told her anything and she'd be lucky to have remembered it. At the knock on the front door, Jess jumped, her heart suddenly hammering in her chest. She looked over to see Jordan standing in the window. Leave it to her sister to scare the bejesus out of her first thing. Jess laughed to herself and unlocked the door, throwing it open. "Come on in, Jordan."

Jordan bounced through the door, her usual perkiness back. "Hey sis, how are you doing this morning?" She glanced around the room. "Alex at work?"

Jess waved her over. "No, she's out having lunch with Jamie."

Jordan cringed. "After what happened? I'd've thought you'd go with her. I didn't want to let go of Tim all night. I'd still be with him if he didn't have to work. You two didn't have a fight or anything?"

Jess couldn't hide anything from her sister. Jordan was like a rabid ferret with a chicken bone when it came to getting information out of her. "It's no big deal, really."

Jordan covered her mouth for a second before slowly dropping her hand from her chin. "If you two had a fight, that *is* a big deal. You didn't let what that bitch said get between you guys, did you?"

Jess quickly shook her head. "No, no. It's nothing like that. For some reason, Alex would rather ignore what the cake lady did and go on like nothing happened."

"Hmmmm." Jordan stroked her chin, looking exactly like Tim when he stroked his imaginary beard. "Maybe it's simply the stress."

"That's what I thought." Jess jabbed a finger at Jordan. It was nice to hear someone else coming up with the same conclusion. "I could tell Alex wasn't thrilled about the situation, but I figured because of her past, because of what her family had put her through, she'd be the first to stand up and fight."

"Eeeek." Jordan winced, her entire face crinkling up. "You didn't say that, did you?"

"Well, not exactly that. I think I said something along the lines of I would have thought she of anyone would see how important it is to stand up for what is right because of her family."

Jordan slapped her hand to her forehead. "Jessie, Jessie, Jessie. I can't believe you said that."

"Why? It's true you know." This was beginning to feel like the inquisition.

Jordan grumbled low in her throat and shot Jess a wry look. "That may be the case, Jess, but to bring up Alex's family? Ouch. It's no wonder you guys had a fight. Alex probably took that as a personal attack. You know how she is with her past."

Jess finally let out a groan. "Yeah, you're right. I shouldn't have brought up Alex's family. But to let that woman get away with what she did? How can we do that?"

Jordan shrugged. "I don't know. You two will have to talk it out, I guess. Just don't bring up her family. You've got to remember, they aren't like ours."

Jess settled back in her chair. "I guess you're right. Alex isn't close to her family like we are."

"No, we're really lucky in that way." Jordan bounced forward and gave Jess a big hug. "We've got an awesome family, especially that sweet, beautiful, awesome sister of yours."

Jess burst out laughing. Leave it to Jordan to give herself such shameless credit. "You're too much sometimes, sis."

Jordan puffed out her chest. "And that's why you love me."

Still chuckling, Jess shook her head. Jordan was truly one of a kind.

"So, what's up, other than what you've already told me?" Jordan shuffled her feet, looking around the room.

"Not much." Jess rolled forward, feeling much better. When Alex got home, she'd sit her down and apologize. Together, they could figure out what to do. But for now, she needed something to take her mind off things. Then it dawned on her. "Hey, Jordan, how would you like to help address invitations?"

Jordan bounced on the balls of her feet. "I'd love to."

Over the next hour and a half, Jordan helped Jess address the invitations. Once the last envelope was finished, Jess sat back in her chair and massaged her hand. She hadn't been in this much pain from writing since she was in high school and had to take a handwritten essay exam. "Finally. Thank you so much, Jordan. I've been dreading this for weeks."

"No problem, sis." Jordan patted the two stacks of addressed envelopes sitting in the middle of the table. The first pile leaned precariously and wobbled dangerously. They were invitations to their side of the family or their friends. The second pile, Alex's list, was considerably shorter, consisting of a mere dozen and a half friends and colleagues. Jordan glanced at the smaller stack. "Are you sure this is it for Alex?"

Jess sighed. "I'm afraid so. You know how private she is. And without family..." She shrugged.

"Bummer." Jordan pursed her lips, her forehead wrinkling deeply, before she suddenly sat upright, startling Jess in the process. "At least Alex will always have our family."

"True. She'll always have us."

Jordan clapped her hands together. "Say, what do you think of running to Starbucks as a celebratory treat?"

Jess smiled. "Sounds good to me." She never needed an excuse to go to Starbucks.

Jordan leaped from her chair. "Great. I've just got to go to the bathroom, and I'll be ready to go. My treat."

After Jordan left the room, Jess continued to stare at the two piles of invitations. Barely a quarter of the height of the other, Alex's looked forlorn and sad. A lump rose in Jess's throat. Alex deserved better than that. If only... Then it hit her. Maybe, just maybe... Jess pulled out her cell and did a quick internet search. Finding what she was looking for, she pulled a blank invitation in front of her and scribbled down the address on the envelope. With a smile, she slipped the envelope at random into the center of Alex's pile just as Jordan came back into the room.

"Ready?"

"You bet. Let's just drop these in the mail on the way." She scooped the invitations toward her. Hopefully, her plan would work.

* * *

Alex waited for Jamie outside the art museum. She didn't feel like walking through the entire museum to find her friend, not today. She wasn't up for large crowds or talking to a ton of people. Alex shielded her eyes from the bright sun that was glaring off the marble as Jamie walked down the steps. Although the sky was clear, there was a haze that promised the possibility of a shower later in the day. Off to the right, two mangy pigeons were fighting over what appeared to be half a bagel, complete with cream cheese. Just as Jamie reached the bottom step, one of the pigeons successfully wrestled the bagel from the other and flew off, barely clearing Alex's head.

"Hey, what's up?" Jamie bounced in front of Alex and threw her arms around her, giving her a rib-crushing hug.

Alex struggled for breath. "Not…not much…" If she weren't so tall, she had no doubt that Jamie would have lifted her off the ground. When Jamie released her, Alex massaged her ribs. "Should we go to our regular place?"

Jamie paused, tapping her foot as she thought. "Maybe not today. What do you say to sushi?"

"Lead the way." Alex waved her arm in front of her as if she were a matador encouraging a bull to charge, eliciting a raucous laugh from Jamie. Together, they walked along Monroe Center toward Nagoya Hibachi Steakhouse & Sushi in relative silence. All around them, people hustled in every direction. The smell of burnt oil and automotive exhaust, especially the diesel fumes from the city buses, filled the air like a noxious cloud. That added to the smell of fresh asphalt from two streets over made Alex light-headed, but such was urban life.

When the doors swung shut behind them at Nagoya's, the sudden reduction in noise level was startling but welcome. A young Japanese woman showed them to a booth and took their orders, a California Roll for Alex and a Volcano Roll, an unholy combination of spicy salmon and spicy crab with an eruption of spicy sauce drizzled over the works, for Jamie. When their orders came, Alex stared at Jamie's plate. "I can't believe you're going to eat that monstrosity. I'd have heartburn so bad."

Jamie smiled as she dug in with a pair of chopsticks. "You get used to it, especially after years of Sue's culinary experiments. I can eat darn near anything without it affecting me. At least it's not lutefisk."

Alex laughed as she dunked a section of her California Roll into a dish of soy sauce doctored with wasabi. Sue would never live that one down.

Jamie paused halfway through her Volcano Roll and jabbed her chopsticks at Alex. "I half thought Jess might join us. What, did she have to work or something?"

Alex groaned, dropping her own chopsticks to her plate. Her California Roll had suddenly taken on the consistency of partially cured concrete in her stomach.

Jamie looked on, a look of concern on her face. "Hey, what's up? Everything okay with you two?"

Alex winced. Her sushi threatened to rise up her throat in one great gelatinous lump. She took a deep breath and slowly relayed the gruesome story about the cake lady encounter to Jamie. The longer she spoke, the redder Jamie's face became, and it had nothing to do with her Volcano Roll. "...and then we got into a big argument."

"*What?*" Jamie blurted loud enough that several people turned to look. She leaned in quickly and lowered her voice. "Why did you two fight? It's that baker's fault, not you guys'."

"I know that. And so does Jess. That's not in question. But it's what to do now. Jess's brother-in-law, the lawyer, came over and gave us all the options. Jess wants to turn the woman in to the City's Office of Equity and Engagement, or maybe even file a lawsuit."

The vein in Jamie's forehead was throbbing at a death metal beat and she looked as if she might explode herself. "That's what you guys need to do. Sue the bitch. Call the media. Get it on the news. Maybe even hold a rally downtown on Calder Plaza. I can call everyone we know."

Alex slumped back against the booth and closed her eyes. She should have known that would be how Jamie would respond. There wasn't a cause that Jamie and Sue didn't embrace. And one involving both her best friend and the gay community together—Jamie and Sue would attack that like a wolverine savaging a bucket of KFC.

"Hey, hey, hey." Jamie snapped her fingers in front of Alex's face.

Alex slowly opened her eyes. Her head was beginning to ache, somewhere deep down where her brainstem attached to her spinal cord. Alex rubbed her forehead. Was it too late to simply jump up and run out the door? "Look Jamie, I know you mean the best, but I'm not sure that's what we should do."

"Are you kidding me? You can't let that baker get away with this. No way!" Jamie seemed to be inflating, as if she might rise out of her seat and begin bobbing about the ceiling.

Alex dropped her head into her hands and massaged her temples. How was she going to explain this to Jamie? Finally, she took a long, harsh breath and lifted her eyes. "Jess feels the same. Well, maybe not the TV coverage and rally on the plaza, but she wants to do something. She doesn't want the cake lady to get away with it."

Jamie held out her hand, palm up, as if to say, *there you go*.

Alex ignored her. "I don't want that awful woman to get away with it either. I'm just not sure if it's a good idea to fight this—"

"But—"

Alex shook her head and held up her finger to silence her friend. She needed Jamie to understand this. "You probably can't see this, but there are times when the best course of action is to turn your back and walk away. That's what I had to do with my family. If I had stayed there and tried to fight everything, it would have ended up destroying me in the long run. It almost destroyed me as it was. That's why I don't feel we should pull out the nuclear option over a frigging cake."

Jamie sat in silence. She bobbed her finger at Alex, obviously in deep thought. Finally, she spoke, this time in a softer voice. "I can see what you're saying, Alex. I hadn't thought of it from that standpoint. I really feel for you. What you went through with your family was horrific. No one should ever have to go through that." She reached across the table and took Alex's hand in hers.

Alex gave Jamie's hand a squeeze. "Thanks." There was a huge lump in her throat.

Jamie flashed her a warm smile. "Now promise not to get mad or anything but there's something you should consider. To Jess, it's not just a frigging cake. It's much more than that. She feels violated and rightly so. She might not be able to turn her back and walk away. For her, the first step to healing might be to do something, anything to get back what that horrible woman took from her, took from both of you."

Alex began to protest. "But she didn't take anything from us."

"Yes, she did. She took away your equality, your right to be treated like anyone else. In refusing to serve you, she in essence is saying that because of who you love, you're not entitled to the same things as others. It's discrimination at its very core. It's hurtful, it's demoralizing, it's dehumanizing, and it's a violation against who you both are. That's why Jess probably feels she must do something to try to right that wrong."

"Crap." Alex slowly shook her head. She hadn't looked at it like that. But still, she didn't want their entire lives turned upside down. "Okay, I hear what you're saying, Jamie, and you're right. Jess wants to fight back, to take back what was taken. But I'm not sure about lawsuits and TV coverage and rallies. That's just going to be one big mess and we already have enough going on."

Jamie bobbed her head with her bottom lip sticking out. "Totally understandable. Nothing says you have to do all that. Maybe think about at least filing a complaint with the City's Office of Equity and Engagement. That would be something and might help Jess with healing. Just talk to her."

Alex found herself nodding along with Jamie. Put this way, this was something she could do. It wouldn't totally blitzkrieg their lives but would be doing something to fight back. "I think I'll do just that, Jamie."

Jamie gave Alex's hand another hearty squeeze. "Excellent. Just remember, no matter what, don't let something like this turn the two of you against each other. If you do, then the hate wins."

A half hour later when Alex climbed behind the wheel of her car, she felt much better. Now all she had to do was patch things up with Jess, and she had an idea of just how to do that.

* * *

Jess sat on their back deck, a venti Caramel Ribbon Crunch Frappuccino sitting on the end table beside her, beads of condensation dripping down the cup and forming a puddle beneath. The light breeze caused the trees to sway, and big tufts of white fluffy cotton from the neighbors' cottonwood tree stirred around their large backyard. Two bunnies (this spring's babies) were chasing each other around the tree line. Jess smiled. They were really blessed to have such a large and lovely backyard this close to town. She glanced at her phone. Alex should be home soon. Then maybe they could talk about last night. There was no reason they should be attacking each other. And if that meant that she had to walk away from what had happened with the cake baker, so be it.

Jess took a sip of her Frappuccino, relishing the thick, sweet coldness as it slid down her throat, especially with the bright sun beating down on her face.

At the sound of the slider opening, Jess spun around. Alex walked out onto the deck.

"Peace offering." She held up a Starbucks Frappuccino.

"Ummm…I appreciate the gesture but…" Jess laughed and pointed to the drink sitting on the table beside her.

Alex burst out laughing too. "What's the odds?"

"Actually, with me and Starbucks, the odds are pretty good." Jess patted the chair beside her. "You could always have it."

Alex sat down and placed the drink beside Jess's half-empty cup. "Too sweet for my taste, but there's nothing that says you can't have both." She grinned mischievously.

"We'll see." Jess felt a weight lift off her shoulders. Alex seemed to have calmed down, and the peace offering was a sweet overture. "Say, Alex, about yesterday…"

"Look, Wheels, I understand." Alex waved her off. "I'm sorry I didn't listen more. Whatever you want, I'll support you. It's just not worth fighting over what that woman did."

A lump rose in Jess's throat. "I don't…I don't know what to say, Legs. Thank you. And I'll always support you, no matter what."

Alex lowered her eyes, looking sheepish. "I shouldn't have gotten so uptight about things. I know what that woman did really hurt you so I'm here for you now. What would you like to do? What course of action do you think would be best?"

Jess swallowed with great difficulty. The lump in her throat felt as big as a grapefruit. Tears threatened at the corners of her eyes. If Alex was willing to support her, she could at least try to support Alex as well. "I'm not sure, Legs. I don't want to go all gung-ho with lawsuits and press and all that crap. We have enough stress as it is." She watched the slight rigidness that only she could notice leaving Alex's shoulders and neck. "But I can't just let that woman get away with it either."

Alex nodded as she listened. "I can certainly understand that. You shouldn't have had to experience that. No one should. So maybe instead of all the lawsuits and press, we could file a complaint with the City's Office of Equity and Engagement. It might not raise as much awareness, but it would be something."

Jess smiled brightly and reached out to take Alex's hand. "I think that's a good idea. Thank you." Her voice cracked at last.

Alex squeezed her hand. "That's why I'm here. When all is said and done, all that matters is us."

Not knowing what else to say, Jess picked up her nearly empty Frappuccino with her free hand and downed the rest of it, causing a sudden pain to race through her head. She dropped the cup back onto the table and grabbed her forehead with both hands. "Arrrrggg."

"Brain freeze?" Alex chuckled.

"Oh yeah." Jess massaged her temples. Served her right—she shouldn't have slurped her drink down so fast. Tears ran down her cheeks but at least they weren't tears caused by the situation with the baker. When the pain subsided a minute later, Jess looked up. "Now that we've gotten that all taken care of, how about we go for a run and a long, steamy shower afterward? I've got to burn off that second Frappuccino somehow."

Alex sat upright, her eyes suddenly wide. "Or we could skip the run and go directly for the shower. Believe me, I can help you work off that second Starbucks." She gave Jess a salacious wink.

"Oh." Jess giggled, her voice a mere whisper. Across the yard, the young bunnies were still chasing each other around. Maybe she and Alex should take a cue from them. "I like the way you think, Legs."

Alex leaped from her chair, calling over her shoulder as she dashed toward the house. "Race you!"

Jess wheeled around to follow but suddenly stopped, grabbing the second Frappuccino. She wasn't going to let that go to waste. Once through the door, she took a second for her eyes to adjust. When she could finally see, Jess spotted Alex's shirt on the floor in front of her. She smiled, her arousal quickly building. Next, she passed Alex's bra, this dangling from the light in the living room. Alex's shoes were scattered pell-mell up the hallway. Her socks were nowhere in sight. Where they went was anyone's guess. Alex's jeans were inside out and draped over the large frame of van Gogh's *Starry Night*. How Alex had got them stuck up there she'd never know. Lastly, Jess found Alex's panties hanging from the bathroom doorknob, the sexy little boy shorts with kittens printed on them and the word "meow" across the butt. Jess plucked them from the doorknob and entered the bathroom. Alex stood there, completely naked, one hand against the shower and the other on her jutted-out hip. Jess held up Alex's panties and twirled them around on her index finger. "You seem to have lost something."

"And you seem to be grossly overdressed." Alex's voice was low, husky, hot. She stared at Jess with her eyes hooded, a pout to her lips.

Jess flung Alex's panties onto the sink where they twisted around the faucet. "Then maybe you had better get over here and do something about that."

"Mmmm. My pleasure." Alex walked slowly toward Jess, one hip at a time, biting her bottom lip seductively.

Jess's stomach flip-flopped. Her heartbeat increased as if she had raced up the trails. When Alex stepped in front of her, her belly button at eye level, Jess sucked in a deep breath of Alex's glorious scent. Alex straddled her, bumping her thighs against Jess's legs as if about to give a lap dance. As fun as that would be, Jess wanted more—much, much more.

Alex sat down in Jess's lap, grinding her hips against Jess. Although Jess couldn't feel Alex with her legs, she certainly could feel the jostling throughout her lower abdomen and upper body. But it was the scent, Alex's intoxicatingly heady, musky scent, that really excited her. She grabbed Alex by her taut buttocks, a hand digging into the flesh of each cheek, and lifted her up. Alex slowly rose, her body rubbing along Jess's the entire way until she stood. Alex threw her right leg over Jess's left shoulder and leaned in, supporting herself with her left leg. She looped her fingers into Jess's hair as if to steady herself.

Jess couldn't take it anymore. Alex's center was only inches away. Jess's eyes crossed as she tried to take in Alex's beauty, the thin strip of whitish blond hair, the darker pink of labia. With Alex's position, her center gaped open. Jess licked her lips and began to salivate. She closed her eyes and buried her nose and mouth in the source of Alex's sweet scent. With the first lap of her tongue, Jess grew light-headed. With the second lap, Alex groaned. Jess wrapped her arms around the back of Alex's buttocks, holding her tight. She wasn't going to let Alex go anywhere.

Jess ran the tip of her tongue up Alex's right labia and back down her left. Back and forth, back and forth. It felt like velvet against the tip of Jess's tongue. She then quickly swirled her tongue around Alex's engorged clitoris. Alex cried out and her leg almost slipped out from beneath her, but Jess held her tight. Years in a wheelchair had made her arms super strong. She could hold Alex up even if Alex couldn't stand on her own. Jess thrust her tongue into Alex's center and worked it slowly in and out, in and out, feeling Alex's heat against her chin as she thrust deeper and deeper. Her top lip brushed against Alex's throbbing clitoris with each driving dive forward. Jess grabbed Alex's buttocks tighter, working that taut, round flesh with her strong fingers, gripping it tight and massaging round and round, round and round.

Alex moaned, her breathing growing more ragged. She sucked in quick breaths that only encouraged Jess more. Her breasts ached, nipples burning against the fabric of her shirt, and her stomach roiled. Even farther below, heat was building. She pulled Alex against her mouth with more pressure and flicked her tongue over Alex's clitoris, causing Alex to jerk again and again. Alex twisted her fingers into Jess's hair, pulling her in deeper. Jess worked her tongue over the super sensitive ball of nerves, grinding her chin into Alex's center, her nose brushing up and down on Alex's little strip of hair. She sucked hard, taking Alex's clitoris between her lips. She squeezed it in her mouth, lightly nipping at the pulsating hardness with her teeth.

Alex cried out louder. Jess sucked Alex's clitoris in and out, in and out, in and out, faster and faster. Alex's moans bounced off the tile walls and floor. The sounds coming from her were raw, guttural, animalistic. Alex's thighs quivered against her cheeks, and Jess held her up, held her center to her mouth, sucking and sucking, in and out. Suddenly Alex clamped her thighs tightly against the sides of Jess's head. She dug her nails into Jess's hair, pulling tight. "Oh God, Jess, I'm coming! Dear God, I'm coming!"

Jess held Alex, supporting her entire weight. Alex grabbed Jess by the shoulders to keep from falling. Her entire body convulsed, again and again and again. Just when Alex's climax seemed to subside, Jess flicked her clitoris again, sending Alex into another round of tremors. Finally, Alex collapsed against Jess, her body bent over the top of her, gasping breath after ragged breath. Jess wrapped her arms around Alex, helping to stabilize her so she didn't fall flat on the floor. Nothing would ruin a moment of intense passion like a trip to the ER, especially if the patient were an ER doctor. Jess fought back a giggle. Poor Alex would never live that down.

After long minutes, Alex was finally able to stand on her own. As she removed her right leg from Jess's shoulder, the cool air brushing her cheeks was a stark contrast to the intense heat of Alex's center. Alex looked down and smiled, her chin quivering with post-climax adrenaline. "Oh my God, Wheels, that was... that was...I can't even find the words to describe what that was." She chuckled.

"Why thank you." Jess smiled back at her. She couldn't think of a better compliment than leaving Alex speechless. She blew on her knuckles and rubbed them against her chest.

Alex burst out laughing. "You should be proud of yourself after that. Wowza!"

Jess began to laugh as well.

Alex suddenly grew serious. "There's just one problem, though."

"Oh?" Her laughter freezing in her throat, Jess felt her chest tighten. Had she done something wrong? Had she maybe been a little too aggressive?

Alex cracked a wide smile and pointed to Jess. "You still seem to be grossly overdressed."

Jess snorted through her nose. "Well then you had better get over here and do something about that, Legs. Immediately."

"Yes, ma'am." Alex stood up straight, her small breasts bouncing, and gave Jess a salute.

Jess held her arms over her head and Alex hooked her fingers in the hem of Jess's shirt and slowly worked it higher, one inch at a time. Jess held her breath. There was nothing more erotic than being undressed by a hot, naked woman, especially when that hot, naked woman was Alex. She bit her lower lip when Alex's fingers lightly tickled her skin. A shiver ran up her spine. Her heart was playing leapfrog in her chest. When Alex paused just under her breasts, teasing the fabric ever so slowly, Jess couldn't take it anymore. "Oh, for the love of God, Legs, just rip off my clothes already."

Alex laughed and quickly pulled Jess's shirt the rest of the way off. Without waiting, she wrapped her right hand around Jess's back and unlatched her bra with just two fingers. As the lace fell from her breasts, revealing dark, swollen nipples that were hard as marbles, Jess sucked in a quick breath and rolled her shoulders so that her bra fell into her lap. This was more like it. There was a time for teasing and a time for action and this was most definitely the latter. She grabbed Alex's hands and clasped them over her aching breasts. She could feel Alex's touch clear down into the pit of her stomach. She arched her back, pushing her chest against Alex's hands, cool against her hot skin. Her nipples were on fire—or was it ice cold? Jess couldn't tell. Her feelings were all jumbled up, as if every nerve cell in her body was misfiring in a gloriously sensual fireworks show.

Jess clenched her teeth as Alex slowly kneaded her breasts with the palms of her hands, grazing her hard, overly sensitive nipples with her thumbs. With each pass, Jess sucked in a quick breath through her teeth. Her head was beginning to spin, as if she had just gone on her fifth ride of the Tilt-A-Whirl at the county fair. Jess looked up into Alex's eyes, pleading—more, more, more. She almost cried out a hearty yippee when Alex moved her right hand from Jess's breast and twisted it into the hair at the nape of her neck, pulling her in closer and pressing her lips firmly to Jess's.

Jess stretched her neck out, seeking more contact. She opened her mouth and pushed her tongue against Alex's teeth. When Alex yielded, she thrust her tongue deeply into Alex's mouth, probing every inch and swirling around Alex's tongue in an erotic ballet—around and around, in and out, over and over. Jess pushed her hand beneath herself, lifting her hips from her chair. She tried to support herself with one arm and paw off her pants with the other, all while continuing to kiss Alex. She wasn't having much luck, but she didn't want to stop. Finally, she pulled back, their lips parting with a sloppy slurp. Jess gasped for breath. Her chest heaved and her heart felt as if it were performing an entire gymnastics routine, Olympic gold medal worthy.

Alex looked down at Jess struggling with her pants and smiled. "Here, let me help." She swept her arm behind Jess, lifting her from her chair, and quickly unbuttoned Jess's jeans. When she tried to slip the jeans over Jess's hips, Jess slapped her hands away playfully and thrust the denim along with her purple lace panties over her hips and halfway down her legs. Alex laughed even more. "Whoa there. Not anxious at all to shed clothing, are you?"

"You've been naked all this time. It's not fair." Jess tried to lean forward to free her legs, but Alex knelt and slid Jess's jeans and panties the rest of the way off, letting them drop to the tile floor between them.

"Better." Alex raised an eyebrow.

"Oh yes." Jess reached out for Alex, her voice low and husky.

Alex inched closer on her knees but before she took Jess's hands, she licked her lips and opened her mouth. "May I pick you up?"

Jess nodded slowly, as if she were underwater in a dream. She appreciated Alex asking. Although it might seem like a small thing to others, it was a big deal for Jess. And Alex's acknowledging that made her even more aroused. "Uh-huh." The words came out as a soft moan.

Alex scooped Jess up, her arms under her bum. They faced each other, their bodies pressing together, Jess's legs dangling on each side of Alex. She could feel the warmth of Alex's chest against hers, the steaminess of Alex's breath against her neck. And even in her center, she could feel something—maybe not what others would feel but it was something, a combination of heat and pressure, and what more did she really need?

Alex walked with Jess clinging to her, her arms thrown around Alex's neck. At first, Jess was expecting Alex to head for the bedroom but instead, she stepped into the shower. Alex gently sat Jess sideways on the wide shower stool, her bum right on the edge. Alex kissed Jess along the neck before pulling away. She looked down at Jess, a fierce determination in her eyes. "Lie back. I've got something in mind."

Following Alex's order, Jess lay back. It was a good thing the stool was so wide because although her bum was on the very edge, the rest of her fit with just the very top of her head hanging off the other side.

Alex once again knelt onto the tile floor, this time sliding in between Jess's legs. Jess sucked in a quick breath. She knew what was coming. And it wouldn't be a moment too soon. She was ready to explode right then.

Jess stared up at the ceiling, biting her lip. She arched her back as Alex slid her hands up her sides, higher and higher. Alex's hot breath, almost like a dragon's fire, puffed against her mons and lower belly. Slowly, Alex began to kiss her sensitive flesh, starting just below her belly button and creeping lower with each subsequent kiss. The muscles in Jess's abdomen twitched and trembled, her back still arched against the stool. She closed her eyes, anticipating, anticipating, any moment now. Her breath quickened. *Please, please, please.*

When the tip of Alex's tongue touched her center, gently separating her labia, Jess cried with a long deep moan. "Oh God, Yes!" This was exactly what she needed, more than she even knew. Her clitoris pulsed with the beat of her heart, a burning, throbbing sensation traveling all through her body. Alex plunged her tongue deeper and deeper, separating her labia until Jess could feel a whisper of cold air hitting her center each time Alex pulled back.

With each flick of Alex's tongue, Jess moved closer and closer to the edge. Her breathing sounded like a steam engine about to take off. She gasped hot breath after hot breath. The tension built in her belly, growing more and more until her entire body felt as if it were about to collapse in upon itself. Her heart galloped as if it were trying to crawl up her throat.

Alex slid her thumb over Jess's trembling clitoris as she continued her oral ministrations. Jess closed her eyes so tightly that tears seeped from the corners. She clenched her teeth, grinding them back and forth. *Any second now. Any second now.* And then it hit, an explosion quickly radiating out from her center to encompass her entire being. Jess opened her mouth and cried out. It went on and on. Jess lost all track of time. Her vision grew dim. Sounds were far off. And then she collapsed, her chest heaving, her teeth chattering, and her body shaking.

She gasped breath after breath as her heart slowly, grudgingly returned to a more normal rate.

Jess tried to sit up, but her abdominal muscles simply shook, trembling under the skin of her belly. She felt as if she had just completed a thousand crunches. Alex quickly helped her into a sitting position and Jess began to laugh uncontrollably, an adrenaline-fueled mania. She laughed until she cried. Finally, slowly, she regained control and wrapped her arms around Alex. "I've got to tell you, Legs, that was amazing!"

Alex pulled back to look her directly in the eyes. "Just amazing?" She grinned widely.

Jess chuckled and shook her head. "Okay, it was *fucking* amazing!"

Alex tilted her head back and snorted out a laugh. "That's more like it."

Jess winked and leaned in close. "Just like you, Legs. Just like you. Now what do you say to that shower?"

CHAPTER ELEVEN

Over the next two weeks, although they were still looking for a baker to replace the antigay cake lady, Alex began to relax. The invitations had all been mailed out and they were receiving RSVPs almost daily. The rest of their wedding plans were in the bag, so to speak. Now all they had to do was wait until the big day.

Perhaps the best thing that had happened was the meeting with the City's Office of Equity and Engagement representative, Nicole Meitzler, a well-dressed, no-nonsense woman in her early thirties with black hair in an undercut. Alex had instantly liked her. Nicole had worked in the Office of Equity for the past five years and had a good handle on the region and the types of discrimination present. She had listened as Jess and Jordan recounted their meeting with Karen Holmes of Cakes by Karen.

Alex had mostly sat beside Jess, offering moral support since she hadn't directly witnessed the incident. Nicole took copious notes, asking question upon question. The biggest surprise had come when Nicole had told them that they weren't the first, nor even the second, to have experienced the same treatment. The city was building a case against the cake lady who insisted making cakes for same-sex couples was against her religion and therefore protected by free speech. Nicole had assured them that they were taking steps to make sure this didn't happen to anyone else. Alex had felt better with the knowledge that they weren't the only ones that this had happened to.

And now she was enjoying a rare afternoon at home by herself. Jess was working at the bookstore and wouldn't be home for another hour. Alex had spent the day taking a run through downtown Rockford and pampering herself with a long, luxurious shower afterward. The only thing that would have made it better was sharing that shower with Jess. After her lonely shower, she'd ordered a triple burger from Bridge Street Burger Shack with everything, including jalapeño peppers and olives, a true gastronomical treat. Jess would pass out if she saw that but what Jess didn't know wouldn't hurt her. To top off the day, she'd binge-watched both *Deadpool* movies. Maximum effort, indeed.

When Jess finally rolled through the door, Alex looked up from the *Bones* marathon on TV. That was another of her guilty pleasures, right up there with *Dr. Who* and sinfully overstuffed burgers. "Hey Wheels, how'd it go at work?"

Jess wheeled herself into the living room. She had a wide smile on her face. "Really good, Legs, but besides that, I think I may have some good news."

Alex raised an eyebrow. "Oh?" It was obvious Jess was bursting to share something.

Jess leaned forward, her entire body vibrating with excitement. "Hold on to your horses, Legs, I think I've found us a cake baker."

"Truly? Who is it?" Alex sat up straight. They had been searching for weeks with no luck. Most bakers were already booked. Apparently, October in Michigan was a very popular time to get married.

"You're never going to believe." Jess burst out laughing. "Cheryl McKinney from the café at the bookstore. She makes cakes for special occasions on the weekends. I can't believe I didn't think of her before."

"Seriously? And she'd be willing to make ours?" Alex slid to the edge of her seat.

"Oh yeah." Jess rocked onto her back wheels, balancing there. "She heard what had happened and came to me. She's super excited to do it, especially since it's for us."

"And she has no problem with making a cake for a gay wedding?" Alex hated to ask but she had to be sure.

"Are you kidding me?" Jess spun in a circle, nearly overbalancing in her chair. "Cheryl knows I'm gay. Her daughter is gay. I think that's why she's so excited to do this for us. She knows how hard it can be for our community, facing all the hatred and discrimination."

"Awesome!" Alex leaped from the couch and threw her arms around Jess, then let go and stood back up. "What we need to do is celebrate. How about we order something special to eat?"

Jess cocked her hand onto her hip and stared at Alex as if she were a teenager trying to pull a fast one over on her parents. "And a burger from Burger Shack wasn't enough for one day?"

Alex gaped. "How…how did you know?"

"Babe, I can smell the jalapeños and olives from here." Jess wrinkled her nose, looking much like the small bunnies that had taken to munching their variegated Hostas every evening.

"Oh. Busted." Alex covered her mouth. So much for trying to keep that a secret. Darn those jalapeños and olives. If they weren't so sinfully delicious… Alex laughed. They were still worth it. "Why don't you order us something for dinner, Wheels? Pizza sounds good."

"Pizza to wash down the burger, huh?" Jess rolled her eyes.

"Yeah, something like that." Alex smiled sheepishly. "Just get our usual. I'll get the mail while you're doing that."

Jess gave a firm nod and grabbed her phone. Alex walked outside through the garage. The day was still nice—one of those rare goldilocks days where it wasn't too hot or too cold. Maybe they could even go for a stroll along the trails later. She walked down the slight incline to the road and the garish mailbox. As shocking as that mailbox had been at first, it was growing on her, not that she'd ever admit that to Tim or anyone else for that matter.

Alex opened the door in the lure's mouth and reached inside. Along with the usual junk mail—an offer to sell their house by a local realtor, a credit card offer for a card she already had, and something about a service to rid their yard of pests (which got a raised eyebrow since come August, the mosquitos in their backyard would be the size of crows)—a bill for electricity and another for internet, there were also a good half dozen RSVPs. Alex stuffed the regular mail under her arm and thumbed through the RSVPs. She laughed out loud at the first—Jamie and Sue—and tore it open. Surprise, surprise, they were coming. The second was from Jordan and Tim. It was marked, "Maybe." Alex shook her head. Jordan, always the joker.

The third RSVP made Alex stop dead in her tracks. "What the…" The return address was simply the last name, Hartway—her name—from her hometown in Indiana. The rest of the RSVPs and the mail tucked under her arm fell to the cement driveway unnoticed. Alex stared at the envelope in her hand. "What the…"

With her hands shaking as if she'd overdosed on very strong coffee, Alex fumbled at the envelope, her fingers not working properly. She was holding her breath. This had to be some kind of mistake or even a cruel joke. When she finally got the envelope opened, she pulled out the RSVP and closed her eyes. She slowly unfolded the paper and took a deep breath before looking down. All that was written there was a check in front of "Not coming," and a short scribble at the bottom of the page. *Lev 20:13.* Alex felt sick to her stomach. She knew exactly what that scribble meant—one of the harshest passages in the Bible condemning homosexuality. It was a personal favorite of her father and she had grown up hearing it almost every Sunday.

As if in a trance, Alex slowly shuffled up the driveway, dragging her feet the entire way, feeling as if she were trapped in *The Twilight Zone*. This simply could not be real.

When she walked in the door, Jess looked up from the couch where she was now sitting, the TV remote resting on her leg. "Pizza's on the way. What would you like to watch to..." Jess quickly trailed off as she took in Alex's stance, her forehead furrowing. "What's up? More RSVPs?"

Alex tried to answer but nothing came out. Her throat was as dry as a bag of cement. It even tasted a bit like cement. Alex paused and licked her lips, trying again. "You could say that." Her voice sounded dead, even to herself, as if she were trying to speak from the bottom of a very deep pit.

Jess leaned forward, a look of deep concern on her face. "Is there something wrong? You look like you've seen a ghost."

At that, Alex laughed, but the sound was filled with anything but mirth. It sounded more like a bunch of gravel rolling around in a large cast-iron pot, grating at the metal. "Something like that. A reply from Indiana."

Jess froze, her mouth in the shape of a small O. She clasped both hands to her mouth. "From Indiana?" Jess's voice was weak. Panic was in her eyes.

"Yeah. From my family, no less." Alex waved the letter and envelope out in front of her. Her entire body was numb, and the sound of the TV was coming from somewhere far away, fading in and out. A loud noise was beginning to echo in her head, like a bunch of static from a dead radio station.

"From your family?" Jess kept repeating her words in hushed tones. Then after a long moment, Jess dropped her hands away from her mouth and scooted closer to the edge of the couch. "Um...what did they say? They're not coming?" Jess bit her lip as she waited for a reply.

Alex shook her head, not really hearing, still trying to process. It felt like one of those horrible dreams in which it was impossible to wake. Everything was turned upside down. Nothing made sense. And just when she began to grasp what was going on, everything would upend itself and begin again with an even stranger reality. Again and again.

Jess winced as she watched Alex. She leaned so far forward on the couch that she was nearly in danger of slipping onto the floor. "They said yes?"

"What? No…here." Alex held the letter out. Her fingers were sweating, staining the edges of the paper. "Look for yourself."

Jess took the reply and scanned over it, her shoulders falling. "Oh. They're not coming." She sounded as if she might start crying.

Alex stared straight ahead. She wasn't one to do hallucinogens, never had been, but she figured it would probably feel a lot like she felt right then. The entire world seemed disjointed somehow, as if some sick person had fucked with the known universe just for shits and giggles.

"What's this mean at the bottom here?" Jess spoke quietly. She looked over the reply again, her eyes narrowing. "L-E-V, twenty thirteen?"

At that, Alex snapped back to the present. Everything came rushing back with the force of a tornado, a deafening wind roaring louder and louder until everything crashed into place with a gargantuan piercing silence. She looked at Jess. "It's a verse from the Bible. Leviticus chapter twenty, verse thirteen. *If a man lies with a male as with a woman, both of them have committed an abomination; they shall surely be put to death; their blood is upon them.*"

Jess clapped her hands over her mouth once again. "Oh God." She looked as if she were about to be sick. The color was draining out of her face. "Oh Alex. Oh Alex, I'm so sorry."

Alex stepped in front of Jess and took the letter from her lap where it had fallen. She held it in front of herself as if it were a giant swirl of dog crap masquerading as an RSVP. She wrinkled her nose at it then turned back to Jess. "You wouldn't by chance know anything about this, would you?" She thrust the letter out and waved it between them.

Jess began to stammer. "Well…I…um…"

Alex held up an index finger to silence her. She should have known. Jess had been bugging her for months. This was just like her.

Jess tried again. "Look, Alex—"

Alex again held up her hand, this time with all her fingers up and turned away. She didn't want to hear it. Whatever the reason, whatever had gone through Jess's head, she didn't want to hear it. Finally, she turned on her heel. "I'm going for a walk. I'll be back later."

* * *

Jess stared at the front door as it swung shut behind Alex. She should never have sent out that invitation. With her stomach churning like a worn-out washer at a laundromat, Jess reached for her chair, transferred herself from the couch, and wheeled to the door. But as her hand touched the doorknob, she paused. Hadn't she already done enough? As good as her intentions had been, maybe the best thing she could do now was give Alex her space.

Jess dropped her hand from the door and rolled backward to the center of the room. She rubbed her temples, trying to soothe the raging headache that was about to tap dance all through her skull. Alex had been right—her family wasn't worth knowing. But instead of hearing what Alex was saying, she had clung to the fantasy that someday they could all be reunited, tears all around, happily ever after to commence with rainbow-colored streamers floating down from the heavens. Had she really been that naïve?

At a noise on the front porch, Jess sat up straight, her heart skipping in her chest. With a quick thrust of her arms, she zipped to the door and wrenched it open, about to beg forgiveness any way she had to. But instead of Alex, a pimply teenaged boy with a Pizza Hut hat turned around backward over his greasy multicolored hair stood there with a blue insulated pizza carrier over his shoulder, chewing a massive wad of gum the color of Pepto-Bismol. At first, Jess couldn't figure out why he was there.

"Large hand-tossed with mushroom, ham, and green peppers." He looked from the slip in his hand to Jess.

"Ah…ah…yeah." Jess swallowed the lump forming in her throat. "That would be ours."

The delivery kid unzipped the carrier over his shoulder and handed the pizza box to Jess. With a roguish tip of his hat, he was gone.

Jess slowly rolled to the couch with the pizza box in her lap. She dropped the box onto the coffee table with dull thud and stared down at it, no longer hungry. Her stomach felt as if it were about to mutiny on her. But she hadn't eaten all day, and if she didn't at least choke something down, the dull ache that was circling her head would turn into a full-blown, five alarm, dumpster fire of a headache.

She transferred to the couch and opened the box. The pizza didn't even smell good. She took a tentative bite and nearly spit it out. It tasted as if she'd tried to eat the box instead. The pizza had a plasticized cardboard texture to it. Jess forced herself to swallow. It hit her stomach like a wet lump of old newspaper. She forced another bite with the same results, then dropped the remainder of the slice back into the box and flipped the lid closed.

Jess leaned back against the couch. She muted the TV and closed her eyes. Unable to sit still, she picked up her phone. She could call her sister. Jordan would know what to do. But she dropped her phone back onto the couch beside her, already knowing what Jordan would say. She shouldn't have sent that invitation out in the first place, especially when Alex had expressly warned her against it. This was a disaster entirely of her own making.

* * *

Alex walked around town, trying her best to calm down. What had Jess been thinking? Hadn't Jess believed anything she had told her about her family? The only good thing about the RSVP was that they weren't coming. At least she wouldn't have to worry about them showing up and causing a big scene, perhaps even carrying signs to protest their daughter's wicked ways. But then someone from their church might find out. They couldn't have that. No, not the good minister and his righteous family.

Alex forced herself to walk even faster. She was stomping along like an angry hippo. She took some satisfaction in that. She wanted to be pissed. She wanted to rage and stomp her feet and scream out to the heavens above. But who was she really angry with? Jess? Yes, but not entirely. She shouldn't have been surprised that Jess would do something like this. Her family? Of course. She had been angry with them ever since they abandoned her. But who she was really most angry with was herself. After all this time, she'd let her family get to her once more.

Rounding the corner onto Main Street, Alex hoofed it along. People were darting out of her way. She knew she must look like a crazed woman, but she didn't care. She needed to burn this negative energy off. If she had to plow down a few unsuspecting pedestrians, so be it. At that thought, she slowed down. She wasn't going to let her family ruin anyone else's evening. She shouldn't have allowed them to ruin *her* evening. They weren't worth it. But still, even after all these years, she could hear her father's booming voice.

"*If a man lies with a male as with a woman, both of them have committed an abomination; they shall surely be put to death; their blood is upon them.* I am here to tell you, the Bible is clear. We are to treat the homosexual, those abominations, as we would thieves and murderers. They should be put to death."

Alex shivered at the memory. That was why she was so angry with herself. She was a grown-ass woman, a doctor no less, and with one tiny, scribbled note, she'd been reduced to being eight years old again.

Alex paused beside the dam. The water crashing over the spillway roared, and a cool mist rose into the air. The mist against her overheated body snapped her out of her thoughts, almost like a slap to the face. She gripped the railing and stared out at the swirling water below that so perfectly reflected what was going on in her head. As she stood there, she began to feel the energy draining from her body, the adrenaline wearing off, leaving her sapped of strength. Before she could collapse where she stood, she found an empty picnic table.

All around her, people were laughing and talking, kids were running around squealing, and bicyclists and joggers were zipping up the trails. Alex propped her head up between her hands and let out a deep breath. A tiny sparrow flitted down onto the picnic table only a couple of feet in front of her. The little brown bird tilted its head from side to side, looking directly at her as if to ask, "do you have anything to feed me?"

Alex smiled. "Sorry, buddy, but I don't have anything for you."

The bird flicked its wings and darted off in search of a meal. Seconds later, her new feathered friend was wrestling a goldfish cracker from another bird—a nuthatch or maybe a titmouse. What she wouldn't give to be free like that little bird, free from her past.

Alex sat up straight and stretched her back. Although it was a lovely evening, she wished she were home, sitting on the couch. Or maybe on their back deck, a cold drink in her hand. There was just one problem. Jess. As pissed as she was, a bigger part of her just wanted to curl up with Jess in her arms and forget about what had happened. But the proverbial cat was out of the bag, and she couldn't see how to jam it back in without getting clawed up from end to end. Alex laughed at the image.

Deep down, she knew Jess had meant well. And arguing about it for the remainder of the evening would do no one any good. They would have to talk about this sometime—sometime very soon—but for now, she would settle for a cessation of open hostilities.

* * *

Jess had taken to pacing the house in her wheelchair. It had been well over an hour, and she'd expected Alex back before now. That was, if Alex was coming back. But she had to. Her car was still in the garage. Unless Alex had called someone to pick her up. Would Jamie have come to rescue her, maybe give her a place to stay for the night? Or had something else happened, something much worse?

Jess spun around quickly, rocking her chair precariously onto two wheels, and made another pass through the house.

The waiting was the worst part. In many ways, she would have preferred Alex to scream and yell at her, get it all out in the open.

On the next pass through the living room, Jess spotted her phone on the corner of the coffee table. She zipped across the living room, transferred herself onto the couch, and was just about to hit the speed dial for her sister when the front door opened. Alex slowly walked in, her shoulders slumped and looking defeated, as if she had just lost a patient. Jess felt the hard lump rise in her throat once again.

They stared at each other from across the room, neither moving. The seconds ticked by, a thick uncomfortable cloud descending between them.

Jess swallowed. The lump wouldn't budge. She tried again. This time she was able to speak, albeit with difficulty, as if every word were forced through a small, raw opening. "Um...Alex... I...I...I didn't mean...well, you know...I just..."

Alex held up a hand. "Look, Jess, I don't want to talk about it. I don't want to think about it. I just want to forget it even happened for right now."

Jess slowly closed her eyes. This was worse than she'd thought. "But...but...Alex...I..."

"Dammit, Jess! I told you, let it go. Haven't you done enough already!"

* * *

As soon as the words were out of her mouth, Alex regretted it.

Jess gaped at her, the hurt obvious on her face. She slowly lowered her head until she stared at her hands, which were tightly folded in her lap. Jess swallowed, once, twice, three times. The corners of Jess's eyes, what little Alex could see, were overly bright.

Instead of racing over to Jess and pulling her into her arms, Alex stood, unable to move. There was even a part of her (a small part, but a part nonetheless, way down in the far reaches of her being in that dark place that no one wants to acknowledge) that relished in Jess's misery.

But the longer she watched Jess, the worse Alex felt. Was she really going to be that petty? Being angry was one thing, but being mean about it was an entirely different proposition. Finally, Alex cleared her throat. "Look, Jess, I didn't mean that. I'm sorry."

Jess looked up, her eyes brimming with tears. "I'm sorry too, Alex. I didn't mean…" She swallowed again.

Alex did her best to soften her voice and remain calm. "I understand that. And I know you're sorry. But I'm still really angry. You had no right—"

"I know, I know. I shouldn't have." Jess pleaded, the words coming out all in a rush.

Alex crossed her arms. "No, you shouldn't have."

Jess stared at Alex, her bottom lip trembling. She opened her mouth and closed it again. She took a breath and tried again with the same results. She then slumped back against the couch.

Alex walked over to the couch. She glanced at the pizza box on the coffee table. She had completely forgotten about that. But now that she was looking at it, she realized just how hungry she was. She pulled out a limp-looking wedge of pizza and took a bite. It was stone cold, but she didn't care. She swallowed the bite and pointed the floppy slice at Jess. "Let's just forget about all this for tonight. I don't think I can take any more stress right now." She ripped off another bite of pizza with her teeth.

Jess looked over and gave a slow, deliberate nod. She opened her mouth. "Okay, Alex, I'm—"

Before Jess could finish what she was about to say, her cell phone rang. They both jumped at the loud intrusion. Jess pawed at her phone, desperately trying to answer it. She finally succeeded and held it to her ear.

"No, Jordan, this isn't a good time…*What?*" Jess sat up straight. "Say that again."

Alex leaned in closer, trying to hear what was being said on the other end of the line. From the tone of Jess's voice, something big must have happened. Her chest tightened.

Jess waved at Alex frantically. She pulled the phone from her ear. "Quick, quick, change the channel to WOOD TV8."

Alex flipped the channel. On the screen, Tina Van Dickson, a field reporter for TV8, was standing in front of the event center they had booked for their wedding. The moderate breeze was blowing her long brunette hair about her head. She talked into the microphone while staring directly into the camera.

"…just this morning, customers arrived to find the doors locked with this message…" Tina held up a piece of paper and began to read. "…Royale Event and Banquet Center will be closed until further notice. Sorry for any inconvenience." Tina lowered the piece of paper. "We have since learned that the company has filed for bankruptcy. But what is to happen to those who have already booked their events and put money down? Wood TV is working hard to find those answers. This is Tina Van Dickson reporting."

Alex looked from the TV to Jess and back again before throwing her arms into the air. "You have got to be fucking kidding me."

CHAPTER TWELVE

Jess stared at the TV, trying to process. She slowly lifted her phone back to her ear. "I'm going to have to call you back, Jordan." She hung up without waiting for a reply and turned to Alex.

Alex stood there, her eyes glued to the TV, unblinking. The half-eaten slice of pizza had slid from her hand and fallen with a loud *splat* on top of the pizza box.

Jess shook her head. This couldn't be happening. There had to be some mistake. She turned to Alex. "What are we going to do?" Her voice was soft, quiet.

Alex again threw her arms into the air. "Hell if I know." She then threw herself onto the couch with such force that Jess bounced into the air.

Jess reached for the remote that sat between them, feeling as if she were moving in slow motion, and pressed *mute*. The living room went dead silent. Jess immediately wished she hadn't muted the TV, but it would seem odd now if she turned it back on. Instead, she spun to face Alex. "What does this mean? What about our deposit?"

Alex snapped out of her fugue, blinking slowly as she turned to Jess. "I haven't the foggiest frigging idea."

Jess tried to wrap her mind around what she'd seen on TV. "How could they do that? We paid money. We sent out invitations. What are we supposed to do now?"

Alex gritted her teeth, her face growing redder by the second. "I don't know, Jess. Your guess is as good as mine. This entire thing has been a disaster."

Jess leaned back, her eyes narrowing. Although she could tell Alex was moments away from blowing up, she had to ask. "*What* thing has been a disaster?"

Alex waved her hand wildly beside her face. Her chest was heaving. "This wedding mess. Jesus, it's like everything that can go wrong has gone wrong. I'm beginning to think it was all a gigantic fucking mistake."

Jess bristled, her jaw set. She glared directly into Alex's eyes. "So, you think getting married to me is a gigantic fucking mistake!" Her nostrils flared with each word. "Well, maybe you're right. It's all a gigantic fucking mistake, all of it!"

Alex stared right back, her shoulders set and her back rigid. "That's not what I'm saying, but now that you mention it, maybe you're right."

"Fine."

"Fine." Alex crossed her arms.

"*FINE*!" Jess wasn't going to let Alex get the last word, no sirree. If marrying her was such a big fucking mistake, then it was probably a good thing that the event center had closed. Jess pulled her chair up to the couch and transferred herself into it. She quickly wheeled around the front of the coffee table and off down the hall. "I'm going to bed. Good night."

* * *

Alex tried her best to get comfortable on the couch, but she was at least five inches too tall. If she faced the back of the couch, her butt hung over the edge. If she lay with her back to the back of the couch, her knees dangled off. And lying on her back, either her feet were propped too far in the air, or her head was, giving her a worldclass crick in the neck. The easiest solution would have been to go climb into bed with Jess, but she was still too angry for that.

Alex rolled over again with little effect. Apparently, she was destined to be uncomfortable tonight. Outside, the breeze had picked up, coming directly from out of the south. Tomorrow was sure to be a scorcher and the ER was bound to be a real madhouse. On top of the cases of heatstroke and other various heat-related maladies, the patients were sure to be extra crabby. One more thing to look forward to. Yippee.

The minutes ticked on, and Alex wasn't even the slightest bit tired. Finally giving up all pretense of sleep, she sat up straight, kicked her feet up on the coffee table and stared out the window. It was pitch black out. Either it was the new moon or close to it, which suited Alex just fine. The only light was from distant heat lightning that left red spots in the darkness after each muted flash.

Maybe she shouldn't have asked Jess to marry her. Everything had been great before then. It seemed as if the moment that she had popped the question, the whole world had conspired against them, beginning with that big storm back in April. However, that storm had also prompted a spur-of-the-moment vacation. Alex smiled in the darkness. That had been a great trip. If only that hadn't ended. It seemed as if everything from that point onward had been wedding, wedding, wedding, interspersed with varying degrees of catastrophe. She hated to admit it, but she was really beginning to question whether it was even worth it. People weren't supposed to feel that way about a wedding, were they? But what could she do about it? What *should* she do about it?

Sometime long after midnight, Alex finally fell asleep with those questions still rattling around in her head.

The next morning she woke just as the sun was peeking through the windows. She hadn't slept well but at least she could say that she had finally slept. After stretching—her back was twisted up like a string of last year's Christmas lights—Alex cupped her hand to her ear. The house was silent. Jess must still be asleep, which was probably a good thing. Alex didn't know what to say to her.

Alex stood. She might as well do something besides sit around and mope, so she quietly slipped on her shoes (her clothes would be fine for another go-around), grabbed her car keys and a bottle of Gatorade from the fridge (the blue flavored one), and slipped through the door to the garage. Even though the news had said that the event center was closed, Alex figured she might as well try to see if she could find anyone to talk to.

Forty-five minutes later, she pulled into the parking lot of the Royale Event and Banquet Center. The lot was completely empty. The lawn was unmown and beginning to burn in the heat—not a good sign. Alex parked and strutted up the sidewalk to the front door. There was the piece of paper taped to the glass that she'd seen on the news. Someone had scribbled the words, "Fuck you, you bastards," on the bottom. Alex smiled, a wicked, devious smile. She could certainly appreciate the sentiment.

Alex reached out and grabbed the door handle. She pulled and it didn't give. She pulled harder. Still nothing. She gave it an almighty shake, causing the door to rattle in its frame, but no luck. Not knowing what else to do, she cupped her hands to the side of her head and leaned forward until her eyes were mere inches from the glass. She couldn't see anyone inside. The entire place looked abandoned with a trail of papers leading from the door into the depths of the facility. Alex knocked, rattling the glass. She waited. Nothing. Finally, she stepped back, gritting her teeth, feeling completely defeated.

* * *

When Jess wheeled herself out into the living room, she wasn't surprised to find Alex already gone. After their row the night before, Jess was glad. But where did that leave them? If Alex felt that their upcoming wedding was a gigantic fucking mistake, was their entire relationship just one gigantic fucking mistake? Jess couldn't accept that. Not after all they'd been through. Since it was Saturday and she had the day off, Jess grabbed her phone and dialed Jordan's number. At the third ring, Jordan picked up.

"Hey, Jessie-bessie, I was just going to call."

"Yeah, sorry I didn't get back with you last night, sis." Jess swallowed. Maybe she should have talked to Jordan instead of Alex. At least Jordan would have understood. "Things went a little off track last night."

"Oh no, you two didn't have another squabble, did you?" Jordan's voice became concerned.

Jess tried to laugh. That was a mistake. She sounded like a cat trying to yak up a furball. Instead, she cleared her throat. "I guess you could say that, but I don't really want to talk about that over the phone. What are you doing today?"

Jordan perked up. "I'm at Mom and Dad's with Tim. Why don't you come over here. I'm sure we can solve all of life's problems."

Jess wasn't so sure about solving all of life's problems but visiting her family sounded a lot better than sitting around the house by herself. "Okay, I'll be there in half an hour. See you then."

Five minutes later, Jess was on the road. After last night, she needed a little pick-me-up, so she popped through the drive-thru at Starbucks for a Caramel Ribbon Crunch Frappuccino. If anything could cheer her up, that would.

When Jess rolled through the front door to her parents' house with her comfort drink, her sister yelled out, "We're out back, Jess." As she rolled through the house, the sweet and tangy smoke from the grill made her stomach growl. Her dad and Tim must be in the mood to barbeque.

Jess opened the slider and slipped out onto the deck. Her mom and Jordan were lounging in the zero gravity recliners while her dad and Tim were busy fussing with the grill. Smoke was billowing out from under the lid. The only thing missing was Alex. But at that thought, a lump rose up her throat.

Jess wheeled up beside Jordan and placed her drink on the end table next to Jordan's, some fruity concoction with just enough vodka to make it flammable.

Jordan turned to face her. "So, what happened last night? I know you two must have been upset about the event center."

Jess rolled her eyes and tried once again to laugh. Now she sounded like a whole herd of cats yakking up all over the house. She immediately stopped. "I'm afraid that's only the half of it."

"Oh?" Linda sat up straight and jogged her chair around so she could face both her daughters. "What else has happened?"

Jess took a deep breath and opened her mouth. For the next fifteen minutes, she detailed all that had been said from the night before. "…and that's when Alex said maybe our wedding was a gigantic fucking mistake."

Linda pursed her lips at the curse but let it slide.

Jordan cocked her head to the side. "Let me get this straight, you sent an invitation to Alex's family, and they sent it back with a Bible verse about killing gays?"

"Yeah, something like that." Jess winced. Hearing it put so succinctly made it sound a hundred times worse.

"Oh, Jess, what were you thinking?" Linda stared wide-eyed, her voice soft.

Jess bristled. It wasn't as if she didn't feel bad enough that her idea had gone so poorly but hearing her mother say it that way made her feel as if it were the stupidest thing she had ever done. "I don't know what I was thinking, Mom. I guess I wasn't. I just wanted Alex to have what I have, what both Jordan and I have, such a wonderful family."

At that, Linda smiled the way only a mother can smile when she hears how much she means to her children. "Aww, Jess. That's so sweet to hear. Thank you. But unfortunately, not every family is like ours. I wish it were. I wish Alex's family was. But sometimes it's just not that way."

"Yeah, Jess," Jordan chimed in. "We won the lottery when it comes to family."

"But…but…what about Alex? Doesn't she deserve that too." Jess was losing the battle with the lump in her throat. Her eyes were trying to mutiny as well.

Linda stood and walked over to her. She kneeled beside her and pulled her into a hug. "Oh, sweetheart, of course everyone deserves that. But that's not how it is. Alex knows that. As painful as it must be for her, she has come to terms with it. As much as you may have meant well, it wasn't your place to try to fix everything. I'm sorry to say that."

Jess began to sob. Her chest heaved against her mother. "I get that now, Mom. I screwed up. I told Alex that. But now we have the stupid event center thing."

Jordan kneeled on Jess's other side and placed her hand on Jess's arm. "I've talked to Tim about that." Jordan turned and called over her shoulder, "Hey, Tim, tell Jess what you told me about that place going bankrupt."

Tim was battling flames rising three feet into the air by pouring his beer on it. Pete had his head in his hands, shaking it as if unable to believe what he was seeing.

Without turning around, Tim called out, "Don't worry about that. I can file a claim for you with the bankruptcy court against the business. You should get most if not all your money back. It'll just take a while."

Jordan spun back around. "There, see, sis, you should get your money back sometime."

Jess appreciated what her family was trying to do. Still, she couldn't see a way out of the mess she was in. "That's all fine but what are we supposed to do now? The invitations have all been sent out."

Linda squeezed her tight. "Don't worry about that. We can send out an update. I'm sure it happens all the time."

Jess wasn't so sure about that. "I don't know, Mom. First the mess with the bigoted cake lady and then the event center going bankrupt. Then I messed up with the invitations and really pissed off Alex. I don't know what to do. Why has everything with this wedding been so stressful and messed up?"

Linda brushed Jess's hair from her forehead and chuckled. "Oh, sweetie, planning a wedding is supposed to be stressful and messed up. If you can get through that, you can get through anything."

* * *

Alex clopped through the ER, mopping the sweat from her brow. She hated being right. Not only were there an inordinate number of heat-related cases but those patients had by and large been cranky, ornery, or just plain pissy. And with the temperature snuggling up to the three-digit range, it was only going to get worse. The real cherry on the cake was the air conditioning not working as well as it should be. All and all, this was going to be a terrible shift.

Alex grabbed a cold bottle of water from the small fridge behind the nurses station and rubbed the cool bottle against her forehead before cracking it open and taking a large drink. The coldness running down her throat lifted her spirits a bit.

Frank, the security officer on duty, walked by. He gave Alex a little salute, as if he were tipping an imaginary hat. "Good afternoon, Doctor Hartway. Staying cool?"

"Good afternoon, Frank. I'm trying. How about you?" Alex smiled. Of all the security officers, Frank was her favorite. He was never afraid to lend a hand where needed and not just in security matters.

"Whew." Frank wiped his forehead with the back of his sleeve. "I'll tell you, Doctor Hartway, it's hotter than a June bride in a feather bed. And it brings out all the crazies, I think."

"I hear you there. Let's just hope it doesn't get too intense." Alex took another pull from her water bottle.

"We can only hope." Frank chuckled and again gave her that little salute before continuing his rounds.

Alex leaned against the wall, propping herself up with one foot behind her, and thought about Jess. She shouldn't have left this morning without telling Jess where she was going. She should probably call, just to make sure she was okay. Or would that make matters worse?

"Hey, doc, we've got another case of heat exhaustion in Exam Four." Maria walked up to the nurses station. She had her salt-and-pepper hair tied up off her neck. Beads of sweat coated her entire face.

Alex rolled her eyes and kicked off from the wall. "Great, more crabby people who didn't know enough to stay out of the heat."

Maria took a step forward and placed her right hand on her hip. "Speaking of crabby, the heat isn't getting to you too, is it, doc?"

Alex winced. She really had been stomping around the ER in a towering mood. That wasn't fair to her coworkers or the patients, no matter how ill-behaved they were. They came to the ER for compassion as much as for treatment. "Sorry, Maria, you're right. I've been a royal bitch today."

Maria waved her off. "No biggie, doc. We all have bad days. What's up, anyway? Anything I can help with?"

Alex took a deep breath, feeling like a total ass. Her personal problems shouldn't have followed her into the ER. "It's no big deal, Maria. Just more wedding crap."

"Oh?" Maria raised her eyebrows, her hand still on her hip. "What happened now? Another nasty baker?"

"No, no, nothing like that." Alex hadn't wanted to get into it, especially at work, but Maria was a dear friend. "We found out that the place where we were having our wedding went bankrupt."

Maria clapped her hands to her mouth. "No way."

"Yeah, and to top it off, the bastards kept our money." Alex waved her water bottle to emphasize her point.

Maria dropped her hands from her mouth and cocked her shoulders, her head bobbing side to side. "That's just not right. Oh, sweetie, I'm so sorry. What are you going to do?"

"Thanks, Maria." Alex's chest swelled. "I'm not sure what we'll do yet. I'm not sure there *is* going to be a wedding."

"*WHAT? NO WAY!*" Several nurses turned at Maria's exclamation, and a patient who had been walking up the hall abruptly turned around and scurried away. Maria leaned in closer, her voice quieter. "Why not? You two are perfect for each other. Just because some place went bankrupt and you've got to find another venue, that's no reason not to get married. Trust me, I know."

"If that was all, you'd be right." Alex shook her head. "Jess and I had a bit of a blowup over the invitations. She sent one to my family in Indiana."

"Oh." Maria stared for a moment with her lips forming a perfect circle. "And?"

Alex tossed her empty water bottle into the trash and shrugged. "And they sent back a reply."

Maria leaned closer. "*And?*"

"And it contained a Bible verse. Leviticus Twenty Thirteen." Alex clenched her jaws, grinding her teeth.

"Seriously? Isn't that the one about putting gays to death? Happy reading, that is." Maria wrinkled her nose as if she'd just sniffed dog poo.

"Yeah, really happy." Alex still clenched her teeth, the muscles along the side of her face tensing like thick coils of rope. "Jess should never have sent something to my family."

"So, let me get this straight. You're mad at Jess because your family are assholes?" Maria waved her hand beside her head.

"Well…no…that's not…I mean, Jess shouldn't have…"

Maria burst out laughing. "Sweetie, you're mad at the wrong person. Jess only sent the invitation. She didn't tell them how to respond. If anything, you should just laugh at the absurdity of their reply. That's the best they can do to try to hurt you—some old verse from a section of the Bible that no one takes seriously anymore."

Alex hadn't thought of it that way. "I see what you're saying, Maria. And of course, you're…"

Before she could finish her thought, she noticed a tall man with a scraggly beard walking up the hall, wearing a long coat that went to his knees, an odd sight in this heat. He had just entered through the ambulance bay, but to her knowledge, there wasn't an ambulance out there. Alex raised a hand, pointing at the man. "Hey. What're—"

Maria had her back to him, a puzzled look growing on her face as she watched Alex. She started to turn around when Alex saw it—something pulled from beneath the long coat, something black in the man's hand.

"*GUN!*" Without thinking, Alex shoved Maria to the side with all her strength. As Maria fell over a chair and onto the floor, Alex stood facing the man. Their eyes met. Everything became completely quiet and slowed to a crawl.

Flash…flash, flash.

Alex saw the blast from the muzzle of the gun but didn't hear anything. It was deathly quiet. Before she could even move, Frank slammed into the man, taking him down like a linebacker on Sunday. The gun flew out of the man's hand as he crashed to the floor with Frank on top of him. Suddenly, sound returned in a cacophony, as if someone had turned the volume all the way up. Alex quickly scrambled over and kicked the gun farther down the hall out of reach.

Maria pulled herself up from behind the nurses station. She walked out slowly and then with a gasp, she pointed at Alex's chest.

Alex raised her hand to her chest and slowly pulled it away, staring at it with morbid fascination. The room was growing dimmer by the second. "Huh. Sonofabitch." Just before everything faded to black, Alex looked to Maria and held up her red-stained hand for her to see. "I've been shot."

* * *

After everyone had eaten, the Bolderson family sat around on the deck, chatting. Jess wiped the sweat from her brow and patted her overly full tummy. The steaks had been delicious, despite Tim charring them with three-foot flames. Maybe it could become a new family tradition—flaming steaks.

As Jess sipped the remainder of her Frappuccino, which had long since ceased being cold, Tim leaped from his chair. "Hey, I'm getting another beer. Anyone else want anything? Chips? Dip? More vodka?"

Everyone laughed at Tim's antics. "No one?" Tim raised his eyebrows comically until they disappeared under his bangs. Getting no takers, he shuffled toward the door. "More for me then."

Jess turned to Jordan. "Your husband is a goof."

Jordan raised her drink into the air as if making a toast. "And that's why I love him."

Less than a minute later, Tim came busting out the sliding door. "Everyone, quick, you've got to see this." He was frantically pointing over his shoulder. "Hurry!"

For a second, Jess thought Tim was making a joke. From the looks on everyone else's faces, they were thinking the same thing. Then it settled in—there was real panic in his voice and his eyes were bugging out of his head. At once, everyone leapt up and darted for the house. Jess wheeled as fast as she could, pausing just long enough not to run her sister down.

"What's going on?" Pete made it to the door first. "You look like the house is on fire or something."

Tim had stepped to the side to allow everyone in. He was gaping wordlessly, still pointing over his shoulder.

"Babe, what is it?" Jordan grabbed her husband by the hand.

Tim finally found his words. They spewed out all at once. "I was checking the TV for the game and…and…" He gasped and pointed.

Jess looked toward the screen. A large heading read, "Breaking News." Sitting behind the news desk, Derrick Headly, the early news host was reading off a teleprompter. "…and now we're going on scene with Tina Van Dickson. Tina…"

"Oh great, now what?" Jess threw her hands up. What could it be this time?

Tina appeared on the screen holding her microphone in front of herself and standing in front of a large glass double door with the words, "Emergency Department."

Jess immediately recognized the ER where Alex worked. Her chest tightened until she could barely draw breath. She couldn't move. All she could do was stare at the screen.

On TV, Tina turned and gestured to the door behind her. "We're downtown here at Crownwell Hospital where we've just been informed that an armed assailant opened fire in the emergency room. We don't know much yet, but we've been told that one person has been injured. We'll keep you informed as more information becomes available. Back to you, Derrick."

As the screen flashed back to the newsroom, everyone stood in shock, their mouths hanging open. Jess felt as if she had been sucker punched. Her thoughts froze in her head. The seconds ticked by. Jess didn't blink. She wasn't even aware of breathing. Then her heart slammed into the top of her chest, and she gasped. "Alex! Oh my God, Alex! I've got to go!" Panic made her nearly incoherent. She wheeled around, about to race out of the living room.

Jordan wrapped her arm around Jess's shoulders, pulling her in tight before Jess could fly out the front door. "Whoa, sis. We're all going."

CHAPTER THIRTEEN

Alex ran along Lakeshore Trail, the eleven-mile loop in Holland that they'd enjoyed on their mini-vacation after that big storm. The sweet fragrance of lilac filled the air, which seemed odd since the lilacs should have been done by now. There was another scent on the light breeze. Alex was pretty sure it was hyacinths combined with the golden yellow forsythia bushes that lined the trail. But wasn't forsythia only yellow in the spring? Surely, they would be bright green by June. Alex scratched her head as she jogged along the path. The sun was beating down on her shoulders, licking her skin each time it pierced the trees overhead. The warmth felt good. Lately she had been cold, chilled as if she were packed in ice. The cool breeze coming off Lake Michigan kissed her face.

Jess wheeled along in front of her, wheels bouncing each time she ran over a crack in the tarmac. Her brunette hair was tousled from the wind. She called over her shoulder. "Are you keeping up back there, Legs?"

Alex ran up beside her, feet pounding the pavement with a rhythmic *slap, slap, slap*. "Of course, Wheels. Just giving you a bit of a head start." She gave Jess a devious grin.

"Oh *really*? Just try to keep up with me." Jess increased her pace.

Alex pushed herself forward, gasping for breath. Her lungs were burning as if someone had poured acid into them. Her side was beginning to ache, but she ignored it. The sounds of the crowd around her were fading in and out. Still, she ran, trying to catch Jess, but each time she got close, Jess increased her pace again, keeping just out of reach.

Alex pushed harder and harder until she couldn't go on anymore. She stumbled off the trail, bent in two, hands on her knees. Her legs were shaking, threatening to give out at any second. The pain in her side was throbbing with the beat of her heart. She had the strangest feeling as she gasped for breath. Hadn't she done this before? Hadn't she stood exactly where she was now? But that time had been different. That time she had been happy, ecstatic even.

Alex looked up, but Jess was no longer in front of her. Where was she? Alex stood straight and cupped her hands to her mouth. She took a deep breath, feeling as if she had sucked in flames. Ignoring the pain, she called out as loud as she could, "WHERE ARE YOU, JESS?"

Her vision dimmed as if someone had thrown a blanket over the sun. She closed her eyes. What the hell was going on?

When she opened her eyes, Jess was beside her. They were under a big cottonwood tree, the cotton drifting around her feet like tufts of stuffing. How had they gotten here?

"Hey, Legs, why do you look so worried?" Jess laughed and rocked up on her rear wheels.

Worried? She didn't have anything to worry about, did she? Now that she thought about it, there had been something. But what was it? Whatever it was, it fluttered just out of reach, like trying to recall a dream. The harder she tried, the more it slipped away. "I don't know what I'm supposed to do, Jess."

"What do you mean, Legs? Of course, you do. You always do." Jess rolled her head back and laughed again but this time it sounded far away.

Alex found herself beginning to cry. The pain in her side burned as if she were being ripped apart from the inside out. "But I don't know, Jess. I don't. Just tell me what I need to do." She dropped to her knees and covered her face with her hands, sobbing like she hadn't since she was a little girl.

The wind was blowing harder and somewhere in the distance, thunder rumbled. The air smelled heavy with rain. It was hard to breathe, as if her lungs were filled with hot, boiling water. Alex gasped. This must be what drowning felt like. Surprisingly, that thought didn't upset her. If anything, a strange calmness settled over her. If this was drowning, it wasn't that bad.

She stopped crying and dropped her hands from her face. She was no longer on her knees under the cottonwood tree. She was instead sitting in the middle of their bed. All around her were RSVPs for their wedding. She picked one up and opened it. It was from her family. Scribbled along the bottom was a Bible verse—Leviticus 20:13. She knew that one by heart.

Alex quickly threw away the paper. She picked up another and opened it. This was from her family also. This time scribbled along the bottom in her father's messy handwriting was another verse—1 Corinthians 6:9-10. She knew these by heart as well. *Do you not know that the unrighteous will not inherit the kingdom of God? Do not be deceived. Neither fornicators, nor idolaters, nor adulterers, nor homosexuals, nor sodomites, nor thieves, nor covetous, nor drunkards, nor revilers, nor extortioners will inherit the kingdom of God.*

Alex gasped, heart beating against her chest. She threw away the piece of paper but when she looked down, another had replaced it, with another verse. What the hell? She threw that paper away. Another took its place. She closed her eyes and screamed. This couldn't be real. The room grew dark. Even when she opened her eyes, she couldn't see anything. But there was someone there. She was sure of it.

"Jess, is that you?"

Jess rolled into sight as if a spotlight was shining down on her. She seemed to glow in the darkness. Heat lightning flashed in the distance, throwing a strange shadow over Jess's face. "What is it, Legs? What's bothering you?" Her voice was calm, comforting.

Alex reached out but Jess was too far away. "Please, Jess, I don't know what to do. Tell me what I'm supposed to do."

Jess smiled, her hand outstretched, grasping the air between them. Even as Alex reached for her, Jess began to fade. "There's only one thing you need to do, Legs—fight!"

* * *

Jess busted through the doors to the ER, her entire family at her heels. Her father had driven, which was a good thing. On the way, she had tried to call Alex on her cell. No luck. She tried again, and again. Still no luck. She had even tried the main switchboard to the hospital, but she couldn't get past the "all lines are busy" message.

Jordan tried her best to reassure her. "You don't even know if it was Alex. It could have been anyone."

But Jess was sure. She couldn't explain how she knew but she did. Alex was in trouble, and she needed to get to her.

Jess raced up to the thick bullet-proof glass separating the waiting room from the ER. She squealed to a halt and pounded her fist on the small shelf in front of the thick glass to get someone's attention. A sign that said, "This is a healing environment. Threatening or aggressive behavior is not tolerated. Criminal penalties may be pursued if you assault our team members or threaten them. Please be kind to everyone," fell to the floor. Jess stared at it, growing angrier by the second. A fat lot of good that sign had done Alex.

Jess could just see over the bottom of the window. On the other side of the glass, people were bustling everywhere. Besides hospital security, it looked like almost every officer from the Grand Rapids police were present. Farther down the hall, Jess could just barely make out yellow tape strung from wall to wall. She beat her fist against the small shelf again.

One of the admitting nurses turned around at the noise. Her hair was falling out of the twist at the back of her head, and she wore dark burgundy scrubs that looked as if someone had hit her center mass with a water balloon. She took a quick step to the window and called through the hole in the center. "I'm sorry but the ER is closed. You're going to have to go somewhere else."

Jess felt as if she were about to explode, but she bit her bottom lip—hard—and took a deep breath. It didn't help at all. She took another and jabbed her finger at the young woman. "I'm not here for that. I'm…look…I need…" A hand clasped her shoulder. It was her mom. At the squeeze, Jess turned, her eyes pleading. She hadn't realized she was crying.

Linda leaned forward, but Jordan beat her to it. Jordan pointed at Jess as she addressed the admitting nurse. "Look, her fiancée works here. Dr. Alex Hartway. We need—"

Whatever Jordan was about to say, she never got a chance. At the sound of raised voices, Maria poked her head around the corner. She was dressed in dark navy scrubs with darker splotches across the front—blood. She quickly turned to the admitting nurse. "Let them in. That's Alex's family."

The admitting nurse pressed a button on the wall beside her workstation. A loud buzz sounded from the locked entry doors to the ER. They swung open, revealing the commotion behind. Halfway down the hall, in front of the nurses station, a group of police, security, nurses, and doctors were gathered. Maria stood with her back to the door, keeping it from closing.

As Jess rolled through the doors, she could see a large puddle of blood still on the floor beside the yellow police tape. She gasped at the sight. Her stomach rolled. Jess came to a slow rolling stop, both hands clasped over her mouth. How could all that blood have come from one person? How could anyone have survived that? How could Alex have survived that?

Maria was saying something, but Jess hadn't heard a word. She stared at the red puddle, unable to tear her eyes away. It wasn't until she felt a hand on her shoulder again that she looked up. This time it was Maria.

"Wha…what happened? Is Alex dead?" Jess felt as if she were standing outside her body as she asked the question.

"No, no, no." Maria was quick to reassure. "She's alive. She's in surgery right now."

Jess's family looked as shocked and scared as Jess felt. Alex had been shot. A hundred questions raced through Jess's head but all she could do was stare dumbly at Maria, her mouth slowly opening and closing.

Maria stepped closer and with a hand on Jess's back, pointed down the hall to the right. "Come. Let's go to the family lounge and I can fill you in on everything I know."

Jess slowly wheeled down the hall, careful not to look at the blood puddle farther on as she rounded the corner. Her family followed closely like a line of ducklings. Maria walked beside her, one hand still resting on Jess's shoulder.

The family lounge was made to provide comfort with calming, tan-striped wallpaper and lakeshore-themed artwork hanging on each wall. A mini-fridge was in the corner and large over-stuffed couches and padded wooden chairs made the room appear more like a luxury resort than a family lounge in a hospital. While Jess rolled to the center of the room, her family sat on the couches—her mom and dad together and Jordan and Tim together. Both her mom and Jordan were leaning against their husbands and holding their hands in their laps, mirror images of each other.

Maria gestured to the mini-fridge. "Anyone want anything? Water, soda?"

Everyone shook their heads. Jess didn't think she'd be able to drink anything even if she wanted to. She finally found her voice, thick and raspy though it was. "What happened, Maria? How did Alex get shot?"

Maria took a deep breath and pulled over a chair so she could face Jess and her family. Her shoulders were drooped, and she looked as if she hadn't slept in a week. She took another breath as if trying to find her words. "I'm probably not supposed to be telling you this, but you deserve to know. Some guy snuck in through the ambulance bay with a gun." She swallowed with difficulty and her eyes were growing bright. "Alex saw him and pushed me out of the way. She saved my life. I know she did."

Jess had no doubt that Alex would do that. She wasn't the kind of person to duck and hide when others were in trouble.

Maria continued, dabbing at the corners of her eyes. "Unfortunately, the guy opened fire before security could take him down and Alex was hit."

Jordan snuffled. Tim pulled her in tight until her head rested against his chest.

Jess leaned forward, afraid to ask, afraid of the answer. "How bad is it?" She clenched her teeth, waiting for the worst.

Maria slowly shook her head, not meeting her eyes. "It's bad, Jess. I won't lie to you. Alex was hit three times in the chest. One shot hit her in the upper left shoulder. Another in the lower right abdomen. That one got her in the appendix and nicked her liver and kidney. But the worst one hit her center chest, just to the right of her heart, giving her a tension pneumothorax."

"A *what?*" Just the sound of the word made panic rise up in Jess.

"That means she has a collapsed lung and air was filling her chest cavity."

Jess gasped, clapping her hand over her mouth. "Oh, dear God."

"We were able to stabilize her in the ER. She's up in surgery right now. Doctor Romanokov is working on her. He's the best."

Jess knew that from personal experience. Doctor Romanokov had saved her life when she'd crashed her wheelchair and spent a night pinned to a concrete slab with a rusty piece of rebar stuck through her leg.

Pete scooted forward with his arm around Linda and asked the question that Jess couldn't. "Is Alex going to make it?"

Tears spilled over Maria's eyes. Her chest hitched. But she straightened her back and looked them all straight in the eye. "I don't know. I'm sorry. I just don't know." Her bottom lip began to tremble, and she dropped her head forward, tears falling fast.

Jess rolled up to Maria. She didn't know what to say. She didn't know what to do.

Maria looked up and pulled Jess into a firm embrace. "I'm so sorry, Jess. I'm so sorry. If only…I don't know…maybe if…"

Jess forced the tennis ball-sized lump in her throat down with difficulty. It felt as if it had become permanently lodged just below her chin. "It's not your fault, Maria. Alex was doing what Alex does. You shouldn't blame yourself."

Maria looked Jess in the eye. Her chin was still quivering.

Jess felt the tears rolling down her own face. Although part of her wanted to scream at the top of her lungs, another part was strangely calm. Jess clung to that part. "This wasn't your fault, Maria. And I know that Alex wouldn't blame you either. You're her favorite nurse. She always says that."

Maria managed a watery, tear-soaked smile. "Thanks, Jess. That means a lot."

After another offer of drinks, for which she got no takers, Maria finally stood. "I can take you up to the surgical waiting lounge." She glanced out the door. Loud voices and commotion were echoing from down the hall. "It'll be quieter there, and we can see if there's any news on Alex."

Jess followed close behind Maria as she led the way through the hospital, avoiding the scene where Alex had been shot, for which Jess was grateful.

Behind them, Jess's family followed in a tight group, holding on to each other. Although Jess was more grateful than she could ever say, she still wished Alex's own family could be there as well. Shouldn't that be what every family would do?

On the fourth floor, Jess followed Maria into another waiting lounge almost identical to the one they had just left except three times as large. Here, the walls sported pictures of Holland during tulip time. There was one large picture taking center stage of the De Zwaan windmill, the only authentic Dutch windmill operating in the United States that still ground wheat into flour. Jess stared longingly. What she wouldn't give to be in Holland right then with Alex, a sequel to their last trip. The longer Jess stared, the worse the pain in her chest became. It was a pain she couldn't remember feeling before, as if someone had reached deep into her chest and ripped her heart physically from her body, leaving a gigantic gaping hole in its place. Jess gulped and tore her eyes away.

Jess's family settled into two overstuffed couches—her mom again huddling with her dad and Jordan with Tim. They looked strangely out of place, as if they didn't know where they were or why they were there. Thankfully the lounge was empty.

Maria jabbed a thumb over her shoulder. "I'll go see if I can get any updates while you get comfortable."

Jess simply nodded. It didn't matter how welcoming the room was, there was no way she would be able to get comfortable, not with Alex in surgery. Instead, she wheeled up to a large photo of a single red tulip to the left of the windmill. She stared at it until her eyes began to water without really seeing anything. But it was better than looking anywhere else. It was better than looking at her family. If she did that, she'd probably break down completely.

Jordan walked up and knelt beside Jess. "Jess. Jess, are you okay?" Jordan's voice was barely above a whisper.

Jess continued to stare at the red tulip, her chin trembling. Of course, she wasn't okay. She hadn't been for a while now. Not since the cake lady incident. Not since the venue canceled. Not since she had caused Alex pain by trying to invite her family to their wedding. It wasn't supposed to be like that, was it? A wedding was supposed to bring a couple together, not push them apart. And now, Jess felt more separated, more alone, than she ever had.

"Jess, look at me." Jordan reached over and took Jess's hand into hers.

Jess swallowed and turned to her sister, and immediately wished she hadn't. Her sister's expression somehow made everything ten times worse. Maybe it was seeing her own fear and worry mirrored on Jordan's face, but Jess couldn't hold it in any longer. Her chest hitched, her shoulders began to shake, then her entire body.

Jordan pulled Jess in tight, their foreheads pressed together. Jess's strength finally gave way and she sobbed. The sound was raw, visceral, like a wounded animal. Jess sobbed. Jordan held her tight. Their family gathered around, each placing a loving hand on Jess, letting her know that she wasn't alone. Everything came pouring out. Jess howled.

"Shhhh, shhhh, shhhh." Jordan lightly rocked Jess back and forth. "We're here for you Jess. We're here for both you and Alex."

"That's right." Pete rubbed Jess on the shoulder, his voice thicker than Jess had ever heard it. "We're family. That goes for you both."

Jess cried harder. She was truly blessed to have the support of her family. And they already considered Alex a part of that family. They didn't need some piece of paper to say that. They didn't need some big shindig to prove that. She had her family and they accepted Alex as a daughter just as much as they accepted Jess. What more did they really need?

* * *

Jess lost track of time. It had been hours and Alex was still in surgery. But as the minutes ticked by, Jess grew more and more apprehensive. Surely, the longer Alex was in the operating room, the worse things had to be.

Every half hour or so, Maria would check for an update. She had taken on the role of family advocate, for which Jess was immensely grateful. It wasn't until the light bleeding in through the windows had taken on a decidedly orangish red hue that they finally got word. Dr. Romanokov slowly walked into the room, looking as if he had just finished a five-hundred-mile trek through the desert. Jess recognized him at once even though his shiny black hair was now liberally streaked with gray.

Jess wheeled up to him. She opened her mouth but couldn't find the words.

Dr. Romanokov stuffed his hands into his pockets and looked down at Jess. "Ah yes, I remember you. Alex's girlfriend—rebar through leg, very messy."

Jess's family along with Maria circled her. Collectively, they all held their breaths.

Dr. Romanokov pulled up a chair and sat facing Jess and the others. He took a deep breath. "I'm not going to lie to you, Alex is in pretty bad shape. She lost a lot of blood. We had to remove her appendix and small part of liver. But really bad is shot to lung. That was difficult to repair. She has chest tube to relieve pressure and help breathe. She will be intubated for a few days too."

"But she'll be okay, right doc?" Even as the words left her lips, Jess's head spun. From everything Dr. Romanokov had said, it seemed like a miracle that Alex was still alive.

Again, the doctor took a deep breath, looking even more fatigued. "Time will tell. We have saying in OR, anything can happen with gunshots. Sometimes nothing happens. Sometimes bad things happen. The next few days will be crucial." He shrugged. The effort seemed to take all his strength. "That's all we can do at moment."

Jess simply stared. That hadn't been the answer she had wanted to hear.

"Sorry I don't have better news." Dr. Romanokov stood, running his fingers through his graying hair. "Alex is being moved to ICU. I can have one of my nurses show you down."

Maria stepped forward. "I can do that. I'll take them to her."

"Good…good." Dr. Romanokov paused as if to say more. After a long moment, he again tucked his hands in his pockets and lowered his eyes. "Sorry again. Alex is good friend." With that, he turned and walked out of the room, his shoulders slumped.

Everyone stood still for a minute, seemingly in shock. No one looked at each other. Jess closed her eyes to shut out everything around her. Nothing felt real.

Finally, Maria cleared her throat. Everyone jumped at once. "Come on, I'll take you down to the ICU. Alex should be there by now."

Together they left the lounge. Again, Maria led the way with Jess following close behind. The rest of her family followed in a tight bunch. Jess lost track of the different hallways. She wouldn't have been able to find her way back if she even tried. The entire place seemed to be one gigantic maze.

But whatever Jess had pictured in her head hadn't prepared her for what she saw when they rounded that last corner. Jess stopped dead in her tracks as she took in the scene. It didn't even look like Alex. Obviously there had been a mistake. A stranger was lying in Alex's bed, covered with wires and tubes. A ventilator rose and fell with each breath. It sounded like some dying animal gasping for breath. The intubation tube was taped to whitish blue skin.

Jess clasped her hands to her face. "Oh, dear God!"

CHAPTER FOURTEEN

Jess slowly rolled through the door and up to the side of Alex's bed. She reached out but her hand hovered over Alex's arm. This couldn't be Alex in front of her. No. Alex was so full of life. This body, this unrecognizable person, didn't look alive at all. This was some grotesque facsimile of a person, surrounded by machines.

But as Jess stared at the body before her, took in the curve of her jaw and the shape of her ears, the color of her hair and the shape of her hands, she had no doubt that this was Alex. This was the woman she loved. Jess finally placed her hand gently upon Alex's arm, careful not to dislodge the spaghetti of wires. Alex's skin was cool to the touch—almost cold. Jess stared through watery eyes. "Oh Alex. Oh Alex." She lowered her head until it rested on the side of the bed. "Oh Alex."

Jess could feel her family standing behind her, watching her silently. The only sound was the beeping and humming of the machines. Jess closed her eyes. She couldn't bear to see anything more. She just wanted to close out the world and when she finally did reopen her eyes, everything would be better once again, none of this would have happened.

Linda stepped forward and placed her hand on Jess's shoulder. "Maybe we should, you know, let Alex—"

"I'm not leaving. I'm never leaving her again." Jess jerked away so fast that Linda jumped. "I'm staying right here."

Maria cleared her throat. "I can make arrangements for Jess to stay. That's no problem." She looked down at Jess with a soft smile. "Plus, I don't think there's any force on heaven or earth that could drag her out of here."

Jess nodded firmly. She stroked Alex's arm gently, the skin still cool—too cool—under her fingers. But that was okay. She could produce enough heat for both of them.

Linda placed a hand on Jess's shoulder once again. Jess didn't shrug it off this time. "Okay sweetie, you stay. The rest of us will go home for tonight but we'll be back early tomorrow morning to see you—to see you both." She bent forward and gave Jess a hug.

Jordan stepped up next and threw her arms around Jess, squeezing her so tight that Jess could barely breathe. She kissed Jess on the cheek. "Everything will be fine, sis. I just know it will."

Jess appreciated Jordan's unfailing optimism and wished she could share it.

Tim and her dad both clapped her on the back. Her dad tried to say something, but his voice cracked. Finally, he patted her on the back again and leaned forward, kissing Jess on the side of her head. "Love you, sweetheart." His voice was raw and gravelly.

Before she knew it, Jess was alone with Alex and the machines. The room felt strangely empty, as if the real world had faded and she was now in the land of in-between. She swallowed, her throat dry. Even the air didn't seem real, as if someone or something had sucked all the life out of it.

At the loud bang behind her, Jess startled and spun around. Maria was maneuvering a bed into the room.

"Sorry to scare you." Maria smiled as she guided the bed through the tight door. "I've got you a portable bed. Thought you'd be a lot more comfortable than sitting in a chair all night. You can sleep right beside Alex."

Jess scooted out of the way so Maria could position the bed. "Thanks, Maria. You're the best."

Maria shrugged off the compliment. "'Tis nothing, Jess. I'd do anything for you or Alex. Let me know if there's anything else you need, especially if there's anything you need because of…" She nodded to Jess's wheelchair.

Jess was touched. Most people didn't consider that she might have different needs because of her chair. "You're too thoughtful. No wonder you're such a good nurse."

Maria blushed.

Jess chuckled at Maria's expression. "The only thing I can think of is locking the wheels on that bed, so I don't crash to the floor when I transfer."

"Do you need help with that?"

"I can do it, no problem. But maybe something to drink. It's dryer than a desert in here."

"You've got it." Maria set the brake on the portable bed, getting it as close as possible to Alex's bed. She then darted back out the door.

Although Jess wouldn't be directly beside Alex, she could still reach over and hold her hand. While Maria was gone, Jess creeped up as close as she could to the portable bed. She set the brake on her chair and with one hand on her chair and the other on the bed, transferred herself as carefully as she could.

Jess had just slipped into the bed and propped the pillow behind her head when Maria came back in. Not only did Maria have a bottle of water, but she also had a can of Coke and two containers of Jell-O. She pulled a side table closer and lined up the drinks and snacks. "I got you a little something to eat as well. I figured you probably haven't had anything since earlier. Sorry I could only find Jell-O cups, but at least they're blue and those are the best."

Jess's eyes welled up again. She swallowed and merely nodded.

Maria reached out and took Jess's hand. "I'll be back tomorrow morning. If there's anything in the meantime, I've talked to the nurses outside and they'll get whatever you might need." With a glance to Alex then back to Jess, Maria offered a warm smile before backing out of the room.

Alone, Jess gobbled the Jell-O and sucked down half the bottle of water as fast as she could. Her eyelids grew heavy and she yawned, her jaw cracking from the effort. She could feel the energy draining from her. Whatever adrenaline had been coursing through her body was now seriously depleted. She rolled onto her side and reached across the gap between the two beds. She took Alex's hand in hers and wove their fingers together. Barely able to keep her eyes open, she gave Alex's hand a tender squeeze. "Goodnight, my love."

* * *

Jess awoke the next morning to the opening of the sliding door. Throughout the night, she had awoken several times as nurses stopped in and checked on Alex. Even with those interruptions and the incessant beeping, ticking, humming, whirling, and *tshhhh…tshhhh…tshhhh…tshhhh* from the ventilator, she had managed more sleep than she would have thought possible. But as she looked up to see who the latest visitor was, she was pleasantly surprised to see Jordan sliding into the room. An even bigger surprise was the Caramel Ribbon Crunch Frappuccino in her outstretched hand.

Jess's eyes lit up. "For me? Oh God, Jordan, you're a lifesaver."

"You bet, sis." Jordan smiled brightly, handed over the cold drink, and flopped onto the bed beside Jess.

Jess took a huge slurp through the straw, closing her eyes. The icy drink tasted great, bringing a sense of normality for the first time since learning that Alex had been shot. Jess slowly opened her eyes. "Thanks a ton, Jordan. There's a reason you're my favorite sister."

"I'm your *only* sister." Jordan feigned outrage. This was a very old joke between the two.

"Still, you're my favorite." Jess laughed, the first genuine laugh since watching the news report.

They sat together in silence for several minutes, Jess slowly sipping her drink. Finally, Jordan scooted closer, looking over at Alex on the next bed. "Have you heard anything new? I mean with Alex since last night?"

Jess lowered her head. "I'm afraid not. Same ol', same ol'." She hadn't received any updates from the nurses or doctors and had been afraid to ask. What if they told her what she didn't want to hear? Trying to push those thoughts from her head, she turned to Jordan and quickly changed the topic. "Hey, where's Tim?"

Jordan winced. "Sorry, sis, but he had to work. He'll be in later though."

Jess could understand that. "What about Mom and Dad? Are they coming?"

"Yeah, they should be here soon. I'm actually surprised they aren't here already." Jordan glanced over at the door as if their parents might materialize at that very moment. Seeing no one there, she shrugged. "Have you eaten?"

"Jell-O. That was last night." Jess wasn't hungry.

Jordan scowled. "You need to eat, Jess. You won't do anyone any good if you get sick."

"I'm not leaving Alex!" Jess was surprised as her own voice echoed off the wall. She hadn't meant to yell. But there was no way she was leaving Alex alone.

If Jordan was surprised by Jess's outburst, she didn't show it. "I totally understand, sis. If it were Tim, I wouldn't leave either. But you do need to eat. Maybe when Mom and Dad get here, I can go with them to the cafeteria and bring you something back."

Jess relaxed and softened her voice. "I'd like that, Jordan. You're the best sister anyone could have."

"Of course, I am." Jordan sat up straight, puffing herself up like a peacock.

Jess laughed and shook her head. "Bless you, Jordan, for just being you."

Ten minutes later, their parents walked through the door. Linda was hiding something behind her back. "Sorry about being late but we had to stop for…" Her face fell as she noticed the cup in Jess's hand. Slowly she pulled an identical cup from behind her back. "I guess this wasn't needed."

Pete smiled. "I told you if there was a way, Jess would find a Starbucks."

"Actually, I brought it for her." Jordan spoke up, trying her best not to laugh.

Jess took the drink from her mom and set it on the side table with her other one. "That's okay, Mom. I've got a feeling this is going to be at least a two Frappuccino day."

Linda pulled up a chair. "Have you heard anything?"

"I'm afraid not, Mom. The doctor hasn't been in yet." Jess wished she had better news, any news. She glanced at Alex, who looked no different.

"Well, I'm sure that you'll hear something soon." Linda sat with her hands folded neatly in her lap.

Jess figured her mom's enduring hopefulness was where she and Jordan got it from. Although remaining positive after everything that had happened was difficult.

After more than a couple minutes of uncomfortable silence, Jordan hopped up from the corner of Jess's bed and turned to her parents. "How about we go down to the cafeteria and bring Jess back something to eat? We don't want her passing out as well."

Jordan chivvied their parents from the room. At the door, she glanced back and gave Jess a smile and a small nod.

Jess smiled back and mouthed silently, "Thank you."

* * *

Jess transferred herself from the bed to her chair, and a friendly nurse moved the portable bed to the side. When her family returned a bit under an hour later, Jess was glad to see them (and not just because they had brought her a big cheeseburger and a large boat of fries) but she had to use the bathroom.

With breakneck speed, she zipped to the bathroom and back into Alex's room, her wheels screeching loudly on the smooth linoleum floor. "Any news?"

Pete answered, standing behind Linda and rubbing her shoulders. "Nothing yet, sweetheart."

Although not surprised, Jess was still disappointed. Why hadn't they gotten any updates? Was Alex so bad off that no one wanted to say? Jess could now fully appreciate that waiting truly was the worst part. And the first person who said that no news is good news was going to need their own hospital bed.

Jess gobbled down the burger and turned to the fries. She didn't really taste anything but at least her stomach felt better.

Linda surveyed the room. "You know, Jess, if I'm not mistaken, this is the same room you were in a few years ago with your accident."

Jess had no idea. It could have been the janitor's closet for all she knew.

Jordan looked around exactly as Linda had. If not for the age difference, they could have been identical twins with their similar expressions. "You know, Mom, I think you're right. I still remember Alex—she wouldn't leave your side, Jess, not at all."

That Jess did remember. Not the part about Alex never leaving her side but *learning* that Alex had never left her side— after she had been a totally unappreciative jerk and booted Alex from her room. Not one of her finer moments.

"No, she wouldn't." Linda smiled, that type of smile only a mother has when thinking about their child, and looked directly at Jess. "I knew right then that you two would be together forever."

If Jess's chest had been tight before, it was completely frozen now. She and Alex hadn't parted on good terms the last time they'd seen each other. But none of that seemed important anymore, just trivial nonsense.

"Yeah, what's up with you two anyway—always ending up in the ICU? Talk about bad luck." Jordan snatched a fry from the paper boat in front of her.

Pete spoke up. Up until then, he had been mostly quiet, offering his calm, strong presence for support. "I wouldn't call that bad luck at all."

Linda spun around in her chair. Jess and Jordan stared openmouthed.

Pete shrugged, looking sheepish. "Sure, it's not good luck to be in the hospital but it is great luck that Jess and Alex have been there for each other when needed the most."

Jess could barely breathe. Her throat had slammed shut on her, blocked by what felt like a raw potato. Her dad wasn't usually one to chime in on emotional-themed conversations. But seeing this from his perspective gave her hope in a way that nothing up to then had. "I think you're right, Dad. We are lucky."

* * *

Maria stopped in after lunch. This time, she wasn't wearing scrubs but a T-shirt that read, "Nursing: It's a calling," and a pair of faded jeans. "How's everything going?" she asked, voice overly bubbly.

Jess lowered the second Frappuccino (now more than half gone), which she'd been sucking on since her family had left for a break an hour ago. They'd be back early that evening. In the meantime, she'd been watching silly cat videos to take her mind off everything—except every time she found a particularly amusing video, her first thought was to share it with Alex. She turned to Maria and shrugged. "Haven't heard anything yet."

Maria frowned, a deep scowl on her face. "That won't do. I'll go find out what's up?" Without waiting for an answer, Maria spun on her heel and marched off down the hall. Five minutes later, she popped back through the door. "Okay, I've got an update although it isn't much."

Jess would settle for any news.

"Don't look so nervous." Maria smiled. "There's not much to report. Alex's condition remains the same but she's doing good.

With all the blood loss, that's to be expected. Unfortunately, that's about all the news there is right now."

Jess tried to let her breath out but failed. She wouldn't be able to relax until Alex was awake—no, until Alex was out of the hospital and safe at home. "Thanks Maria. Thanks for everything. Are you working today?" Although part of her wanted to be alone, an equally large part of her was afraid. What if something happened to Alex? What if she were the only one there?

Maria pulled up a chair. "Nope. I'm off today, sweetie. ER's closed, something about investigating the breach in security. In the meantime, they're sending everyone across town to Crownwell East. Anyhow, I'm taking some time off after…you know, what happened."

Not wanting to picture why the ER was closed, Jess turned back to her Frappuccino. She was about to take another sip of her lukewarm drink when something dawned on her. "What happened to the shooter? Where is he?" Sudden panic set in. Was he still nearby? Was he somewhere in the hospital at that moment?

The smile faded from Maria's face, replaced with a dangerous, predatory glare. "Oh, he's gone, locked up. Cops dragged him off. Trust me, that asshole will never see the light of day again."

"Good." Although she rarely took pleasure in another's misery, Jess hoped the evil bastard that had shot her girlfriend would suffer a long and massively painful life in prison. Then he could rot in the seventh circle of hell, the circle reserved specially for violence.

After Maria left, Jess leaned back in her chair and closed her eyes. She was about to nod off when an almighty commotion came from the hall outside. She opened her eyes to Jamie and Sue scrambling into the room. When they saw Alex lying in the bed, trussed up with enough wires to do a Thanksgiving turkey proud, they both froze.

Jamie clapped her hands to her mouth as if to stifle a scream, then raced up and threw her arms around Jess. "Oh God, Jess, we just heard. It's all over the news."

"Yeah, we raced down here as fast as we could." Sue joined the hug until both were squeezing Jess tight.

Jess could barely breathe. If they didn't let up, and soon, she'd pass out.

"Let the girl get some air." Jamie slapped Sue lightly on the arm as if she hadn't just been smothering Jess herself a second earlier.

"Okay, okay. Sorry." Sue let go and stood back up. Her eyes were watery.

Jess tried not to notice. She'd cried so much that she didn't think she could anymore. "Thanks for coming, guys."

Jamie took the empty chair that Maria had been sitting in earlier. She leaned forward, her voice quiet. "What the hell happened? How's Alex?"

Jess filled them in. Anytime she paused, either Jamie or Sue would gasp and clamp their hands over their mouths again, sometimes both at the same time.

After Jess finished filling them in on the details, Jamie spoke up. "Sweet Jesus, it's a miracle Alex's still alive. Oh Jess. Oh Jess."

Sue shook her head. "I can't believe it. You two—you've got to stop this hospital shit. I tell you. If it's not one, it's the other."

Jess smiled, agreeing whole-heartedly. But like her dad had said, it was great luck that they had each other during these times.

The final visitor of the afternoon didn't come empty-handed. Terra carried a get-well card, signed by the entire staff at the bookstore in her right hand and in her left—a Caramel Ribbon Crunch Frappuccino.

Jess burst out laughing. "That's the third one someone's brought me today."

"Three? Holy shit, Shaggy. That's a fuck-ton of coffee." Terra also laughed.

Still, Jess wasn't going to look this particular gift horse in the mouth. "Thanks Terra. I can certainly use the pick-me-up." She took a sip. They really were best when still icy.

Terra walked over to Alex. She looked down for a long moment, as if trying to force her brain to believe what her eyes were telling it. Finally, she turned around. "I hate to ask…I'm sure you've already answered this a hundred times…but…"

"…how's Alex doing?" Jess wished there was a way she could record it so she wouldn't have to relive it each time.

"Yeah." Terra lowered her eyes.

Jess filled her in, starting with the shooting and ending with the latest update. For her part, Terra gasped and cried, scowled and swore, at all the right places. Finally, when Jess finished, Terra sat looking stunned. "I just can't believe this. I mean, I can't believe this. Oh my God. I can't imagine what you're going through, Jess."

"Thanks Terra. Can you do something for me?"

"Anything, Jess. Just name it."

"Could you tell your parents that I won't be in for a bit?"

Terra immediately waved her off. "Please, Jess. You don't have to worry about that. Take all the time you need. Everyone at the bookstore is there for you."

Once again, Jess was reminded of just how lucky she was.

* * *

Over the next four days, Jess remained at Alex's side. Or was it five days? Everything was running together. Visitors came and went, came and went, again and again. Jess's family arrived every morning at eight, like clockwork. They brought breakfast then waited around, talking about Alex, the weather, or nothing at all. Other times, they sat in silence. Then they'd get Jess lunch before leaving for the afternoon. Jess used the time to sit beside Alex, holding her hand. If she were lucky, she could catch a nap. Then her family would show back up around six with dinner. Cheeseburger and fries. Jess wasn't sure her stomach could take anything else. And that was how the days went. Lather, rinse, repeat.

Evenings were the busiest. That's when most of the visitors came—Maria, Jamie and Sue, Terra, others. Always the same question—how was Alex doing? Jess had grown accustomed to her role as information giver. When the nurses or doctor came into the room, Jess asked all the questions and took notes so she could pass information along to all those who loved Alex.

The only minor change had come on the third day. The intubation tube had been removed. No more constant *tshhhh… tshhhh…tshhhh…tshhhh*. It left the room strangely quiet. Jess hadn't realized how much she'd grown accustomed to the sound, how much she took comfort in hearing it in the background. That sound meant Alex was still alive and fighting.

But nighttime was the worst, after all visitors left and the ward settled down for a good night's sleep. It was during these times that Jess felt the loneliest, the saddest, the most hopeless. All she could do was stare at Alex, lying unconscious before her. It was during these times that Jess missed Alex the most.

"Hey babe, wish you were here."

At first, Jess felt silly speaking. Alex certainly couldn't respond. But Jess talked to her, nonetheless. If she didn't, she might just explode in one gigantic outburst of unspoken conversation. So, Jess spoke to Alex during those dark and lonely nights. She talked and talked. Didn't matter about what. She just spoke.

"Jamie and Sue came in again today. They give you their best and wish you a quick recovery."

Jess wished the same. She wished it like a little girl—star light, star bright, first star I see tonight, I wish I may, I wish I might, bring back to me my future wife.

Sometimes she talked about nothing, just filling in Alex with the day's events as if she hadn't been in the room the entire time.

"Jordan brought me another Frappuccino today. I swear, babe, if you don't wake up soon, I'll OD on caramel and caffeine."

But other times, she shared more important thoughts, thoughts she wouldn't dare speak during the light of the day.

"I miss you like hell, Alex. I'm so sorry I hurt you by sending that stupid invitation. Please forgive me."

Jess lay in the portable bed beside Alex, her arm bridging the gap between them. She held Alex's hand. The darkness hid a lot. It hid the tears. It hid the anger. It hid the guilt.

"I haven't ever told you this, Alex, but you make everything in my life better, even the not-so-great stuff. You make everything about *me* better, even the not-so-great stuff. I don't know if you know it or not, but the highlight of any day is when I get to see you. That's something I look forward to. Even when you're not with me, I still feel you there. Oh, and while I'm confessing, I'm the one who put that big scratch in the side of your car."

Jess smiled in the darkness. Confessions could be cathartic. She wondered if Alex had done the same when she had been the one in the hospital bed. What had Alex shared with her?

"Before I met you, I wasn't a very happy person. No one really knew. I tried to hide it. But I was miserable on the inside. I was angry all the time. I hated everyone. But then you came along. Wow, did you come along. And you changed my entire life. You brought out the best parts in me and I'll forever be grateful for that. Just saying, 'I love you,' will never fully express what I feel inside. Please come back to me."

Jess fell asleep like that, her hand in Alex's. She dreamed of Holland. What she wouldn't give to be back there now. In her dream, they were huffing it along Lakeshore Trail, both laughing, pushing each other faster and faster. The air was filled with fragrant scents from the flowers as if she were running through the world's largest bouquet. Her wheels bounced over each crack in the pavement. People were jumping out of their way but still they laughed and sped on. These were good times, perfect times.

They finally pulled off the trail, gasping for breath, either from their exertion or from their laughter. Perhaps both. Alex was bent in two. Her legs were shaking.

Once she'd recovered enough to speak, Jess called to Alex, who still stood with her hands on her knees. "Are you okay there, Legs?"

Alex stood and let out a loud whoop of triumph, pumping her fists into the air. She looked happier than Jess had ever seen her. "Whoo-wee, Jess! That was *awesome*! I've really missed you these past few months."

Jess woke as the light began to twinkle through the window. Her arm felt as if it had been folded in two and not at the bendy parts. If only she could have stayed in that dream forever. Jess yawned and turned her head to the side. She was met by intense light blue eyes and a smile.

"Good morning, Wheels. Up for a race?"

CHAPTER FIFTEEN

Alex tried to sit up but winced and collapsed back on the bed as a sharp, ripping pain shot through her chest. She sucked in a quick breath, which only intensified the feeling.

Jess sat up, her eyes flying wide, and screamed. Her voice echoed about the room and down the hallway. "Help! Someone help! Hurry! Please hurry!" She scrambled to the edge of her bed and grappled for her chair.

"Babe, babe…" Alex called, but Jess couldn't hear her. Her throat was dry and raw. She tried to move again but was held back by the tangle of cords and hoses. She looked down her body. "What the hell?"

Jess was in a panic. She fumbled with her chair, moving it so she could transfer.

Alex turned just in time to see Jess disappear from the opposite side of her bed, falling face-first onto the floor. The last thing Alex saw was Jess's butt vanish over the edge. Jess's chair spun away like a car caught in a tornado. There was a metallic clamor as things collided and showered down onto the hard linoleum floor. Alex's brain felt as if she were walking through the mental equivalent of mud. She tried to wrap her thoughts around what was happening. "Oh my God! Jess! Jess!"

"*Fucking hell!*" Jess's voice drifted up from the floor. "*Goddammit!*"

Alex still couldn't see her, but she could hear Jess struggling. Her wheelchair spun around again, this time knocking over the stainless-steel side table. That crashed to the floor with another yelp from Jess.

"Jess! Are you okay?" Alex tried to sit up again only to feel that terrible pain shoot through her chest. Her vision dimmed as if she were about to pass out. Suddenly, a whole host of alarms blared like a dozen sirens going off at once as Alex inadvertently dislodged several of her monitor leads.

By the time the nurses arrived, it was pandemonium. Jess flopped on the floor, trying her damnedest to climb into her chair. Alex's head spun and her vision kept fading in and out. She knew full well that a patient in her condition shouldn't exert themselves. But dammit, she had to know that Jess was all right. She clawed at the bed railing. She had to see Jess. She had to.

The first nurse in the room, a young woman who looked as if she might have graduated from nursing school that very morning, slid to a stop, her shoes squelching on the smooth floor. She took in the scene, looking more shocked than either Jess or Alex. "What the…"

The second nurse, an older woman with short-cropped red hair and a stocky build, at least had the fortitude not to look so surprised. Alex recognized her at once. Pamela something or other. She had worked with her during the height of the COVID crisis.

The third nurse was Maria, wearing street clothes and there for a visit. When she took in the scene, Maria clapped a hand to her mouth to stifle a laugh. "What on earth happened in here?"

"She's awake!" All Alex could see was Jess's hand floating in midair and pointing at her.

"I see that. And from all the commotion, I think everyone else on the floor is probably awake." Maria sprang into action, righting the end table and wrestling Jess's chair over to her.

Meanwhile, the younger nurse pulled the portable bed out into the hall while Pamela moved to Alex's side and began replacing the leads that had pulled loose in the excitement. "Settle down, sweetie. We've got to check you out."

Alex was having none of that. "See if Jess is okay, dammit." She grabbed Pamela's hand, but the effort was too much, and she crashed back against her pillow, fighting for breath.

"You're going to have to calm down or we'll have to give you a sedative. Now, I have to check your vitals, Doctor Hartway."

The use of her professional name above all else got Alex's attention. She did her best to seem calm while trying to peer around Pamela, finally relaxing when she saw that Maria was helping Jess into her chair.

"Wow, you two really know how to draw attention."

Jess scowled at Maria as she settled into the seat of her chair and released the brake. "What was I supposed to do? Alex woke up."

"Sweetheart, everyone knows that by now thanks to you." Maria clapped her on the shoulder.

After what seemed like an hour, Pamela stepped back. "There. Looks like everything is good. All your vitals are right where they should be." She crossed her arms, a stern look on her face. "But you are going to have to remain calm and relaxed, Doctor Hartway."

Maria stepped up to Alex's bed. "Doctors make the worst patients." She exchanged a knowing look with Pamela.

Sometime during all the hullabaloo, the younger nurse had disappeared. Hiding in a closet somewhere reevaluating her career choice? That image made Alex chuckle softly.

Pamela turned to her and eyed her with pursed lips. "Just so you know, Doctor Hartway, laughing is *not* remaining calm and relaxed."

With the room back in order, Pamela walked to the doorway, but before leaving, she turned back to Alex and with her index and middle finger going from pointing at her eyes to pointing at Alex, mimed that she'd be watching her. Alex could care less. She wanted to talk to Jess, to see if Jess was okay. She tried to roll farther onto her side with no success. Finally, she settled for turning her head.

Jess had rolled up to the side of the bed. Maria took a step back and hooked a thumb over her shoulder. "I think I'll get a cup of coffee. Let you two…" Whatever it was that she was letting Alex and Jess do she never said but instead quietly slipped from the room.

"I'm so…"

"Are you…"

"No, you go…" They both said at the same time.

They stared at each other. Jess reached out and gently took Alex's hand.

"Are you…are you okay?" Alex's chest hurt, and her lungs felt as if someone had pulled them out, thrown them on the floor, and stomped on them in stiletto heels for good measure.

Jess smiled and rolled her eyes. "Of course. I just got a bit excited to see you awake."

"A bit, huh?" Alex raised her eyebrows.

Jess blushed and lowered her head, looking so cute that Alex wished she could pull her into her arms, but she was quickly losing energy. Still, she had to know one thing. "What the hell happened?"

Jess looked up, meeting Alex's eyes. Jess took a deep, labored breath. "You were shot, babe."

Alex nodded. That she did remember, or at least part of it. She remembered pushing Maria out of the way, flashes from the muzzle but no sound, seeing her own hand covered in blood, and a whole bunch of disjointed images that didn't make any sense.

Over the next fifteen minutes, Jess filled Alex in with all that she knew. Alex listened with a strange professional detachment, as if hearing about a patient, though the tangle of leads, the chest tube, and the dull, hollow pain throughout her chest that spiked with each breath spoke of the truth. When Jess finished, there were tears in her eyes. Alex tried to smile, to reassure and comfort her, but it turned into a wince instead. Finally, she lifted her hand, the effort as much as if she were trying to climb a mountain, and covered Jess's hand, squeezing it as tightly as she could. "It's okay, Wheels. I'm going to be fine."

Jess snorted and hiccupped at the same time. She wiped her eyes and shook her head. "I thought…I thought you were going to die, Alex. I thought I'd…I'd lost you."

Alex ached for Jess. She knew that feeling. When Jess had been injured, Alex had thought the same. It was the worst feeling of her life, even worse than she felt now. At least she could heal from the bullet wounds, but losing Jess…that she didn't think she could ever recover from. "Shhhh, shhhh, babe. It'll be all right. I'll be all right."

"But…but…but…" Jess blubbered as she cried.

"Come here, Jess." Alex tried to pull her close, but she might as well have been trying to lift a truck. "Come."

Jess rolled closer and lowered the railing separating them. She leaned forward until she was barely sitting in her chair and laid her head against Alex's side. Even though she was being as careful as she could, she still bumped Alex's chest tube.

Alex winced at the jostling. That damn chest tube was going to be the first thing to go the next time the nurse came in. But for now, Jess was more important. Alex stroked her hair. Jess cried. They held hands. There would be time enough to talk later. Minutes later, they had fallen asleep still holding hands.

* * *

Jess couldn't have been asleep for more than ten minutes when one of the ICU doctors walked into the room. Still with the same short spiky gray hair she remembered, Dr. Harris, or Becky as she liked to be called, hadn't aged a day since Jess's own hospital stay. Besides caring for Alex for the past week, Becky had been an invaluable comfort to Jess as well. Jess nudged Alex to wake her.

"So, I heard there was a bit of excitement earlier." Becky chuckled lightly.

"Yes, Alex woke up!" Jess nudged Alex again.

Alex stared around the room, blinking blearily. "Hey, Becky. Long time, no see. What brings you in?"

"Hardy har har. Always the joker, aren't you, Alex? Let's see how you're doing, why don't we?" Becky walked up to the bed and examined Alex, checking her wounds and the chest tube. After a cursory exam, Becky checked the computer, reading the notes and test results.

Jess held her breath.

"Hmmm. Everything is looking good." Becky turned from the computer.

"What are the numbers, doc?" Alex was completely alert now.

Becky smiled. "Always the doctor, huh?" She went over the various numbers and results with Alex.

If not for Alex lying in the bed, the two of them looked as if they were having a consultation for any other patient. Jess didn't understand most of what was being said.

Alex continued to nod as she took it all in with a strange detachment, as if talking about the unseasonably hot weather over a tall glass of lemonade.

When Becky finally finished with all the medical jargon, she smiled and clapped her hands together. "The good news is that I think we can get you out of here this afternoon and moved to a more comfortable room."

"Great." Alex winced as she tried to sit up. "How about we get rid of this chest tube while we're at it?"

"Whoa now, let's not get ahead of ourselves. That tube is there for a reason, as you well know." Becky scowled.

Alex grumbled. "I could just remove it myself." She made as if to pull away the tape holding the tube in place.

Jess gasped. She wouldn't really do that, would she? Then Jess reconsidered. Of course Alex would do something like that.

"Hey, hey, don't you dare." Becky admonished, her voice stern. "I'm not above having you restrained."

Jess laughed at the idea of Alex being tied to her bed. "You'd better listen, babe. She'd do it too."

"Darn right I would." Becky crossed her arms and glared at Alex. "I swear, doctors make the absolute worst patients."

Alex grumbled again and pouted. "Fine."

Becky finally smiled. "I'll see what we can do about getting you moved to some better accommodations but only if you behave."

Jess laid her hand on Alex's arm to prevent more grumping. "She will. I'll make sure of it."

Becky left the room, calling over her shoulder as she went. "No self-doctoring now or I'll be back."

True to her word, Becky arranged for Alex to be transferred that afternoon. The new room was much more inviting. It reminded Jess of the hotel in Holland, only one-third the size. Perhaps the best part was the foldout bed, which was a lot more comfortable than the hard, lumpy contraption she'd had the dubious pleasure of sleeping on for the past week.

After they settled in, Jess transferred herself to the couch so she could stretch out. She looked over at Alex, who looked much different without all the leads bird-nested on top of her. Also, it was a nice change not to have all the beeping, whirling, buzzing, and humming machines as a constant background noise. "How are you feeling, babe?"

She took in Alex's appearance. Her skin was pinking up more, a definite improvement over the bluish-white pallor that had alarmingly been the norm since her surgery.

Alex yawned and blinked slowly. "Other than being tired, I'm ready to go home. Just have to get rid of this damn tube." She looked down at her chest.

"Don't you dare! You heard what Doctor Becky said. I'm not afraid to rat you out." Jess jabbed a finger at Alex. She didn't remember being this bad of a patient when she was in the hospital, although Jordan would probably disagree.

"Fine." Alex yawned again. "In that case, maybe a nap is in order. Being a patient is exhausting."

Jess leaned back and stifled her own yawn behind her hand. A nap might be just what the doctor ordered.

* * *

Alex was ready to get out of the hospital. By now, she'd settle for anywhere but here. At least she was able to get out of bed and walk a bit since her chest tube had been removed. However, it was slow going. Every step sent stabs of intensely sharp pain through her. The only highlight had been the visitors. Although exhausting, it was nice to see people and chat for a bit. It broke up the monotony. The most surprising visitor had been Dr. Ron Primeau, the president of the hospital.

"Doctor Hartway, it's so good to see you up and recovering." Dr. Primeau, a tall, distinguished man with curly white hair, popped into the room just after breakfast the morning after she awoke. His voice boomed in the room.

"Ah, ah. Thank you, Doctor Primeau." Alex grabbed the hospital gown she was wearing and pulled it tightly closed under her chin.

"Please, call me Ron. And please relax. We're all friends here." Ron smiled broadly. He turned toward Jess. "And who's this? Your sister?"

Alex bit her lip. "Actually, Ron, this is my fiancée, Jess Bolderson. We're getting married this fall."

"Oh excellent." In two mighty steps, Ron crossed the room and offered his hand to Jess. "Congratulations. I'm so glad to meet you, Jess."

"Um, thank you, sir." Jess looked like a deer in headlights.

Ron turned back to Alex. "You better not forget my invitation." He let out a room-filling bark of a laugh.

"Don't worry, Ron. I'll make sure you get one." Alex mentally made a note to send an invitation as soon as she got out of there.

Ron pulled up a chair, suddenly serious. "I just want to say that we're all very sorry about what happened to you. I mean, for someone to get shot, one of our own even, in this hospital, it's a real tragedy. Everyone has been rooting for you to recover. We're all here for you...for both of you." He glanced over to Jess and gave a firm nod.

"Thanks, Ron. That really means a lot." Alex swallowed, fighting down the grapefruit-sized lump in her throat.

Ron smiled gently. "Unfortunately, I have the unenviable task of telling you that someone from legal will be down later to talk with you."

Alex sat up straight. The lump made a spectacular crash into her stomach. Jess gasped beside her. "I'm not…I'm not in trouble or anything, am I? I mean…"

"No, no, nothing like that." Ron waved off her concerns. "I know, I hate lawyers too. But we need you to tell legal everything you remember. It's all part of the charges against the shooter."

Alex let out a sigh of relief. Jess did the same.

Ron placed his large hand reassuringly over Alex's. "Believe me, you have nothing to worry about except getting better. Consider yourself on paid leave, so take all the time you need. As far as everyone is concerned, you're a real hero."

After Ron left, Alex turned to Jess. With her index finger clamped between her teeth, Jess had a strange look on her face, as if she had broken Alex's favorite coffee mug and was afraid to tell her. "What's up, babe? Was it the lawyer stuff?"

Jess slowly shook her head. She popped her finger from out of her teeth. For a moment, she looked as if she might jam the finger back in. She lowered her eyes. "You told Doctor Ron that I'm your fiancée."

"Yeah?"

Jess stared at her hands in her lap, not raising her eyes to meet Alex. "It's just…I don't know…before you got shot…are we still?"

"Oh." Now it made sense. The night before she'd been shot suddenly came rushing back. "Hey, Jess, look at me."

Jess slowly, reluctantly raised her head. She chewed on her bottom lip.

Alex's heart went out to Jess. What she must have been going through the past week or so. But Jess had never faltered. She had been there the entire time. Finally, Alex reached out to Jess. She twisted their fingers together. "Do you still want to get married? I mean, I understand if you don't."

Jess gasped. "Of course I want to get married. I just didn't know if you still wanted to."

Alex smiled widely. "Of course, I do, Wheels. I'm not letting a little thing like an argument or getting shot put an end to that. If I've learned anything from all this, it's that life is too short to let the small shit get to us."

"Are you sure, Alex? I mean, with everything…all the crap with the wedding…I don't want you to have any doubts." Jess didn't look completely convinced.

"I don't. I won't." Alex leaned forward and cupped Jess's cheek in her hand, looking directly into her deep, dark brown eyes. "Tell you what, Jess, will you marry me…again?"

Jess finally smiled as well, a visible weight lifting from her shoulders. "You bet, Legs, I'd marry you again and again."

* * *

"What's the first thing you want to do when you get out of the hospital?" Jess rocked onto her back wheels as she looked over at Alex, who had just finished a lap walking up the hall and back.

Alex sat on the edge of her bed, gasping for breath and clutching at her side. "Get rid of this damn gown, that's what I'm going to do."

"I don't know babe—I kind of like the view, especially when you catch a little breeze." Jess raised an eyebrow, a mischievous grin on her lips.

Alex scowled. "That only happened one time and it was an accident."

"Sure it was, babe. Sure it was." Jess laughed loudly, her chair crashing back onto all four wheels. "You won't hear me complaining, I can guarantee that."

"I bet." Alex threw Jess another scowl but couldn't quite hide the smirk underneath. "I can't wait to get out of here. All this prodding and poking, nurses and doctors popping in at all hours, I'm ready for some peace and quiet."

Jess shook her head. As much as Alex might like to gripe, Jess knew it was mostly an act. Alex was grateful to everyone, even if she hid it behind scowls and complaints. "Any updates on when that might be?"

"Doctor Becky thinks maybe the day after tomorrow." Alex scooted back until she rested with a pillow behind her. She tried to cross her legs in the bed and thought better of that. With a wince, she clutched at her side again.

"That's good news then." Jess narrowed her eyes as she watched Alex. "Still really hurting, huh?"

Alex grumbled under her breath. She glanced down at her side. "Yeah, it's mostly when I move. Feels like someone's jamming a rod through me."

"Ironically, I know exactly how that feels, Legs." Jess stuck her tongue out.

"Oh yeah, I vaguely remember something about that, Wheels." Alex chuckled. "I just wish it'd stop hurting when I move."

Jess picked up a napkin from the bedside table, wadded it up, and threw it at Alex, who easily ducked it as it flew over her head. "Geez, Alex, you've got to give yourself time to heal. You've had three holes punched through your body, two of which were through vital organs. It might take a little while to get over that."

"I know. Believe me, I know." Alex crossed her arms over her chest, her bottom lip pooched out, making her look all of twelve years old. "But I've got stuff to do. And there's the wedding. We've still got to find a venue. And God knows what else is going to come up there. This sucks!"

Jess tapped a finger against her temple. "You know, Alex, I've been thinking…"

"That's a dangerous pastime, Wheels. You'd better be careful."

Jess rolled her eyes. That was one of Alex's favorite jokes. "Yeah, I know. Still, I've been thinking. About our wedding. What if we just said fuck it to all these plans?"

Alex turned serious. "You're not wanting to get married now?"

Jess shook her head. "No, nothing like that." She watched as Alex relaxed. "But this entire wedding thing got super stressful. Everything was going wrong. I mean, isn't getting married supposed to be fun?"

Alex nodded vigorously. "You'd think so, wouldn't you?"

"Yeah, which is why I got to thinking…why don't we bag the entire idea of a big, fancy wedding? We can have it in our backyard. Go potluck. Much easier, and we'd also save a ton of money."

Alex leaned forward. "You'd really be okay with that?"

"Of course." Jess was getting excited. She hadn't felt like that concerning their wedding since Alex had initially popped the question. "That's kind of what I was thinking to begin with, but then we got all wrapped up with planning the perfect wedding. You know, we're only—"

"—getting married once. That's what I've been telling myself all this time, but it seems like too much." Alex stared at Jess. "All I care about is being with you."

Jess slapped herself on the forehead. "Seriously, Legs? That's all I want too. We don't need all this elaborate crap."

Alex bounced on her bed then quickly winced. When she recovered, she threw her arms wide. "No, I think you're on to something here, Wheels. Let's say fuck it. Let's just go for simple. We should have done that in the first place."

Jess rocked up again on her back wheels and spun around. This was great. They would focus on what was truly important— the two of them.

Alex pointed directly at Jess, fixing her with her eyes. "I love your idea, Jess. This will be so much better. I can't wait until October."

Jess dropped back on all four wheels again. It was all she could do not to go racing up and down the hallway. Alex looked happier than Jess had seen her in months.

Jess froze, another idea suddenly coming to mind. "Tell you what, Legs, since we're saying fuck it to everything, let's say fuck it to the date as well."

"So, not do it in October?" Alex gaped, total confusion on her face. "Then when?"

Jess rolled quickly to the side of Alex's bed. She took Alex by the hand. "As soon as you get out of here. Next week!"

Alex burst out laughing. "Next week? Are you crazy? How can we possibly do it next week?"

Jess gave Alex's hand a squeeze, leaned in close, and gave a sly wink. "Just you leave that to me."

CHAPTER SIXTEEN

Alex slowly walked up the hallway again, holding her right side with each step. Although it had been well over a week, it still hurt a lot to move, especially the wound that felt as if her lung was being pulled through an itty-bitty hole and then flapped about the room. It was an experience she wouldn't recommend to anyone. But if she didn't regain her strength and mobility, she would never be discharged.

She paused at the corner, wheezing and holding herself up with a hand against the wall. She grumbled under her breath, something that she found herself doing a lot lately. How many gunshot wounds had she treated in her career? A hundred? Two hundred? Way too many. But she never thought she'd be one of them.

Alex rested, breathing slowly. No matter what she did, she couldn't quite catch her breath. It only made sense—she'd had a large caliber lead slug take a leisurely stroll through her pulmonary system. Just her luck, the gunman had decided to use a forty-five. No measly little nine-millimeter for her, no siree. Her real fear was that this might become her new normal. And if it did, how was she ever to run again, let alone function normally on a daily basis? But she couldn't let herself fall down that rabbit hole. If she did, she might never be able to crawl back out and Jess didn't deserve that.

Alex took a deep breath (it burned like hell) and pushed off from the wall. She could do this. She had a wedding to get ready for and she'd be damned if she wasn't going to wear that amazing dress.

When she got back to her room, she collapsed on the bed, gasping. Her mouth was dry. She wasn't sure if that had more to do with her injuries or the dry hospital air. Probably a little of both. As she leaned back, she grabbed a water bottle from the side table—beads of condensation covered the plastic and left a puddle on the table surface. She lifted the bottle to her forehead, rolling it against her overly heated skin. She closed her eyes and let out a long, low sigh. Dear God, that felt good. Even the droplets that landed on her chest, trickling slowly between her breasts, felt like heaven. If Jess were there, she could help mop up the dampness running down her chest—maybe even get in a playful squeeze as well—but she had sent her home that morning. To say Jess had protested would be a gross understatement. She'd flat-out refused until Alex had pointed out that if they were to pull off their expedited wedding plans, Jess would need to get started right away. Jess had grudgingly acquiesced but with the stipulation that Alex work extra hard to get discharged. That was a challenge she had gladly accepted, even with the pain it would entail. She wanted out of here, the sooner the better.

Alex finally opened her eyes, twisted the cap off the water bottle, and took a long slurp. Sweet, sweet nirvana, but that was magnificent—which might have to do a bit with the pain meds. Although Dr. Becky had cut her back to the point that she was no longer tasting sunshine, she could still feel the effects, not that she was going to admit that. She would probably never get out of the hospital if she told anyone she was still fighting the urge to break out into a raucous chorus of "Zip-a-Dee-Doo-Dah" every time the meds kicked in.

After drinking nearly half the bottle in one swig, Alex recapped it and set it aside just as Dr. Becky entered the room.

"Good morning, Dr. Alex. How's my worst patient doing?"

"Good morning to you too, Dr. Becky. So, when am I getting out of here?" Alex chuckled. This was an ongoing joke between them.

"Hold on, hold on. I've got to check you out first. You know the drill." Becky walked up to the side of the bed.

"*Hrupphh.*" Alex pulled her gown open so Becky could examine the angry red divots in her chest, held together with tiny black sutures that looked as if she were growing whiskers from her wounds. Although the wounds looked to be healing well, Alex had no doubt she'd be left with substantial scarring.

Becky nodded to herself and stood back up. "Okay Alex, I need you to lean forward now so I can check those exit wounds."

Alex leaned forward. She hadn't seen the exit wounds yet and wasn't sure she wanted to. From her experience, bullets, especially from large bore weapons like the one she was shot with, tended to make a right mess out of flesh when they exited the body. Alex winced as Becky gently probed the spots with her fingers, causing sharp, hot stabs of pain to shoot through her.

"How's it looking, doc?"

Becky prodded a bit more then stood up. As Alex wrapped herself back in the gown, Becky smiled brightly. "Everything is looking good. I don't see any signs of infection. I am very happy with how it's healing. We should even be able to get those sutures removed today."

Alex sat up straight. This was unexpectedly good news. "So does that mean I'm getting out of here soon as well?" She held her breath.

Becky put her index finger to her cheek, holding her chin in her hand as if thinking it over. "I think you might be ready to be discharged today."

"Hallelujah, doc, I'm out of here!" Alex threw her legs over the side of the bed, ready to run for the door.

"Whoa, whoa, Alex." Becky motioned for her to relax. "You're not quite ready to go yet. We need to get those stitches out, get your paperwork around, and get a ride here for you."

"*Phhhftt.*" Alex waved Becky off. "My car is still here. I can drive myself home."

Becky stood back, her arms crossed, giving Alex a stern glare. "I don't think so, Dr. Alex. You know as well as I do that even if—and I am going to emphasize the *if*—you are ready to be discharged, that doesn't mean you're ready to do everything you want. That means no driving yourself home from the hospital. No ride, no discharge. I'm not afraid to keep you here another week."

Alex scowled. "Fine. I'll get a ride."

"Good." Becky relaxed, her shoulders dropping. "I'll have a nurse come in and remove those stitches and we'll see about getting you out of here in an hour or two. Call that ride."

Alex could barely contain her excitement. She was heading home. Sweet Jesus and all his carpenter friends, she was heading home. "Thanks, Becky. For…for everything."

"No problem, Alex. Just take it easy, get rest, and don't overdo it." Becky walked to the door but before she disappeared, she called back over her shoulder. "And you really are my worst patient. Get better soon."

* * *

Jess pulled up the drive as the garage door rattled up along its tracks. It was nice to be home after so long staying in the hospital. As she parked the car, she looked to the empty spot where Alex's car was usually parked with a deep sigh.

Jess threw open her car door and heaved her wheelchair from the back seat, surprised Jordan wasn't there already. The squeal when she told Jordan she needed help with an exciting change to their wedding had left Jess partially deaf in that ear for a least a half hour.

Jess rolled down the driveway to the mailbox while she waited. Overhead, squirrels were chattering loudly in some great disagreement in the treetops. The fuzzy little bastards could really make a ruckus sometimes, but she liked watching their antics, especially in their large backyard. Once she hit the street, Jess looked at the giant fishing lure-shaped box mailbox and shook her head. It was a good thing she loved her brother-in-law as much as she did.

"Holy crap!" When Jess opened the mouth to their mailbox, she found it stuffed to the gills. She dug the mail out of the box, dropping it into her lap. Jess closed the mouth of the box and pawed through the large pile. There was the usual junk mail and bills, a good two to three dozen RSVPs—she'd have to go through those. There were no less than ten credit card offers—those could go directly in the bin. But halfway through the stack, a plain white envelope caught her eye, addressed in a wide flowing script to both Alex and her, with no return address. Jess stared at it, her brow furrowing. "What the hell's this?"

Jess ripped open the envelope with her finger and shook out the single-page letter. She quickly unfolded it and read the first line. "Oh my God!" She clapped her hand to her mouth. "I don't fucking believe it!" She read down the page, her hand still clasped tightly over her mouth. When she finished, she read it again...and again. Even after the third time through, Jess still had problems believing her eyes. Of all the people. "Oh, my fucking God!"

At the bottom of the letter, just below the missive, was a phone number. Jess pulled out her cell, nearly dropping it into the street in her haste. She punched in the number, holding her breath. Someone answered on the third ring. When Jess hung up ten minutes later, her head was spinning. It still didn't feel real. How was she going to keep this a secret? She stared down at the letter once again, smiling from ear to ear. She clapped her hand over her mouth again. "Oh my God! I don't fucking believe it!"

Jordan pulled up in her new Geyser Blue Wilderness edition Subaru Outback while Jess was still staring at the letter. She hopped out with a typical Jordan-esque bounce and trotted up to Jess. "What's up, sis? Find a chain letter or something in your mailbox?"

"Not quite." Jess was still in a daze. She held the letter out to Jordan, her hand shaking. "Check this out."

Jordan snatched the piece of paper and quickly read, her eyes growing wider and wider until she looked as if she had been goosed from behind (a favorite pastime of her husband). When she finished, she dropped her hand with the letter in it and turned to Jess. "Son. Of. A. Bitch. You've got to be kidding. This is *awesome*! How? When? Why?"

Jess shrugged. "I just got it now. As for everything else, I have no idea."

Jordan leaned in conspiratorially and cupped her hand to her mouth, her voice a low whisper. "So, are you going to tell Alex?"

"Are you *nuts?* There's no way I'm telling her about this." Jess grew suddenly stern, glaring at her sister in a way that would have frightened away a mama bear. "And neither will you, Jordan."

"Yeah, yeah." Jordan nonchalantly waved her off. "Whatever."

"Jordan, I'm serious. You are not to tell Alex, no matter what." Jess knew Jordan's ability to keep secrets ranged from slim-to-none to not-a-chance-in-hell. She was hoping for at least slim-to-none.

"Fine. I won't tell." Jordan clasped her right hand to her chest, trying to look innocent. She failed miserably. "You have my word."

Although not totally convinced, Jess could dream. "Okay, then. Let's go inside. I've got a lot to fill you in on about our new and improved wedding plans."

Jordan looked as if she were in the transports of pure ecstasy. She rocked up on her toes and let out a squeal that caused all the squabbling squirrels overhead to go silent.

Once inside, Jess offered her sister a Diet Coke and grabbed a Cherry Vanilla Dr. Pepper for herself. Lordy did it feel good to be home.

Jess rolled into the living room. Jordan took a seat on the couch while Jess faced her in her chair. She cracked open her drink and took a long sip before starting. She needed to wet her whistle as her grandmama used to say. "So, I talked it over with Alex and we're wanting to adjust the timeline, especially since the venue screwed us over. Thing is—I need your help."

Jordan took a sip of her Diet Coke and nodded. "Sure, sis, no problem. When were you guys thinking then?"

"Next week."

Jordan blew soda halfway across the room in the spit take of all spit takes. "*NEXT WEEK? Holy shit, Jess! Are you shitting me?*" She tried to catch the Diet Coke running off her chin with zero luck then thumped the can onto the coffee table, trying to mop soda from the front of her T-shirt.

Jess laughed and tossed a paper napkin at Jordan, who blotted at her shirt and wiped her sticky hands. "Nope, I'm serious. We want to get married as soon as possible."

"But…but…"

It was fun seeing Jordan speechless. That didn't happen very often, and Jess was going to savor the moment. "What do you think?"

"I think…I think you're insane." Jordan tossed the soiled napkin back at Jess, who batted it away.

"So, do you think it's possible?" Jess took another sip.

"Well, yeah…I guess…if I had an army…" Jordan looked punch drunk.

"Good." Jess leaned back in her chair. "And as for an army…I think I can help you there." For the next half-hour, Jess went over her plans.

Jordan passed from shocked, to incredulous, to cautious optimism, and finally settled on giddy, all in the span of minutes.

When Jess finished, she leaned forward and looked Jordan directly in the eyes. "So, think you can do it, sis? Because I'm putting you in charge."

"Really?" Jordan puffed out her chest, a wild, manic look entering her eyes. "I love the smell of weddings in the morning."

Jess chuckled and shook her head. Talk about a truly Jordan response. But before she could reply, her phone went off in her pocket. She grabbed it and looked at the screen. "Oh, speak of the devil, it's Alex." Jess answered and listened. Her heart skipped a beat. "Say that again…"

Jordan sat across from Jess, taking in the one-sided conversation. She leaned farther and farther forward until her bum rested on the very edge of the couch. She slid completely off when Jess shouted.

"I'll be right there." Jess jammed her phone back into her pocket as Jordan scrambled to pick herself up from the floor. "Sorry Jordan, but I've got to go. Alex is being discharged!"

Jordan stood. She looked as excited as Jess felt. "Do you need any help? I could go—"

"Nope, thanks Jordan, I've got this." Jess wheeled around and sped toward the door. Just as she threw open the door to the garage, she called over her shoulder. "And hey, sis, thanks for taking on our wedding. I owe you one—we both do."

* * *

Alex sat on the edge of her hospital bed, waiting on her discharge papers. As the minutes ticked by, she fidgeted with her phone. Just as she was about to go find out what was holding everything up, there was a rattle at the door.

Maria came in, pushing a wheelchair and holding Alex's discharge papers.

"What are you doing here?" Alex stared in disbelief. Although Maria visited nearly every day, Alex had no idea that she would be the one to give her her walking papers.

"Are you kidding, doc? I wouldn't miss this for the world." Maria wheeled the chair up to Alex and fastened the brake. She handed over a large stack of papers.

"Thanks, Maria." Alex tucked the papers under her arm and stood. She nodded toward the wheelchair. "But I won't be needing that."

"Now why did I think you were going to say that?" Maria laughed with her hand still on the chair.

Alex tried to walk past Maria, but she blocked the way. "Come on, I want to walk out of here."

"Nice try, doc. But you know the drill." Maria glanced from Alex to the chair and back. "*All* patients—and yes that includes you—have to be wheeled out of the hospital." She crossed her arms, planting herself firmly between Alex and the door.

"Oh, for crying out loud." Alex stared but Maria wouldn't budge.

"Don't make me call security because you know I will." Maria was smiling an I-dare-you-to-call-my-bluff smile.

Alex stood for another half minute, continuing to stare down Maria, before she threw her hands in the air. She knew a losing battle when she saw one. "Fine. I'll sit in the damnable chair." She flopped into the chair harder than she should have, causing all three wounds in her chest to ping like a shot of lightning.

"Now that's a good patient." Maria chuckled.

Alex twisted her head around and scowled. If it were anyone else, she didn't care how much security was called, she wouldn't sit in the chair. "Okay, let's go."

If Alex had thought she would be able to make her exit quietly, she was grossly mistaken. As soon as she was wheeled through the door, she was met with hospital staff lining the hallway. As one, they all began to clap. Someone wolf whistled halfway down the hall. Besides the long line of nurses, orderlies, and even security, she also saw Becky Harris from ICU, Johnathan Bryce and Emil Januzelli from the ER, her surgeon Andre Romanokov, and even hospital president Ron Primeau, in a dark navy suit and red tie with the hospital's logo embroidered on it. Alex was immediately overwhelmed. Why had all these people come to see her off? Surely, she didn't rate such treatment. As she gaped at the crowd, a tear spilled from the corner of each eye. Alex wiped them away with the back of her hand only to find them replaced by more.

Maria slowly pushed her down the hall. People were still clapping and cheering. Alex raised her hand, waving a heartfelt acknowledgment as she passed. Tears flowed freely. She mouthed the words, "thank you," over and over though no sound came out. When they reached the end of the hall, Maria spun Alex around as she punched the call button for the elevator. The staff had closed ranks behind them until Alex couldn't see down the hall. She tried to swallow with little success. Finally, when the elevator *dinged* and the doors slid open, she bowed her head to the crowd. "Thank you." This time she was able to get the words out but just barely. As the doors slid closed behind them, shutting the staff from view, Alex turned to Maria. "You knew about this?" Her voice was still thick.

"I don't know what you're talking about, doc." Maria wore a smug grin.

All Alex could do was wipe her eyes again with the back of her hand and smile. Once the doors opened on the first floor, she was greeted again with clapping and cheers. All manner of staff crowded the lobby—from nurses to doctors (many of whom she didn't know), to housekeeping and food service. Even the old gentleman who volunteered to play the baby grand piano in the lobby every Tuesday was there.

Again, the tears flowed. Alex raised her hand in a grateful wave. Here she was being given a hero's welcome. But what for? Deep down she knew. She had survived. She was one of them and she had survived. That was why they were all there, clapping and cheering, because it could have been any of them. It was as much for them as it was for her.

Once through the front glass doors, Alex turned to Maria. "I wasn't expecting that. Why didn't you tell me?" Her voice was still thick.

Maria chuckled. "Because if I did, you'd try to sneak out, doc." She pushed Alex closer to the patient loading area. With a grand, wide swing of her arm, she waved to the street as a car pulled up. "Your chariot awaits, m'lady."

* * *

Jess pulled off Michigan Ave into the hospital pickup area. When she spotted Alex sitting in a wheelchair with Maria behind her, she almost crashed her car. Jess gaped out the side window. How on earth had Maria gotten Alex to sit in that chair?

Edging up to the curb, Jess threw the car in park and opened her door, but as she spun around to grab her wheelchair from the back seat, Maria stepped forward and opened the passenger door, leaving Alex scowling in the chair like a grumpy toddler.

Maria poked her head into the car. "No need for you to get out, Jess. I've got this."

Jess shut her door and leaned over the center console, holding herself up with an elbow. She looked beyond Maria for a moment and then back to her. Silently, she mouthed, "How?"

Maria stood up and let out a loud, braying laugh. Several pedestrians along the sidewalk turned and looked. "I threatened to call security on her. She griped quite a bit but finally gave in."

Maria stepped to the side so Jess could view Alex better. Jess called out the door, "Hey, nice ride you've got there, Legs. Care to trade?"

"Funny one, Wheels." Alex stood, wincing from the effort. She slowly edged to the car, still holding her paperwork under her arm.

Before Alex could slip into the car, Maria pulled her into a gentle hug. "Now you get better soon, doc. I'm going to miss you in the ER." When she released Alex, Maria dabbed a tear from the corner of her eye.

"Thanks, Maria, for…well, for everything." Alex nodded back toward the building. "And tell everyone else thanks as well."

"Will do, doc. Will do." Maria stepped back as Alex gingerly slid into the passenger seat. Once Alex was completely in, Maria closed the door with a final smile and wave.

Before pulling away from the curb, Jess reached over the center console and patted Alex on the thigh. "It's so great seeing you outside the hospital, Legs. There were times when…times when…" Jess's throat closed off, cutting off her words. She held up a finger as she fought to regain control.

Alex covered Jess's hand with hers. She looked directly into Jess's eyes, a soft, almost shy smile on her lips.

A good minute or two passed before Jess could speak again. When she did, she raised her hand to Alex's face and brushed her cheek with her thumb and index finger. "Sorry about that, Alex. I'm just so happy to see you going home. There were times when I…when I thought you might not ever leave the hospital."

Alex leaned into Jess's hand. She closed her eyes. "I'm sorry, Jess. I'm sorry for what you've been through, what I've put you through these past few weeks."

Jess jerked up. She didn't want Alex to get the wrong idea. She waited until Alex opened her eyes and looked at her. "Alex, you haven't put me through anything these past few weeks. None of this was your doing. You were shot by some deranged gunman. It was a really shitty thing that happened, but you don't have to feel guilty in the least. I would go through it all again a thousand times over, just to be there for you."

Alex blinked rapidly. She smiled, lips closed, and nodded—once, twice. "You're the best, Jess. Thanks."

Jess pulled Alex in close, careful not to aggravate her injuries, and kissed her tenderly on the forehead. "No thanks needed, babe—ever." She straightened up and threw the car in gear. "So, what do you say we get you home?"

Alex looked as if she were about to bounce right out of her seat. "Now, that's the best thing I've heard in a long, long time." She pointed out the windshield. "Onward!"

* * *

When Alex walked through the door from the garage into the house, she stopped and closed her eyes, taking a deep breath. Although it had only been a couple of weeks since she had last been here, it felt like a lifetime.

"Everything okay there, Legs." Jess wheeled up beside her.

Alex took another deep breath. Even the air in their house was different, better, as if each breath were a sweet second chance at life. She opened her eyes and looked down at Jess. "Yes, Wheels, everything is okay—more than okay. Just feels so good to be home."

"I know, babe. I know."

Alex walked slowly to the couch. She still tired easily whenever she stood for long periods—and since being shot, five minutes constituted a long period. She sat, propping her feet up on the coffee table.

Jess rolled up beside her. "Anything you need? Soda? Water?"

Alex shook her head.

The house was unusually quiet. Even when they talked, the sound seemed to bounce off the walls and fade away in a way that it didn't before. She looked around. Nothing had changed. But still the house felt as if it were a stranger's. Perhaps that was normal after a long absence. Perhaps deep down, she wasn't sure she would ever see their home again.

The silence continued, becoming an almost unbearable weight pressing down on her. As she looked around, gathering her thoughts, Alex realized what the problem was. The last time she'd been here, the last time she'd sat in this very spot, they'd had a fight. Things had been said. Bad things. Things that should never be said in a relationship. She startled at the hand on her arm.

"Are you sure you're okay, Alex?" Jess leaned in closer, concern furrowing her brow.

Alex hesitated a moment. "I can't help but think of the last time we were here together, Jess. All the things I said. How it all seemed like such a big deal at the time."

"But that's all in the past, Alex. We can't beat ourselves up about things from the past. We just have to move on."

"I know. But I don't want to move on without first saying how much it means to me that you were there for me through all this." Alex reached out and took Jess's hand in hers. Now, their house was beginning to feel like home again. "And, Wheels, I can't wait to start the rest of our lives together."

Jess leaned in until their foreheads were pressed together. "Me either, Legs. Me either."

CHAPTER SEVENTEEN

The big day had finally arrived. Jamie had shown up early that morning to help Alex get ready. Sue was floating around, overseeing last-minute preparations. Alex sat on the edge of the bed in the spare bedroom. She still didn't see why she couldn't get ready in the same room as Jess, but Jess had been adamant (along with everyone Alex had questioned on the topic) that the brides weren't supposed to see each other on their wedding day—it was tradition. It may be tradition, but they did bend the rules a little. Alex had seen Jess for less than five minutes that morning before they were chivied to their separate rooms.

"I don't see why we have to get ready so early. I mean, we've got another couple of hours before the ceremony." Alex stretched gingerly. The pain in her chest had slowly gotten better since she'd been discharged from the hospital a little over a week ago, but she still couldn't make sudden movements without her chest feeling as if it might tear in two.

Jamie flopped onto the end of the bed. "Those couple of hours are going to fly by. Plus, it's going to take you that long to get ready."

Alex rolled her eyes. Never in her life had it taken a couple of hours to get ready and she didn't see why today would be the exception. "But the rehearsal didn't take long at all."

"That's because you weren't wearing a dress, silly. That makes all the difference." Jamie sighed. "I didn't know being your best woman would be so exhausting."

"Bah." Alex laughed, thankful she had Jamie to keep her company. She didn't like to admit it, but she was more nervous than she'd ever been. "Maybe we should check on the arrangements in the backyard."

"Don't you dare!" Jamie sat up straight. "Jess would skin you…and *me*…alive if she caught you fussing around out there. There's plenty of people here to take care of all that."

That was a gross understatement. For the past two days, there had been an army trudging back and forth to their backyard. It was all Alex could do to sit and watch them pass by the windows. Jess wouldn't let her see what was going on out there. She was still recovering and therefore had to take it easy, which in Jess parlance was doing nothing more strenuous than sipping a cold drink.

"So, what do you think Jess is doing right now?" Alex fidgeted absently with the sleeve of her dress that sat beside her on the bed.

Jamie laughed and shook her head. "I'd imagine she's as nervous as you are. It's a good thing she has Jordan to calm her down."

Alex snorted through her nose and let out a loud chuckle. "Jordan calm Jess down? I'd imagine Jordan's the one who's having kittens about now."

"You're probably right, but at least she'd take Jess's mind from things."

Laughing, Alex pictured Jordan running around the room and flapping her arms like a ginormous flightless bird. "Jordan would be good at that."

Jamie pulled out her phone and checked the time. "Okay, Alex, we should probably start to get you ready. You don't want to be late for your own wedding."

"Fine."

By the time she'd fixed her hair and put on a little makeup (she very rarely wore any, but this was a special occasion), Alex was ready to step into her dress. Other than the initial fitting, she hadn't worn the dress. Everything was taking twice as long as she'd thought since her hands were shaking so bad.

Jamie was already decked out to the nines in a black tux, looking very debonair with her golden blond hair slicked back. "Calm down there a bit, Alex. You look like you're about to blast off."

"Believe me, I'm trying." Alex shook out her hands, trying to release some of the excess energy. How was she supposed to calm down when her nerves were revved so high that she felt as if her head might pop off at any moment?

"Deep breaths, darling. Deep breaths." Jamie came over and laid a hand on Alex's shoulder. "Let me help you into this thing." She inclined her head toward the wedding dress as if afraid it might jump up and bite her.

Alex looked at herself in the full-length mirror on the back of the door. She was wearing her favorite green lace panties and matching bra. With her light skin, the green really stood out. On her upper thigh, there was a matching garter. But it was the three deeply red wounds across her chest that drew her attention. They had healed a lot, but it would be months before they no longer looked so angry, and she would always have the scars. As strange as it may sound, she was glad. They were a reminder of how things could have turned out much, much worse, a testament to how precious and fragile life was. And now she was going to share that life with Jess. Nothing could be sweeter than that.

"Are you okay, Alex?" Jamie leaned in, her eyes narrowed, looking concerned.

Alex smiled and turned to her best friend. "Yeah, Jamie, I couldn't be better."

* * *

"Are you sure this is going to work, Jess?" Jordan cocked her head and stared at Jess, a skeptical look on her face.

Jess smiled. "Of course. Jerome and I have everything worked out." She had been planning this surprise for months. It had been hard to keep this particular secret, but Jess was sure she had succeeded.

"I can't believe you're doing this, sis." Jordan reached down and helped adjust things. "This is going to knock everyone's socks off."

Jess chuckled. Not exactly the response she was going for. "I don't know, Jordan. I'd settle for pleasantly surprised."

"Oh, there's going to be surprise, believe you me." Jordan stood back, inspecting her work. "I wouldn't be shocked if there were people passing out in the aisles."

Jess grinned. The response she was most looking forward to was Alex's. "What do you think?"

Jordan took her chin in her hand, inspecting everything as if she had just assembled a RAKKESTAD armoire from Ikea and was surveying the finished results. "Looks good, sis."

"Great." Jess shifted on the bed. "Now, help me with this dress, won't you? We're running out of time."

"We're doing fine on time." Jordan scooped the white dress from the end of the bed. "Just relax a bit. You've got the jitters."

Jess wasn't sure about the jitters, but her entire body *zinged* with pent-up energy. She could do with a quick zip up the trail in her racing chair to burn off the excess adrenaline.

But it wasn't just this surprise that had Jess so keyed up. She had another—she just hoped they would show. They'd talked on the phone more than once. They seemed as excited as she was. But still, there was always the possibility that things could go horribly, horribly wrong. She had learned that the hard way.

Jess fidgeted with her hands in her lap. She was only wearing a black lace bra and matching panties, Alex's favorite.

Jordan stood in front of Jess with the dress in her hands. She took a deep breath. "Ready?"

"As I'll ever be." Jess leaned forward with her arms outstretched. "Let's get this show on the road."

Jess closed her eyes as the dress slid over her head. The fabric tickled her cheeks and nose. She could feel it pooling around her on the bed, leaving her in an island of sleek, white material. When the dress fell to her shoulders, she opened her eyes, glanced across the room at the mirror and smiled. Alex was going to love this dress. "Hey, Jordan, can you help lift me up?" As great as the dress looked, it was a bit difficult to maneuver in.

"Sure, sis." Jordan leaned over and threw an arm around her back.

Jess wrapped her arms around Jordan's neck.

"Ready?" Jordan whispered, her cheek again Jess's.

"Yep." Jess prepared, her stomach tightening. When Jordan stood, lifting her from the bed, she quickly swept the dress under her bum. "Okay."

Jordan gently lowered her back to the bed. She stepped back, eyeing Jess up and down. Her eyes were overly bright, and her chin quivered ever so slightly. "Absolutely beautiful."

Jess blushed. "Thanks, sis. Just one last thing." She picked up the white leather gloves from beside her on the bed and slipped them onto her hands.

The doors suddenly opened, and Jess tried to hide herself without success, but quickly relaxed when she realized it was her mother.

Linda froze on the spot. "Oh, my sweet daughter." Her eyes filled with tears, and she walked over, taking Jess's face in her hands. She kissed Jess on one cheek and then the other.

"Come on, Mom, you're going to get me all messy." Jess squirmed in her mom's grip.

Linda finally let go, stepped back and smiled, still looking weepy. "It's not every day one of my daughters gets married."

Jess smiled back. "Where's Dad?"

Linda laughed. "He's in the kitchen trying to look tough but you know how men are. He's a basket case, not that he'd admit it. Same for Tim."

Jordan shook her head. "Figures. Tim cried at the end of *Avatar*."

Jess took a deep breath. Time was getting short. They'd better hurry. It would be bad luck for one of the brides to be late. "Okay. Let's do this."

* * *

Waiting in the hallway outside the guest bedroom, Alex took Tim's arm as he held it out to her. "Are you ready for this?"

Alex sucked in a quick breath and nodded. She didn't dare speak. She didn't dare even open her mouth. She gripped Tim tightly with both hands.

"It's time, sis." Tim looked down at Alex, a bright, warm smile on his lips.

Alex glanced over, trying not to look surprised. "I'm not your sister—not yet."

Tim chuckled softly. "Alex, you've always been a sister to me. You don't need a piece of paper to make it official."

Alex's eyes prickled with tears, but she couldn't let herself cry. Not right now.

Together, they walked through the living room toward the slider to the back deck and large yard beyond. The deep orange glow of the sun setting over the line of trees at the back of their yard blinded her as they stepped outside. Thankfully, the trees should shade the giant fireball in the sky in a few more minutes. She gripped Tim's arm tighter as her eyes adjusted. When she was finally able to see, she gasped.

Where there was once a vast expanse of green grass, there was now a scene straight out of a fairytale. Two rows of chairs lined a smooth temporary parquet pathway to a giant flower-covered arbor. All through the yard, Japanese lanterns were strung. Come evening, they were sure to be breathtaking. Beyond the chairs toward the tree line was a huge tent with numerous tables, each with bottles of wine along with a large floral centerpiece in the center and a temporary parquet dance floor to the right.

Alex stood dumbfounded. How could all this have been put together in only a matter of days? How had their friends pulled this off? What's more, how in the name of all things holy and just had Jess kept all this a secret? She glanced at the crowd. Both sides were completely full. Alex smiled as she read the sign posted at the back of the chairs. "*Take your seat on either side, either way it's for a bride!*" She snorted out a laugh. It must have been Jordan's doing. As she looked out at the familiar faces staring back at her, she was suddenly overwhelmed by the love she saw. She hadn't expected many to be there for her, but she'd been wrong. Maria was front and center, a great weepy smile on her lips. Beside her was Pamela. She could see Dr. Johnathan Bryce and his wife, Vicky, along with Dr. Emil Januzelli. Dr. Andre Romanokov sat beside Dr. Becky Harris. And true to his word, Dr. Ron Primeau sat with his arm around a striking woman who had to be his wife. Alex could even make out Frank the security guard. In the very front, Sue was dressed in an identical tux to Jamie's. Together, they stood under the arbor, looking more serious and dignified than Alex had ever seen them. On the opposite side, Jordan was talking quietly to Linda, who sat in the front row. Linda looked as if she might break out in tears at any moment.

Alex recognized many from Jess's list. The easiest to spot had to be Jerome in full Roxy Rocket drag persona. She was impossible to miss. Alex also recognized several from the bookstore, including the owners, Bob and Liz Veenstra. But as Alex glanced from face to face, her head begin to spin. All these people, all these friends, were there for both Jess and her. This was her family. These were the people who loved and accepted her, no judgment, no condemnation, no strings attached at all.

Suddenly from the right, beautiful classical guitar music filled the air. Alex turned to find Jodi Price, the tall guitar player from Terra's band, Blind Pariah. She was propped up on a stool, playing "All of Me" by John Legend. Alex swallowed hard. The song perfectly summed up her feelings for Jess.

Tim gave her a small nudge to break her out of her daze. "Here we go."

Alex took a deep breath and put one foot in front of the other, staring at the ground a few feet in front of her. She felt as if she were walking through a dreamscape. But no dream could be as wonderful as where she was now. She had a strangely pleasant floaty feeling. Her heart in her chest felt like a crazed ferret doing the weasel war dance. The faces flowed together until they were nothing more than one big blur. If not for Tim, she probably would have passed out somewhere around the midpoint of the procession.

When Alex reached the front, she looked up and her eyes flew wide open. Terra stood before her, white dreadlocks pulled back in a long ponytail. She wore a flowing, medieval-looking robe. Alex leaned in. "I didn't know you were doing our ceremony, Terra."

Terra waggled her eyebrows with a bright smile. "Trust me, doc, I wouldn't miss this for the world. That's why I got ordained."

Alex couldn't think of anyone better to perform their wedding ceremony.

Tim led Alex to the right, stopping in front of Jamie and Sue. When Alex pulled her arm from Tim's, he grabbed her hand and placed a tender kiss on her forehead. "Welcome to the family, Alex." He gave her hand a firm squeeze before walking over to stand behind Jordan.

Jamie leaned forward and dropped a hand to her shoulder. She gave Alex a firm pat. "Remember, deep breaths, Alex. Deep breaths."

Breathing in general seemed to be the issue. Her heart was swapping places with her kidneys. The rest of her internal organs were bouncing around like overly stimulated teenagers at a sock hop. Her stomach had taken up residence somewhere in the vicinity of her larynx and the two were duking it out. Alex stared forward, not seeing anything. She listened to the guitar, focusing on the melody. That seemed to help.

Suddenly, the music stopped. Alex jerked as if she had been poked. The silence drew out. Alex looked up, glancing over the crowd. Many were looking about as well. After a minute or so, Jodi began to play "I'm Yours" by Jason Mraz, and Alex smiled. Another perfect song for their wedding. Alex turned her head

to the left, gazing down the parquet pathway. A collective gasp
filled the air. At the back, Jess sat beside Pete. Alex sucked in
a breath between her closed teeth. Jess was so beautiful. Her
dress seemed specially tailored to flow with her chair. It almost
looked as if Jess were floating. Beside her, Pete was dressed in a
tux, the black contrasting vibrantly with the white of Jess's dress.
He stared straight ahead, his jaw set and his chin raised, clearly
doing his best to hold it together. She knew that feeling well.

Slowly, Pete led Jess up the aisle, his hand on her shoulder
the entire time. Jess was halfway down the aisle, and then three
quarters. Only a few feet now. Then another inch or two.

Jess came to a stop in front of Alex. She looked up and smiled.
Alex smiled back. In all the time that Alex had known her, she
had never seen Jess look so happy. She felt the same way. They
stared into each other's eyes and it was as if they had slipped
into another world. Time slowed down. The crowd faded away.
Even the music grew quieter, finally dwindling completely into
the background. The only thing that existed in that moment
was Jess and her.

"Hi, Legs."

Alex chuckled. "Hi, Wheels."

Somewhere from a long distance away, Alex heard someone
ask, "Who presents these women for marriage?"

Alex glanced over to Pete. He gave her a wink and waved
his arm out toward the people gathered there. He cleared his
throat. "Their family does—all of us."

Alex gulped. She looked out over the smiling faces. In all
ways that really mattered, this was her real family.

Alex turned back to Jess. From the look in her eye, she felt
the same way.

Pete remained at Jess's left side, and Tim walked up to Jess's
right side. They both leaned in, offering an arm under each of
Jess's and stood, bringing Jess with them.

Alex covered her mouth as she mumbled under her breath.
"Oh my God. Oh *my* God." A loud rustle rose from the crowd.
Murmurs and gasps filled the backyard as Jess stood. Alex
blinked and rubbed her eyes.

Jess reached out, taking both of Alex's hands in her white gloved ones as Pete and Tim stepped back. "Hey, Legs, surprise." Jess lowered her eyes slightly, her cheeks growing rosy.

All Alex could do was shake her head. She gulped, trying to find her words, then gulped again. "But…but…*how*? How is this possible?"

Jess laughed softly and squeezed Alex's hands, first one then the other. "Jerome helped with the braces. I know it probably seems silly, but I wanted to stand to get married to you, Legs."

Alex had told herself she wouldn't cry. But that was before she'd witnessed this miracle. "It's not silly at all, Wheels…or should I call you 'Legs' now?" Her voice was thick as the first tear spilled over her eyelid, but she didn't dare let go of Jess to wipe it away.

Jess giggled softly, looking directly into Alex's eyes, and shrugged. "Naw. I'll always be 'Wheels' to you, Legs."

* * *

Jess leaned in until her forehead touched Alex's. No one else existed but the two of them. "I love you, Legs."

"I love you too, Wheels." Alex's voice almost purred.

"Beautiful day, huh?"

"Yes, it is, especially with you here with me." Alex chuckled.

"Wow. It looks like these two are in their own little world." Terra laughed as she addressed the guests. "I'm not sure we're even needed here."

A roll of laughter rose from the crowd.

"We're really doing this." Jess still leaned against Alex's forehead. She never wanted to move.

"Yes, we're really doing this." Alex confirmed, her voice dreamy.

Terra cleared her throat. "So, are we ready, you two lovebirds?"

Another roll of laughter from the crowd.

Jess didn't hear much of what Terra was saying. She continued to stare into Alex's eyes. As Alex stared back, Jess's heart quickened. They had been through so much to get here. Now that they were standing in front of their loved ones, it felt as if they'd been building to this moment from the very first time they met. This was where they belonged—together.

Terra's raised voice snapped Jess back to the present. "What?"

The crowd laughed and Terra chuckled. "It's time to slip a ring on Alex's finger."

Jess shook her head. "Oh, yeah, right."

Jordan handed over the ring, but before she let go, she leaned in close and whispered in Jess's ear. "You've got this, sis. Now marry that woman!"

Jess nearly snorted a laugh through her nose. She tilted her eyes down to Alex's hand (it was shaking ever so subtly in her own) and gently slipped the golden circle onto Alex's long, slender finger.

Terra nodded. "And now, Alex, if you would put your ring on Jess's finger."

Alex didn't need told twice. She took the ring from Jamie, and after Jess pulled off her white leather glove, deftly slid it onto her finger.

This time, Jess wasn't sure if it was her hand or Alex's that was shaking—probably a bit of both. It was almost official. They were almost wife and wife.

Terra stepped forward, holding a long, olive-green strip of cloth ribbon about two inches wide and a good three feet long. "Now, Alex, if you'll place your left hand over Jess's left hand. And Jess, place your right hand over Alex's. And finally, Alex, place your right hand over Jess's."

With their hands stacked together, Jess looked up and smiled at Alex, who smiled and winked back.

Terra draped the cloth over their hands "The origin of the phrase 'tying the knot' comes from medieval times with the tradition of handfasting." She took the two ends of the cloth in her fingers. "The first knot symbolizes Alex's love for Jess." She tied a knot under Jess and Alex's hands.

Jess felt the ribbon snug their hands together.

"The second knot symbolizes Jess's love for Alex." Terra tied another knot.

The ribbon snugged a bit tighter.

"The third knot symbolizes Jess and Alex's love for everyone who has come to witness their wedding today." Terra tied a final knot.

Jess glanced out at their loved ones. There didn't seem to be a dry eye in the bunch. But she didn't dare look for too long or she'd start crying herself.

Terra paused, placing her hand atop Jess and Alex's bound hands. "At this time, the lovely couple would like to share their vows with you. Jess."

Jess cleared her throat. She teetered, but Alex held her firmly, helping steady her as she stood. Jess cleared her throat again. "Alex, you have always been there when I needed you most, through good times and bad. You have been my strength when I've been weak. You have shown me happiness when I am sad. And you've given me confidence when I've felt unsure. So, I make this vow to you, today in front of all those who love us, that I will be your strength when you need me, your happiness when you're sad, and your confidence when you're unsure, from now until the day I die."

Terra turned to Alex. "Alex, your turn."

Alex rocked up on her toes. She squeezed Jess's hands. "Wow. How am I going to be able to follow that?" The crowd laughed. "As many of you here know, I've recently had a brush with mortality. A lot of people say that can change a person. But through it all, this amazing woman—this beautiful, kind, sweet, loving woman standing in front of me today—never left my side. She was there for me when I needed her most, when I wasn't even aware. If that's not love, I don't know what is. So therefore, my vow to Jess is to never leave her side—through sickness and health, through the good times and not so good—I vow to always be right beside her whenever she needs me, for now and forever."

Terra raised her hands high above Jess and Alex. "And with the power vested in me, I pronounce these two wife and wife." She nodded to Jess and Alex. "You may kiss your bride!"

Jess and Alex leaned in, and when their lips touched, the crowd sprang to their feet, clapping and cheering.

* * *

Alex walked alongside Jess, who had returned to her chair after the ceremony, greeting guests and sharing well-wishes. Everyone had retreated to the large tent and gathered around the many tables, sipping wine and snacking on a whole host of finger foods. The Japanese lanterns swayed in the soft breeze, filling the darkening yard with a fantasy-like glow that cast moving shadows across the grass. Fireflies flitted along the tree line, adding to the ambience.

If it were up to Alex, they'd already be on their honeymoon where it was only the two of them. But that would have to wait—just not too long. She had a lot of plans for the night when they were finally alone—plans that would require room service the next morning. Alex smiled to herself.

"Hey, Legs, there's someone I'd like you to meet." Jess tugged her arm.

"Huh?" Alex turned around, a guilty blush rising on her cheeks. "Sorry, what did you say, Wheels? I was…" She waved her hand vaguely around her ear.

Jess didn't seem to mind her distraction. She pointed to a young couple standing in front of her. "I was just saying, there's someone I'd like you to meet."

Alex looked from Jess to the couple, not really seeing them at first. Then she focused on the young woman. Something about her seemed familiar, as if from a long-forgotten dream. Alex squinted as she stared, her mouth dropping open. It couldn't be. But the more Alex stared, the more she couldn't deny the resemblance. Finally, she gathered her breath. "Abigail? Abby? Is that you?"

"Hi, sis. Been a long time." With a cute shrug, Abigail smiled brightly.

Alex's head began to spin, as if the earth had suddenly rolled over on its side in one great mind-twisting flop. Her knees grew weak, and she dropped into a chair. She gulped at the air. Finally, she managed a single word. "How?"

Jess rolled over and placed her hand on Alex's knee. "Abby contacted me. She heard that you were getting married from your parents and that you were living in West Michigan. We've been talking."

Abby pulled up a seat beside Alex. "Yeah, I heard all about it as you can imagine. You know what Dad's like." Abby wrinkled her nose. "But don't worry, I'm not like that at all."

Alex nodded numbly. She turned to Jess. "Why didn't you tell me?"

Jess chuckled. "I wanted it to be a surprise. You *are* surprised, right?"

"Ah, yeah." Alex snorted through her nose. "I wouldn't have been more surprised if the pope showed up."

Abby laughed along with Jess. "I wouldn't have missed this for the world, Alex." Her voice grew thick, and her eyes teared up. "All these years, we were told that you ran off with some cult and probably died. I never thought I'd see you again. And then your invitation came…" Abby smiled at Jess.

"I never thought I'd see you either, sis." Alex dabbed her eyes. "Oh my God, I can't believe it. You've gotten so big."

"I was just a little kid the last time I saw you. Now I'm a professor of anthropology at Grand Valley State University, and I'm married to a wonderful man. Here, I want you to meet him." Abby reached out and pulled the young man standing nearby toward her by the hand. "Alex, this is my husband, Rodney Kirk. Rodney, this is my long-lost sister, Alex."

Rodney stepped forward and took Alex's hand, giving it a firm shake. "It's a pleasure to meet you. I'm excited to have you as my new sister-in-law."

Sister-in-law. Alex's head spun faster. "I'm…I'm…glad to meet you…too. And this is my wife, Jess."

"We've met." Rodney smiled toward Jess.

"Looks like you've got a lot of other guests to see." Abby stood. "So, we'll let you be for now."

"Wait!" Alex sprang to her feet. "I…I don't…I don't want to lose you again."

Abby chuckled softly. "Don't worry, sis. We'll have a lifetime to catch up. I'm not going anywhere, and I'm not letting you disappear again either."

Tears ran freely down Alex's cheeks. She didn't know what to say. Finally, she threw her arms wide and wrapped them around Abby. "Thanks for coming. Love you, sis."

Abby sniffled, her nose running and her cheeks wet. "Love you too, sis."

After Abby walked away, holding her husband's hand, Alex turned to Jess. "I don't know how to thank you, Wheels. This is the greatest wedding gift ever!"

Jess rolled up and pulled Alex down into a deep embrace, planting a kiss on her lips. "No thanks needed, Legs. No thanks needed at all."

EPILOGUE

"I can't believe we've been gone a whole month." Alex dropped the suitcases from each arm onto the couch. They had spent their honeymoon in Holland, Michigan. This time was even better than the last. Although she wasn't up for running—not while she was still healing from her injuries—they'd had a great time walking along the lakeshore and shopping.

"It certainly didn't seem like a month." Jess rocked up on her back wheels. "Maybe we should take another honeymoon."

Alex ran over and kissed Jess deeply on the lips. "I like how you think, babe. Maybe we could start with a shower?" She waggled her eyebrows salaciously.

Jess burst out laughing. "You know what happens when we try to take a shower? We are often overcome."

"Exactly." Alex lowered her voice and gave Jess a playful wink.

"Easy. Down, girl!" Jess giggled wildly. "I've got a better idea."

"Oh?" Better than messing around in the shower? Alex was intrigued.

Jess sat up straight and threw her shoulders back and forth. "Oh yeah. Tim helped with it. It's a big surprise."

"Oh God, not another fishing tackle mailbox or something?" Alex groaned.

"Nope, better." Jess took Alex by the hand and led her out the slider to their deck.

Alex's mouth dropped open. There on the corner of their deck was a brand-new hot tub, just waiting to be used. "Oh my God, Wheels. How?"

"Tim was able to get the money back from the venue. That along with the money we saved on our ceremony, I figured we could use something special for us." Jess smiled ear to ear. "Besides, you said a hot tub would be good for my injuries. Now it will be good for yours as well."

Alex continued to stare from the hot tub to her new wife and back. What had she done to deserve such an amazing woman in her life? If she lived to be a hundred, she would still be asking that question. But even if it took a lifetime, she would never stop asking.

"So, what do you say we break this bad boy in properly, Legs?" Jess reached up and ripped her shirt and bra over her head in one swift motion. She then quickly removed her shorts and panties with equal gusto.

Alex pulled off her own shirt and bra, tossing them somewhere over the edge of the deck into the flowers. She'd find them later. She then dropped her shorts and panties around her ankles and with one great kick, flung those high into the air. They landed on the roof. That was going to take a bit more effort, but she didn't care. She stood there naked, taking in her beautiful—and equally naked—wife. "Last one in, Wheels…"

Jess rolled forward like a streak. "Yeah, last one in, Legs…"

Bella Books, Inc.

Women. Books. Even Better Together.

P.O. Box 10543
Tallahassee, FL 32302
Phone: (800) 729-4992
www.BellaBooks.com

More Titles from Bella Books

Hunter's Revenge – Gerri Hill
978-1-64247-447-3 | 276 pgs | paperback: $18.95 | eBook: $9.99
Tori Hunter is back! Don't miss this final chapter in the acclaimed Tori Hunter series.

Integrity – E. J. Noyes
978-1-64247-465-7 | 28 pgs | paperback: $19.95 | eBook: $9.99
It was supposed to be an ordinary workday...

The Order – TJ O'Shea
978-1-64247-378-0 | 396 pgs | paperback: $19.95 | eBook: $9.99
For two women the battle between new love and old loyalty may prove more dangerous than the war they're trying to survive.

Under the Stars with You – Jaime Clevenger
978-1-64247-439-8 | 302 pgs | paperback: $19.95 | eBook: $9.99
Sometimes believing in love is the first step. And sometimes it's all about trusting the stars.

The Missing Piece – Kat Jackson
978-1-64247-445-9 | 250 pgs | paperback: $18.95 | eBook: $9.99
Renee's world collides with possibility and the past, setting off a tidal wave of changes she could have never predicted.

An Acquired Taste – Cheri Ritz
978-1-64247-462-6 | 206 pgs | paperback: $17.95 | eBook: $9.99
Can Elle and Ashley stand the heat in the *Celebrity Cook Off* kitchen?

Printed in the USA
CPSIA information can be obtained
at www.ICGtesting.com
JSHW021210200324
59570JS00001B/3